THE LOCKE BOX

JENNIFER DANIELS NEAL

SemiTone
BOOKS & MUSIC

DEDICATION

The Locke Box is lovingly dedicated to my own Locke who has been kind, and sturdy, and sexy for decades now. Thank you, Jeff, for making room in our home for all of my imaginary friends.

CONTENTS

Preface   ix

1. The Locke Family Plot   1
2. Annabelle   11
3. At the Station   19
4. The Locke Homestead   29
5. Playing House   41
6. The Balancing Act   55
7. From Aaron's to the Woodshop   79
8. Let's Just Love Each Other   95
9. You Belong to Me   111
10. At the Hospital   123
11. Out of the Loop   133
12. Church Day   145
13. The Letter   157
14. What Could Possibly Happen There, Indeed   171
15. Identical but Different   193
16. The Genie's Bottle   217
17. I Will   227

Author's Notes   235
About the Author   237

Landon, I'm not really sure how to begin this letter. It's one of those: If you're reading this, I must be dead, so...I'm sorry about that, Bro.

I need you to do two things for me.

THE LOCKE FAMILY PLOT

"This is why you keep pedaling. Because occasionally…this."

With a foot planted on either side of my bike, I remove my helmet to congratulate myself on what lies at the end of this trail. An old cemetery, peculiar in its beauty, and remote. So remote, I suspect it has fallen into disuse.

It seems indecent to ride into such a place. I leave the woods on foot, blinking against sudden sunlight, wading knee-deep through the grass of several solemn acres. Mammoth brown headstones mark the graves, some of them ancient—by American standards—and amassed in groups according to kin. At least, that's what I'm gathering from the clusters of common surnames. There are several dead Lockes.

As I explore, the garden's quietude begins to seduce my imagination. The tips of the grass tickle my palms and spread gossip about me from hill to hill. Morning light filters through the sprawling oaks like ethereal stairways—yeah, I'm really getting into it. I envision winged angels ascending to the heavens, having just plucked the recent dead. Oh! And the Spanish moss that drapes from the branches? Tangled snakes. Silent guardians of the reapers' process.

When I come upon the next gravestone, Annabelle Locke's, I begin to wish that my imagination had *not* become such an active participant, and that I had just stuck to considering the dead people's names as potential options for future children. Despite the serenity of the place, or maybe because of it, I find myself quite jumpy. So, in an effort to ground myself, I chide the grave's unfortunate tenant out loud. "It was creepy of you, Annabelle, to die on my birthday."

Annabelle is not arguing. Even so, I make my sternest teacher face to tell her that, "Yes it was."

Now that that's settled, I amble to the next outcropping. BUT... when something unnatural slinks into my periphery, I spin my whole body around to confront it. A man's head has appeared over the top of Annabelle's stone. And I shriek.

"Maybe it was creepy of you," the head says, "to be born on her death-day."

I choke back the flare of annoyance that follows the embarrassment, that follows the fright. The head is clearly amused. It says, with some effort at decorum, "I didn't mean to startle you. I was sitting back against the stone when you spoke. She was my great-great-grandmother."

By this time, the head's whole body has risen into view, and the gravestone, which is nearly shoulder height for me, is hardly chest height for it. It holds out a hand for me to shake.

Broad frame. Nice cheekbones. Strong evidence that it hasn't held a razor in days. I feel slightly more agreeable. I concede that it is certainly and solidly a living man. I think that, before the spark of laughter—at my expense—grey clouds had overcast his late-summer-green eyes.

"It's a lovely name," I manage, but I do not shake his hand.

"I haven't told it to you yet."

He bestows a suggestive nod at the hand I am not shaking.

"I mean Annabelle," I say. "Your great-great-grandmother."

"Oh. Right. And I'm Locke." Locke combs back layers of shoulder-length, brown hair with the hand in contention. Then reaches it out again. "Well, Landon," he corrects, "but everybody calls me Locke."

I've always wanted hair like that. My wild mane is nearly untamable. And it is certainly orange. I'm annoyed all over again.

"In Texas," Locke says, as if he's educating a foreigner or a child, "we shake hands when we meet. I put mine out, so. And then you grasp it. It's a sign of good faith."

I regard the outstretched appendage and shake my head. "No, I'm not going to. Not till you can give me a good excuse for walking around with hair like that."

"What?" he laughs. He's unused to being declined. Of course, he is. Look at him.

"All shiny and obedient and showing off your bone structure." I wave my water bottle at that bone structure and peruse it with a scowl. "Anyway, we can't become acquainted with your great-great-grandmother's gothic headstone standing between us. It's bad luck."

Locke lifts his head up but points his attention down at my feet. "It's only bad luck for the person standing right on top of her," he says.

I take a decisive step sideways and cut my eyes at him in a way that makes him chuckle.

It's a really nice sound.

After a moment, I say, "You're not here to visit Annabelle. You couldn't be old enough to miss her." The cloudiness I'd noticed before, now spreads across Locke's whole face. He makes a slight, seemingly involuntary motion that draws my gaze to a newer marker standing behind him.

NOW WE KNOW IN PART;
THEN WE SHALL KNOW IN FULL,
EVEN AS WE ARE FULLY KNOWN.
AARON ALEXANDER LOCKE

"My brother," he says.

"I'm so sorry."

Locke nods upward in acknowledgement.

"August twenty-fifth," I note. "He died a year ago today."

He doesn't reply.

This is what he looks like. When he's not trying. He's exquisite. I have to make the conscious decision not to stare.

Locke redirects the conversation. "What are you doing roaming around a graveyard?"

"I just stumbled upon it. I moved here a few weeks ago to teach sign language at the college, and I was out exploring on my bike." I thumb toward the trail that runs to campus, then I step forward to offer my hand. "Emma Caine."

"A quick study!" Locke bloats the words with exaggerated delight. He clasps my hand and regains what I interpret as a pompous and possibly *minutely* attractive, if also infuriating air. He resumes his instruction: "Now I say, 'It's nice to meet you.' And you say—" He raises a hand to his heart. "'Sir, believe me, the pleasure is all mine.'"

I wait, straight-faced, for Locke to get over himself.

"Nothing?" he asks. He appraises me from head to toe and back again. "OK," he says. But it doesn't mean, *OK*. It means, *I accept*.

"I like old cemeteries," I say, to better explain why I'm out here roaming. "I enjoy reading the markers and wondering about their stories." Hesitantly, I add, "It's probably more romantic when you don't have a face to go along with the name."

Locke is quiet. I worry that I've upset him until he says, "It didn't sound like you were wondering about their stories. It sounded like you were reprimanding them."

I bite back a smile. "I was not reprimanding them. Well, I was kind of reprimanding *that* one."

"You were totally reprimanding them."

"Your granny deserved it."

Locke leans forward against Annabelle's stone and rests his chin in his hand. "How do you figure?"

"She died on my birthday...Locke. And that was rude."

"But like, a hundred years before you were born."

"Not the point." I whip my head to the side, my unruly hair flying along, and I keep my face cast away. Until there is no response, and I fall out of character to check on his reaction. His eyes are smiling at me in a way that makes me want to continue this ridiculous conversation for another few days. So, I do. "I got distracted from my *real* task," I say, "of finding names for my baby, before I'd found *any* that would fit him. Or her. And, by the way, I didn't realize I had an audience. I was enjoying the solitude."

I haven't finished my tirade before Locke's demeanor does a one-eighty. "Ah," he stalls. "I misjudged this." He wags a finger between us. He consults his watch. "I should get back to work. It was nice to meet you, Emma."

Doesn't sound like it.

"Congratulations on the new baby and all that."

What just happened? "Oh, I'm not—" I begin. Does he think I'm pregnant? He's already moved past the stone and past me, when I realize, too late, that I've completely shut him down. I hadn't pegged him for the type to just forfeit. Of course, he *is* here to visit his deceased brother. And he obviously thinks that I'm otherwise committed.

Before I can call him back to correct the misconception, the sound of hurtling rocks and spinning tires draws my focus away. An ivory-colored sedan appears, fishtailing as it comes, and speeds over the country lane toward us, generating a deluge of dust.

It leaves the lane altogether, bumps onto the grass—narrowly missing the gravestones of two Houstons—and cuts close enough to the low branch of a live oak to take some Spanish moss for a rodeo ride.

It then careens right at me! Like it's aiming for me! I think the driver still has a foot on the gas! I make the instant decision to vault over Annabelle's grave marker to keep from being demolished. When the car crashes, it splits the stone into three great chunks with titanic noise. It stops just feet from where I've landed, inelegantly, on my backside.

The muted echoes of Annabelle's splintering stone pulse through my head, and for a moment, I'm sure I've gone deaf again. Even though I vaguely know it to be an odd thing to do, I lie down to welcome the quiet, but from what seems a long way off, one noise sinks through to me: the panic of Locke's voice as he sprints toward the place where I lie. I don't want to be the reason for that. He's ordering me to open my eyes, so I do.

Locke nearly falls on top of me in his haste to make sure I'm alright and runs his hands over me to check for damage. He searches my eyes with such ferocity, that it has the effect of steadying me. He nods, as if we've shared words, and rushes out of my orbit again. I swallow, rise to my feet, and follow.

The front of the car is crunched. The hood is crumpled onto itself, and the windshield is a spiderweb of cracks. Wrenching the driver's door open, Locke comes to an abrupt halt. He goes ashen, glances into the backseat, glances at me, and moves to block me from view.

"I may be able to help," I protest. "I was an EMT for a few years."

"Then come quickly," he says, and moves out of the way. "It's not good."

The woman in the driver's seat is going to die. I do not say this out loud. But her skin is purpling, and her lips are turning blue. When Locke steps out of her view, her eyes rove for him wildly, and she babbles a frantic mixture of phrases in English that keep slipping into Spanish—like she can't keep the English turned on right now.

I'm fluent in American Sign Language. Spanish, not so much. But the woman slaps at me when I try to assess her. It becomes clear that she's distressed about the well-being of her backseat occupant. Locke's already stretched across, fumbling around with car seat latches. He brings out a small pink bundle of a baby. Dead. Or unconscious. Or asleep. I don't know.

"Let me see her," I insist. He places the infant into my arms, then bites his thumbnail while I work. The pulse is strong. There's no blood. No sign of trauma. The child opens her dark, almond-shaped eyes, and reaches for my cheek. I honestly think she slept through it. How?

"Here she is, Mama," I tell the woman. "Look. She's doing fine." I smooth the child's wispy black hair. Her head nearly fits into the palm of my hand. I try to remember how old my nephews were when they were this small. Five months? Six? "We're going to take good care of her, OK? Now let me take care of you." Locke reaches for the baby so that I can help the woman, but, as I said, she is going to die. I'm sorry she's going to die. I reach in to try to help her, and she grips my arm.

"Him," she pleads. "Him." A litany of slurred Spanish phrases tells me she's about to lose consciousness. Locke nudges me aside and presses the baby to her chest. The woman is crying. She's so beautiful. Dark hair. Dark skin. She tries to wrap an arm around the baby, but she's losing control of her motor function. Locke positions the woman's arms around the baby and physically embraces both mother and child. The woman leans her head back to gaze at him. The muscles around her eyes relax. Like Locke is her final consolation. And then she dies.

"No!" I cry. "Your baby!" I tug Locke out of the way. I unlock the woman's seatbelt and drag her out of the car. I swear she's already going cold. I start CPR. I plead with her to wake. "What did you take?!" I scream. There aren't any real abrasions. I don't think she died from the wreck. She's more purple now than before. "Don't leave your baby!"

Three minutes. Five. I'm heaving mightily into the chest compressions as if I can force the life back into her. I feel a strong arm around my middle. Locke is pulling me off of the woman with one arm and holding the baby with the other. Even so, I struggle against him. "She has to stay!" I tell him.

"Emma?"

I can't break his restraint.

"She's gone. Let her go."

I surrender with an exasperated exhale, and he releases me to sit back on my heels. I'm staring at the woman. I drop my head.

"Take the baby," he says, and I do. He fishes his phone from the pocket of his jeans. While I cradle the child, he dials 911.

The hot, sticky morning is becoming a hotter, stickier day. I seek relief in the shade of a tree, but my legs are unsteady, and I stumble, drawing a sharp look of concern from the man who's now asking for assistance. He exhibits amazing poise. I carefully sit down with the baby and rock her, willing my voice to remain calm and sweet. I keep stealing glimpses of the bizarre scene: Locke pacing among gravestones, phone to his ear, in front of the crushed hood of a car, beside which this child's mother— I draw a stabilizing breath and wonder if the feeling that I'm floating means I'm in shock.

Locke ends the call and comes to kneel before me.

"How is she?" he asks. His voice anchors me back to Earth.

"She's fine as far as I can tell. Alert. Responsive."

As if to disagree, the baby begins to cry.

He presses a long finger into her tiny hand, and she latches onto it with all of her own.

"You're not hurt?" he asks. When Locke lifts his face to me in question, I realize he's asking me, and not simply placating the child. "Your own baby's OK?" he prompts.

"Oh." A moment of levity. "Locke, I didn't mean to imply that I had a child on the way. I'm not pregnant. I'm not even seeing anybody. I just like to consider names in case, you know, *someday*." I wave a hand when I say "someday."

He gives me another once over, his eyes landing on the bike shorts that leave little room for an expanding uterus. "Yeah, you don't look pregnant." He shakes his head. "I mean—"

"Yes?"

"No, you just look—" He searches for an appropriate phrase and comes up with, "the opposite of pregnant."

"What is that supposed to mean?"

Locke puckers his lips in consternation, or maybe to stop them from making more words. It makes me laugh outright, if only to ease my nerves, and that makes him laugh too. "You know good and well what I mean. And yes," he hurries to say, "you would still be attractive if you were pregnant as a peach." He balances his forehead on his fingers. "I think the trauma has made me stupid."

"Did you hear that, Baby?" I coo to the child. "Landon Locke is not so full of clever words right now." I lean closer to confide, "It can be intimidating to have strong and capable women like us around." The baby grabs hold of my mouth, and Locke rolls his eyes, but there's a smile in them.

It doesn't take long for the severity of the situation to reassert itself. "How long do you think it will take the police?" I ask. "I can't bear for that woman to have to lie there."

"Let's sit on the other side of the tree," Locke suggests. He hops up and helps me to my feet. Standing before him, I take a moment to scrutinize his handsome face. "What is it?" he asks.

"Did you see the way she looked at you at the end?"

2

ANNABELLE

It's a long time before we're allowed to leave. The medical examiner has to deal with the body, so an ambulance has to be driven to the site. We spend the time trying to pacify the baby. That would be a lot easier if the police hadn't immediately snatched the diaper bag we'd found in the car. Pretty sure milk and baby wipes aren't going to help them solve any mysteries. But anyway, when the baby finally falls asleep, I lean my own head back against the tree and close my eyes.

I've just dozed off when Locke says, "That's Sheriff Dunn." At first, I don't know to whom he's referring. The sheriff stands away from the blur of his officers' activity without garnering much attention. I consider him.

"My brother was one of his officers," Locke says. "In fact, the last time I saw him was Aaron's burial. He was standing on that very spot."

That very spot isn't that close to Aaron's grave.

"I kept watching him through the service," Locke continues, "wishing I could walk around too, or that I could just be *any*where else."

It's Locke who approaches the sheriff and not the other way around. He introduces me as his friend, which I guess is true.

"Hell of a day for this," the sheriff says. "Tell me about the driver."

"I don't have anything to tell," Locke answers. "She wasn't making any sense. She died in a matter of minutes."

"How did you know her?"

"No, I didn't know her. I'd never seen her before."

"You don't know anything at all about the woman," the sheriff confirms.

"Right." Locke quirks his brow. "Should I?"

"Just making sure. Miss Caine, *you* tell me about her." Sheriff Dunn examines me, and then the baby in my arms. He eyes her in a way that makes me think the infant is under suspicion. I realize that sounds lunatic, but that's what I see. Maybe he just doesn't like babies.

"I didn't know her, either," I tell him.

"No connection at all? She wasn't coming here to meet with the two of you for any reason?" He looks from me to Locke and back again.

"Actually," I point out, "we weren't even meeting with each other. We didn't know each other before today."

Sheriff Dunn frowns. "I thought you said you were friends."

"We are." Both Locke and I say it in unison. "But we only became friends today," I add.

The sheriff seems chafed by this.

"So, you're here, why?" the sheriff asks me. He glances around. "You have people?"

"What?" I look to Locke for guidance. "No. I do not *have* people."

Locke starts to smile. "He wants to know if any of your family is buried here," he says.

"Oh. Is that a Texas thing? No. No family here. I'm from Michigan." I display on my right pinky where I'm from along the state's mitten shape. "I just happened upon this place."

The sheriff nods in comprehension, but his eyes reserve judgement. He asks us to stick around until the scene is processed, so we return to the trunk of our tree where we watch the police take pictures and bag items from the car.

It shouldn't be taking this long. There's hardly anything to sort. I went through the car myself—couldn't even find an ID. When one of the officers painstakingly processes the contents of the diaper bag and finally sets them among the other items, I offer the baby to Locke and stalk over to retrieve it.

"We need that," I say.

"No Ma'am. We can't release anything here. It has to be cleared first. Somebody died."

"Well, she didn't die because of diapers."

The officer ignores me, pacing over the ground to continue his search. I pace right along with him.

"The baby hasn't eaten in hours," I tell him. "She's very young. Please."

The officer gets to his knees to search under the car. So do I. "About the diaper bag," I say.

I'm already adamant when I hear the baby start crying, and that revs up some latent maternal instinct in me. "We need it right now," I insist.

"This is an investigation, ma'am, and whatever is in that bag may be connected."

"*Or*"—I raise my voice—"whatever is in that bag could keep a baby from being hungry and in pain!"

The man darkens, and his tone brokers no more discussion. "I'm not giving you the bag," he grunts. "Child Services is on the way."

When I open my mouth to use more words about what kind of sense that makes, and possibly to remark on the man's intelligence, Locke intervenes. I suppose he's familiar with the officer because of his brother's role with the police.

"Anderson," he says calmly. "Would it be possible to clear that bag now? And if a diaper could be spared, for the sake of the child's comfort—"

"And health," I interject. I urge Locke on with a meaningful nod. He needs to make it clear what's at stake here. "They get very raw when they're left in their own urine," I add. "We'll need wipes too."

Locke's expression is hard to read. Somewhere between *I find your candor amusing* and *I got this*. He steps slightly in front of me to take back the conversation. I don't think anyone has ever done that to me before. I'm not sure how to feel about it.

"Don't you think that's fair?" he's asking the officer. Locke has drawn the consideration of others as well. He has a way of commanding attention with his posture and his voice, though he hasn't spoken above a conversational volume, and he's holding an infant in his arms. The infant, by the way, has also quieted and is now gazing up at him.

"Yeah, that's fair," another man says. "Anderson, if the bag's been checked, then give it over. For goodness' sake." The same man speaks out to a younger officer, or maybe an intern, further away. "Can we get some water over here? These folks have been here all day."

As the group breaks up, one of them mutters something about Locke's little firecracker of a woman, and Locke grins at the ground.

Another two hours pass. The sun has trekked to the other side of the cemetery, and the shadows from the large, old stones have stretched long by the time we are finally asked to relinquish the baby to a Ms. Vaughn from Child Services. It's a task I can hardly stomach.

We watch as our little, self-imposed charge is carried away, looking even smaller against the woman's meaty shoulder than she had in Locke's strong arms. What will happen to her now? Does she have family? Anyone worrying about her? I fold my arms around myself because they feel conspicuously empty and fatigued.

I can't stand it. I go after the woman. "Can we check up on her?" I call out. "I don't want her to get lost. Or neglected. Can't I just keep her until this is all sorted out? I keep my nephews all the time." My nephews live back home in Michigan, so *all the time* may have been a stretch.

Ms. Vaughn is sympathetic, but there is strict protocol for the child's safety. She secures the baby into a car seat and digs through her purse for a business card, which she hands to me. From the back seat, the baby begins to wail.

"She probably needs to be changed again," I say. "She has to eat every few hours." Ms. Vaughn climbs into her own seat, closes the door, and starts up the engine.

I feel a hand on my shoulder. "She'll be OK, Em," Locke speaks softly. "The lady's trained for this."

I stare after the car as it wobbles over the uneven ground and onto the dirt road. A tow truck waits to take its place. "We don't even know her name," I say.

Locke thinks about that. "Annabelle," he suggests. My response, which surprises me as much as it does him, believe me, is to twist around and start sobbing into his chest. He slowly puts his arms around me. I feel him inhale, hold it, and lay his cheek on top of my head to let it out.

When I begin to quiet, I become aware that Locke is using the heel of his hand to rub circles into the small of my back. And also, that it feels really good. At length, I mumble into his T-shirt, "How does this work? Are we just supposed to go back to our own lives now?"

"I think we collided too hard for that," he says. "Pushed right past get-to-know-me, into bonded-for-life."

"You do know that *feeling* bonded for life and *being* bonded for life are two entirely different things."

He looks down at me, clinging to him like a koala. "You're holding on to me pretty tightly to be making such distinctions."

"So?" I tighten my grip even more.

"We should stick together," Locke says. "Come home with me." His rumbly voice, close to my ear, sends a shiver down my spine.

I can think of several reasons that make going home with Locke a bad idea. The pleasure of those little circles he keeps pressing into me, for instance. And the responsiveness of my spine to the vibration of his voice (the memory of which initiates a little after-shiver).

"I'll be a gentleman," he insists. He raises both hands to confirm his innocence, but without pulling the rest of himself away from me. "Even though you don't look pregnant." I can hear him smiling. "I'll make you dinner." Locke searches the sky above his head as if he can see into his kitchen cabinets. "It may have to be peanut butter."

I consider him through what I know are red-rimmed eyes. I don't want to leave him. I'm not even sure I can. But that's also why I have to. "We should process this tonight," I say. "Separately."

"It doesn't have to be peanut butter," Locke counters. "We could stop at the store."

"Peanut butter sounds perfect," I assure him. "I just—I need to clear my head."

"No, don't clear your head. That's a terrible idea. You'll wipe me right out of it. I want to know you're OK. I want to have a debrief. And...to go on dates."

"Tomorrow," I promise.

"You're not just going to try to forget all this ever happened?"

I hand him my phone. "Call yourself, and you'll have my number." He does. When it rings, he hands it back, but I don't hang up. Instead, I hold up a finger to let him know I intend to leave a message.

"Hey. It's me." I mean to make a joke, but my voice sounds too fragile to fake it. "You were brilliant today," I speak into the phone but peer into his eyes. I try for a stronger tone. "Thanks for letting me cry all over your T-shirt." Pause. "And for your self-inflated sense of humor and your shameless hair." His lips pile to one side. "I don't have much faith in bonded for life," I say, fragile again. I bow my head. "So, you'll have to...if you still feel like it tomorrow..." I hesitate. I've said both more than I want to and less than I need to.

Locke's watching me with his cloudy face. That's the one that's going to get me hurt. This time I allow myself to keep staring. Finally, I draw the phone down from my ear and end the call.

"What else did you want to say?" he asks.

I shake my head, but then, because I can't help myself, I sign a phrase with my hands. Locke cocks his head in question, but I don't explain.

"You are an interesting woman, Emma."

We find my bike, and I decline his offer to drive me home. When I turn my helmet upside down, to sort out the straps, Locke informs me that there's something caught in my hair.

"That does not surprise me," I tell him. "Elflocks collect things. There's no telling what you'll find in there."

"I *like* your hai—"

"Don't." I raise a hand to cut him off. "I made peace with it ages ago."

"I really *do*." This awards him a full-on glare, so he adds, in a tone that means he's puzzling me out, "think that it resembles that nest of Spanish moss." He points behind me, and I smile broadly. "In a *good* way," he tacks on with triumph. "You don't mind your hair at all, do you? You just think it's funny to be self-deprecating."

I make a non-committal shrug.

"May I?" Locke asks. He uses both hands to free the object. A silver chain. A tiny bracelet with a charm in the shape of an old-fashioned skeleton key.

"The baby's?" I ask.

It sparks a memory for Locke, about his brother. "Aaron was all into skeleton keys. He even had one tattooed over his heart." Locke traces his finger in a line over his chest, from sternum to side. "It wasn't delicate like that. Had a skull that's jaw seemed to be biting into the rest of it. It was wicked."

I offer him the bracelet.

"No, you keep it," he says.

"Well, now I have a Locke. And a key." I pocket the chain, wondering if I'll ever have the chance to return it to Baby Annabelle. Then I put my hand to my ear in the shape of a phone. "Call me maybe," I tease.

"Call you definitely. Pick up maybe. When's too early?"

I blink a smile and hit the trail before I can allow myself to get swept up in this gorgeous man's unapologetic pursuit.

Once out of his company, alone on my bike, I feel the darkening of the wooded trail like gloom descending. I refuse to give audience to my wilder imaginings. Instead, I think of how Annabelle stared up at Locke as he petitioned the officers for her diaper bag.

It couldn't have all been coincidence, right? The fact that Locke and I converged upon his brother's grave at the very same moment that car ran off the road?

My mom believes that life is full of appointments. That even seasons of struggle and sorrow are not accidental but are full of purpose. That we are *called* to them. I've never been able to manufacture that kind of faith. It's one of the reasons I bike so much. To give God a chance to show up.

And what showed up instead? A car that nearly annihilated me. A woman who died too soon. An orphaned infant who surprisingly burrowed into my heart. And Landon Locke. With whom I bonded. In what way and for how long, I can't be sure.

I come to the crosswalk between the bike trails and my apartment with a head full of questions. An unfamiliar car is parked on the pad in front of my door, and two men are walking—sneaking?—around the side of my porch. I watch them, trying to suss out what I'm actually seeing.

One of the men stretches up to push on a window. Is he trying to enter my apartment? The other one notices me and slaps his partner's thigh. A moment lapses. The two men begin to move in my direction. No way are they just here to check the water meter. Not after the day I've had.

It's a busy road, and there's enough fast traffic to keep the men from being able to traverse it. They're both poised on the curb. "What do you want?" I yell.

"Stay there," one of them says. He's watching the line of vehicles for his chance to dash across. The other man jogs back to their car.

"Tell me who you are and what you want with me," I call.

I don't get an answer. He's found his opportunity and he darts forward.

My bike is already pointed away. My system bursts with adrenaline, and my faith proves stronger than I realize when my first instinct is to silently pray for help.

3

AT THE STATION

My second instinct, on the heels of that one, is to pedal. Hard. Chancing a glimpse over my shoulder, I see that the car has surged onto the road. It's loud in short bursts, the way boys back home used to soup up their muscle cars to show off. I'll never make it to campus if they follow me by car. I'll have to get back to the bike trails.

The car slows to retrieve the man who is chasing me on foot, and then it's beside me. The passenger window slides down. I hear my name. How do they know it? How do they know where I live?

"We just want to talk."

I doubt the veracity of that statement, because before I can react, the car swerves toward me, running me out of the bike lane, down a grassy embankment.

Not the police, then. I had been holding out hope that maybe these guys were cops needing to follow up with me, or, even better, just wanting to confirm that I'd made it safely home. I now relinquish that. The police are good guys. The police definitely don't run innocent people off the road.

I'm an experienced rider. I keep my mount and jump my wheels over the ditch. I know exactly where the narrow trail picks up, and I make for it, grateful for the compulsion that has driven me over every inch of these trails since I moved in. The car has no chance of following me there. The trees are too close together.

Once I safely rejoin the path, I plow ahead, my mind singly devoted to the act of putting distance between myself and whoever is in that car. But at some point, I'll have to decide where to go. Many of the trails lead too far into the wilderness. I'm not stocked for that kind of ride. Other paths quickly loop back to the start. No way.

There's a connector trail. A hub that feeds into several different outlets. One leads to a major highway. Is that where I want to go? I decide to make for the connector and call the police once I get there. Hopefully, my phone will still work, that far into the country.

About thirty-five minutes later—man, I must have flown!—I arrive at a signpost where several paths converge. I pull my bike off the trail and listen to the woods for any sound that could be human. When I'm satisfied that no one is around, I withdraw my phone. Six calls from two numbers and one of them has left a text. *Em, please call right away. Locke*

The other number is the sheriff's office. They've left a voicemail. "Miss Caine, Sheriff Dunn. I need to speak with you right away. Please call me at…"

Since when does anyone need to speak to me *right away*? I decide to call the sheriff directly. When he answers, I speak with nervous intensity. "Sheriff, it's Emma Caine. There were two—"

"Miss Caine, thank you for calling back. We need to go over a few more things. Could you come by the station?"

"Sir, when I got home, there were two men trying to break into my apartment. They chased me in their car. They ran me off the road."

After finding out how I've fled and where I am now, the sheriff asks me to meet his deputy where the connector trail joins the highway. I hang up, a clear objective helping to focus my mind and calm my nerves.

I dial Locke.

"Are you safe?" he answers pointedly.

"How did you know something was wrong?"

"*Is* there?"

I quickly recount what has happened and my plan of action.

I hear him breathe out. "You must be one hell of a cyclist," he says. "I wish I could be the one to pick you up. OK, well, hang up and get yourself to the deputy. I'll see you at the station."

"Why are *you* going to the station?"

"They called me too."

"What more could they possibly need from us?"

"Emma, the woman from Child Services was attacked."

"What?!" I feel slightly hysterical. "What are you saying? Annabelle?"

"She's OK. The police have her. Just get yourself to the deputy. I'll see you soon."

The deputy retrieves me without incident, buys me a huge bottle of water, and bids me to wait in the rigid seats of the station's lobby. My foot is tapping incessantly. I mess with my bike. I take a few sips. I scan the area repeatedly. What I'd like to know is what happened to all the *right-aways*?

Really, I've only been there about ten minutes when the front door is propelled inward, and Locke appears, his broad shoulders threatening to test its frame. His eyes land on me and—I am not going to lie—I feel warm from head to toe by the way he says my name. Like the fact of me fills him up.

He smells like the bike trails. Like the trees themselves. Actually, he smells like the logs my daddy used to chop for firewood when we'd go camping. Back when my daddy still loved me.

I start to greet him when a passing officer whips his head in our direction like he's been struck. He's about as towheaded of a man as one could be, with eyebrows the same impossible white, over eyes of light blue. An awkward silence ensues while the man rubs at his forearm and peruses Locke's whole body. Then, in what would have been a brotherly gesture, except for the way his thumb presses into the pulse point at Locke's throat, he grips the back of Locke's neck. "Landon. I'm sorry, man. I—"

"No need." Locke cuts him off and swipes the man's hand away. "I do it to myself in the mirror. I do it to my mom sometimes. It's why I haven't cut my hair since he died."

Locke introduces the officer as Chris Michaels, his brother's old partner, and I surmise why Chris has acted like he's seen a ghost. When he leaves, I say, "You were twins, you and Aaron."

Locke indicates that they were.

"Identical?"

He can't answer me, because, at the same moment, a woman wraps her long arms around his chest from behind. She's pretty and tall, with thick hair as silky and obedient as Locke's—whom she is now embracing. I'm not sure we're going to get along.

Locke looks over his shoulder and backstrokes to pull the beauty to his side. He kisses her head and greets her with an intimate, "Hey, Baby."

It's just that I've met my quota of new friends for the day and there's really no more room for Baby in it.

"You know I hate it when you call me Baby," Baby says. She nods upward in my direction. "Who's the little hard-body?"

"The little hard-body is Emma," Locke responds. "We bonded for life today."

Baby takes this news in stride, with a hum of acceptance.

"Em," Locke says, "allow me to present my little sister, Sarah."

Little sister. Well, I suppose I could make room for *family*.

Locke covers his mouth and leans over to say, too loudly to be secretive, "You remember how this works, right? The whole hand shaking thing?"

I shove him away to greet Sarah.

"I'm sorry you guys have been through such an ordeal," she says. "I wanted to come help, but they told me to stay put."

"Are you an officer?" I ask. Sarah isn't wearing a uniform, but that's not conclusive.

"No, I'm just working the desk till I get through business school.

Someday..." She eyes her brother meaningfully. "I'm going to take over the family business."

"Just as soon as Dad retires," Locke confirms. His tone holds irony.

"Because...he's never going to?" I guess. I'm rewarded with one large nod from each of them.

"But he should," Locke says. "Sarah's got a good head for business and Dad could use a fresh perspective."

An interior door opens halfway as the sheriff waves us in. "Sorry for the wait. There are a lot of moving parts here." He ushers us into his office where the walls around his metal desk are a slick beige. Three of them have windows that run from shoulder height—my shoulders, Locke's chest—to the ceiling. He gestures to two rusty-hinged folding chairs and shimmies around the desk to his own swivel chair, which whines under his weight.

"OK, so obviously I can't fill you in on all the details. The woman driving the car—"

"Have you found her family?" I ask.

"We have not."

"But you know who she was."

The trajectory of the sheriff's chin goes askew. "We know that she shot up with heroin before driving a car," he says. "And that's about it." He doesn't invite me to follow up. "Skip to—"

"Hang on," I butt in. "With her well-cared-for infant in the back seat? That doesn't make any sense."

Sheriff Dunn glowers at me. "Junkies often don't," he says. That's probably true.

"How do you know she shot up?" I ask. *I* didn't know. I thought she may have swallowed something. It's not really my field of exper-tise. Sheriff Dunn doesn't answer.

"How do you know she shot up?" Locke says.

This time Dunn does answer. Did I not just ask that same thing?

"The syringe that was found was pretty conclusive," Dunn says.

Locke is frowning. We went through that car. I didn't see a syringe. I'm betting he didn't either.

"Where was it found?" I ask. For the first time, it occurs to me that the woman's death was more than an accident. I blurt out, "Wait! Was that woman *murdered*?!"

"No. There is no indication of that. Skip to Ms. Vaughn." And that distracts me.

"Is she OK?" I ask. "The baby?"

The sheriff rubs his forehead with enough pressure to affect the shape of his eyes, but he nods that both Ms. Vaughn and the baby are fine. Then he relaxes against the back of his chair and begins to twiddle his thumbs. That's annoying. I purposefully track the sheriff's twiddling thumbs with my eyes. When he notices, he stops.

"What were they looking for at Emma's house?" Locke asks.

"That's a good question." The pointed statement comes from the doorway where Aaron's old partner, Chris Michaels, has decided to stick his towhead in.

"OK, how about this one?" Locke's voice takes on an edge. "How would anyone," he begins, "outside of the police," he pauses, "have Emma's name and address?"

Boom! Did he just call the police into question?! If he feels me ogling him, he doesn't let on.

"The same way they had Ms. Vaughn's," the sheriff says.

"Which was?" Locke gives him ample time to respond and when it's apparent he's not going to, Locke cuts to the chase. "Sheriff, just what do you need us here for?"

"We need to rule you out," Chris says. "Well...we need to rule her out." His icy blue eyes land on me.

"Rule her out for what?" Locke asks. "She was nearly obliterated by that car this morning and has done nothing but take care of its only surviving occupant ever since."

Chris makes a vague gesture. I guess it means he's unimpressed.

The sheriff addresses me. "Miss Caine, I'm told that you worked very hard on that woman. We'd like to know what stake you have in this."

I wipe my mouth with the back of my hand when he brings it up. We're trained to use a protective barrier when we do mouth-to-mouth, but I wasn't exactly prepared. I wonder how they know how hard I worked. I probably broke her ribs doing compressions.

"I just wanted to keep her here," I say.

"A woman you don't even know?" Chris asks.

"Yeah," I snap. "A human being. A *mother*."

"The diaper bag was clearly an issue of contention earlier," the sheriff says. "Was there something you were trying to find?"

I puff out a breath to tell the sheriff he's out of his mind, but that doesn't satisfy me, so I say it directly. "You are out of your mind. Of course, the bag was in contention. Your officers were keeping me from changing an infant's dirty diaper! What did you think I was trying to find? Drug money?"

I feel, rather than hear, Locke's calming shush. Perhaps drug money was an unwise choice for an unlikely example. Sheriff Dunn rests his elbows on the desk in front of him. He steeples his fingers under his chin and lifts his eyebrows in question.

"It's just too big a coincidence," Chris says. He's still looming in the doorway. We have to crane our necks to look up at him. "You two being at that exact location at the exact time of the crash."

"Chris, you know good and well why I was at that exact location on this exact morning, and if anyone should be questioned for the circumstances that put me there..." Locke sounds downright dangerous. He lets that sentence hang.

Color spreads up the officer's cheeks. He straightens out his left arm the way someone might crack their neck in a tense situation.

The sheriff checks Locke with, "Landon, do not go there."

Obviously, the three men share a history of which I am ignorant. I try to dial back the energy in the room. "OK, Locke had a reason for being at the cemetery. What can I do to put your minds at ease about me? I ride my bike over those trails almost every day, and today's trail led me to the cemetery. Anyway, somebody ran me off the road! Isn't that proof enough that I'm innocent?"

"I'd say just the opposite," Chris suggests. Locke begins to rise to his feet, but I stay him with a touch, and it occurs to me that we're acting as counterweights for one another.

Sheriff Dunn says, "Those men were looking for something they couldn't find on Ms. Vaughn or the baby. Maybe they thought you had it."

A light goes on for me. "Maybe I do." I reach into the pocket of my bicycle shorts, and in that moment, I command the attention of all three men present. I bring out the tiny bracelet. "This was caught in my hair. It belongs to the baby."

Sheriff Dunn takes the chain on the tip of a pencil, but only Chris sharpens his focus. The fingers on his right hand press into his left forearm again, at the crease in the elbow. What is up with that arm? Is he injured? Maybe *he's* a junkie. He sees me scrutinizing him and lowers his arms to his sides.

"Well, I doubt that this is what anyone's after," Dunn says. "But we'll catalogue it." He steps around me and shoulders Chris out of the room. Before the door closes, I hear him say, "I chose not to bring you in on this case for a reason."

I turn on Locke. "What was *that* about? Do you blame Chris for what happened to your brother?"

Before he can reply, a baby's cry goes up, shrill and close-by. We both jump to peer through the windows, but all we can see is part of the empty hallway. Locke's voice takes on a conspiratorial urgency.

"Do you still feel the way you did, about keeping the baby till this is sorted out?" he asks.

"Yes. But I don't know how I would do it now, even if they'd let me. I don't feel very safe going back to my apartment."

"I've been thinking about that." Locke faces me full-on. "My mom's a schoolteacher. Teachers here have automatic certification as foster parents. If she would go for it, and if Dunn would go for it, and if he could convince Child Services—"

"That's a lot of ifs," I tell him.

"Yeah but, *if*...would you foster Annabelle with me?"

"Really?"

"I don't know much about babies," he says. "You'd have to coach me. We'd probably have to agree to stay at my folks' house. Who knows for how long? You don't even know them. But they're great. Annabelle would be safe there. And you would be safe there."

My wheels start turning. What would it mean for my classes? What would it mean for my practicum students? What would it mean for— "I have an accidental cat," I say.

Locke stares at me blankly. "Well, of the many unexpected things that have come out of your mouth today, that was the most."

"And it's pregnant."

"I stand corrected," he laughs. "Bring the cat. We have a huge ranch. What do you mean *accidental*?"

"You know. It just showed up. And now it depends on me."

"There's a lot of that going around," he says. The clouds in his eyes threaten to come out in force.

"Dude, you have to stop looking at me like that," I tell him.

"Like what?"

Like you need to be kissed. "Never mind," I say aloud. "Do you think it'll work?"

Sheriff Dunn reenters the room, so Locke flashes his eyebrows to say, *Let's see.*

In a humble voice—which has resumed all the easy friendliness I've grown accustomed to—Locke says, "I'm sorry for what I insinuated before, Sheriff." Dunn makes a motion that tells him not to bother about it, and Locke nods his appreciation. "Do you really suspect either of us?"

"No, Landon." Dunn sounds weary. "Of course not. But I'm an investigator, and I have to ask. I've seen stranger things."

"I've got a stranger thing for you." Locke presents his scheme in such a convincing way, that the sheriff, amazingly, comes to accept it. He gets his mom on board, and somehow, having procured paperwork and signatures, I find my arms full of Baby Annabelle again, walking next to Landon Locke into a hot, breezy night.

4

THE LOCKE HOMESTEAD

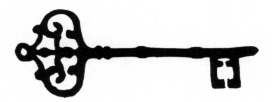

"Of *course*, you have a big, ole, beat-up pickup truck, Texas," I croon.

Locke has tied my bike down in the back, and since there's only one seat in the vehicle, a bench seat, the baby's carrier is now buckled between us.

I am trying—and failing—to stop fixating on the way the man's forearm works as he grips the steering wheel. As he casually and masculinely— How many muscles can a forearm possibly have? I make a fist and wriggle my fingers to flex my own. Definitely not as many. No, not at all the same effect.

Locke glances over to see what I'm doing, so I fold my arms and look away.

"It was my grandaddy's," he says.

"What was?"

"The…pickup truck?"

Oh yeah. That's what I'd commented on before his clever muscles befuddled me. I narrow my eyes at them.

"I have to move a lot of furniture."

He has said words, Emma. Think. Speak. What is wrong with you?!

"Is that what you do?" I ask.

Locke chuckles. "Feels like it sometimes. I make the furniture, so I have to move it."

I position myself away from his devious muscles to watch the night fall over the hills. It's like driving through ocean waves, with the moonlight and the breeze working in tandem upon the long grass. I stretch my legs out, feet on the dash, hands between my thighs. The moment my head relaxes against the seat, I feel heavy with exhaustion. "Well, we're going to have to invest in a family car now," I say.

When Locke doesn't answer, I roll my head across the seat back to find him admiring my legs. His eyes dart back to the road. "Nah," he says. A quirky grin tells me he knows he's been caught. "You look way too good stretched out in my truck."

This is the strangest day of my life. And that is saying something.

"So, how are we going to nab this accidental cat of yours?" Locke asks. This opens a new line of scheming. The police have asked us not to reenter my apartment without their assistance, but they didn't say anything about grabbing something off the porch.

"I put the cat out this morning before my ride. I'm hopeful she'll be waiting at the door to eat. And there's a crate on the porch that I borrowed the other day when I took her to get fixed."

Before Locke can ask the question that's forming, I say, "That's how I found out. Doc felt around and told me I was too late. Said she counted at least four kitten heads inside."

Locke laughs at me outright. I really like it when he does that.

"I gotta tell you, Em, there is no one I'd rather endure a horrific trauma with."

"Awww, thanks buddy," I sing. "The feeling is mutual."

One uneventful cat-napping, a few state highways, and several miles of wooden fence line later, Locke stops the truck before a massive iron gate that would have impressed even the most ostentatious cattle rancher. It extends up and over the driveway where it displays the Locke family name in prominent black letters. I lean forward to marvel at it through the windshield.

"Yeah," Locke admits. "My grandparents nearly divorced over that thing. You should have seen how much bigger Granddaddy *wanted* to make it." With that, he hops out into the beam of headlights to deal with the gate.

Never, until this moment, have I fully appreciated the real merits of back pockets on blue jeans. But more importantly, when Locke pulls us through the marquee and secures the gate behind, it feels like he shuts out all of the scary bad stuff in the world. The long gravel driveway winds through peaceful pastures and past a paddock where, even in the dark, I can make out several elephantine creatures standing in front of two large barns. I bolt upright to get a better look.

"You have longhorns!" I exclaim. "You actually do. And little donkeys alongside them. Oh my gosh. Could you *be* more Texan? I love this."

"Wait till you meet the armadillos," he says.

I know he's joking and yet I still turn my head to confirm it. Whatever that looks like on me makes him laugh again.

"I knew you were joking," I say.

"I'm not," he refutes.

"You have a herd of armadillos."

"Oh no, don't call them a herd," he rushes to say. "They get very indignant. The appropriate term is a fez."

"You have a *fez* of armadillos." I double check. Locke nods. "Shut up," I say.

Once we round the next curve, a spacious farmhouse comes into view. It has several A-frame rooflines that contrast the moonlit sky. The house is wrapped in a deck with a slanting metal roof and niches set with rustic wooden furniture, the kind you have to special order.

"Wait. Did *you* make the table and chairs?" I ask. "They're gorgeous."

Locke clunks the long lever on the steering column into park. "Yeah, Granddaddy and I made those. He said that table was my first real achievement." By the satisfaction framing his mouth, I can tell his grandaddy's praise means the world to him.

"He's the one who taught you, then?" I ask.

Locke nods. "He was a master. Seems like every family for miles owns something of his. Mom used to call me his little shadow when I was a kid. I followed him that close."

That makes me smile. I wish I'd known Locke when he was a kid. "Is he still around?" I ask.

Locke shakes his head, and there's some sadness in the move. "He died three years back. He was sick for a while."

Suddenly, Locke lunges across my lap to roll down my window. It's the old kind that you have to crank, so for the while it takes, I am, at once, amused and unnerved by his familiarity. I pound my fists against his back. "What are you doing?!" I laugh.

Once he's finished, he motions for me to notice something.

"You want me to look for—"

"Don't look," he cuts in. "Smell."

So, I sniff the air outside my window and am instantly rewarded by a scent so sweet and pervasive I try to keep inhaling past my capacity. "That is intoxicating! What is that?"

"Night-blooming jessamine." Locke reaches across me again, this time to point out a vine that's growing over a trellis in front of a vegetable garden. "Can you make out the tubular flowers? They only open at night. You can't smell them during the day."

"How? It fills up everything."

"When we're rested, I'll take you exploring. This place has lots of secrets that can only be discovered in the dark."

I'm ruminating on that offer when a suspicious thought occurs to me. "Did you just feed me a line? Do you say that to every woman you bring home?"

"What? No."

"It sounds very...romantic."

"Does it?"

"Oh, whatever, Locke. Secrets that can only be discovered in the dark?"

I know he gets my meaning when a mischievous gleam comes to play in his eyes. "Hey, if you don't want me to show you..." He opens his door, but then looks back for my response.

"I didn't say that," I mutter. And if I sound coy, it's because I'm trying to cover the sound of my heart hammering out the possibilities.

Warm light spills from the home's wide windows and falls through the front door as a slender, middle-aged woman hurries down the steps to us. Locke rises from his driver's seat into her strong embrace. Her hands press his back, then the tops of his shoulders, then his biceps, like she needs to feel the mass of him to confirm his wellbeing.

"I'm fine, Mom. I'm sorry to worry you. This is Emma."

I've walked around the hood, and now Locke's mom hugs me too. She's maybe four inches taller than I am. Sharp brown eyes. Short wavy hair.

"Welcome, Emma," she says. "I'm Ardea." She stares full at my face for a few seconds, then nods. Just the way Locke had done when he was convinced that the car hadn't harmed me.

"And the baby?" she asks.

Locke stretches across the steering wheel to release the carrier and presents its occupant, sound asleep inside. "We're calling her Annabelle," he says.

"Poor little thing."

He hands me the carrier, and his mom touches Annabelle's small hand. "What can I carry?" she asks.

"There's not much else," Locke says. "Sheriff Dunn told us to wait to go inside Emma's place. But we *did* manage..." He disappears around the side of the pickup and reappears with the pet crate. "An accidental cat."

"Yeah." I cringe an apology. "And she's going to have kittens any day now."

Ardea claps her hands once and barks out a laugh that endears me to her forever.

"Thank you, Mrs. Locke," I say. I wave in a circular motion. "For all this."

I've barely finished the words when I have to blink against the unexpected sting of tears. I swallow them down. Despite all the blathering I did earlier at the cemetery, I hate to cry in front of people. And their moms.

"You're alright," Locke says against my head. It's the same voice he'd used to shush me with, back at the police station. The one I can feel more than can hear.

"Come inside, you two," his mom says. "Sarah's gone to the store for all things baby, and dinner's waiting for you."

Somehow, I move forward. But I'm thinking about what Locke said earlier. It *is* like we were forged together today. I mean, who else could possibly understand the impact of everything that's happened? What if he hadn't been there? Where would that leave me right now, instead of pacing across the front path, up the steps, and into the door of Locke's childhood home?

"That's Landon and Aaron at their first swim meet," Ardea says. "The boys were probably five years old."

I'm visually grazing on a shelf of photos, when I stop at the one she means. Two young boys who are mirror images in team shorts, ready to dive in from the edge of a pool, identical expressions of concentration from behind goggles.

"Landon was always the better swimmer," his mom adds. "Aaron liked games where he could attack people." Locke makes a face to say it's true and hands me a photo from higher up.

"This is Grandaddy," he says. "That's us at the woodshop, here on the property where I work."

A door to the side of the kitchen opens, and Sarah comes in from the garage. "Hello, hello!" she calls. Locke disappears out the way Sarah came in.

"Hi, Emma. You made it. Ooohh, is that the baby?!" Sarah ditches her purse and rushes to the carrier to unhook the sleeping infant.

"Sarah Locke, do not wake that child up," her mom chastises. "She needs rest." Her voice goes soft as Sarah lifts the saggy bundle. "God love it," she says, and the two adore Annabelle from her tiny fingernails to her eyelashes and her button nose.

Locke returns with his arms full of grocery bags, which he unloads onto the counter. "Where's Dad?" he asks.

There's a small hesitation before Mrs. Locke answers. "He went to the cemetery."

Sarah glances at her brother and away again.

"I'd hoped he'd be back by now," their mom says. She checks the clock on the wall.

"This is a big anniversary for you, Mrs. Locke," I say. "I hope we're not too much of a burden right now."

She visibly bolsters herself. "You and this baby are just what we need. Something to focus on. Some real way to fight the bad in this world."

Locke catches my eye and winks. When he returns his attention to the items his sister has brought, he says, "Sarah, there are enough tiny clothes here to dress all the children in the Lone Star State." He flicks through the bags. "Why in the world would a baby need four pairs of shoes? She can't even walk." He picks up the four pairs, one at a time in an exaggerated arc, and exhibits them altogether in his large hand.

Sarah snatches the shoes in question. "Our little Annabelle is a fashionista," she says.

Locke digs around again. "Um, I think she's too young for these." I cover my mouth when Locke holds up a lacy purple bra and matching panties to himself. He slides one foot across the wooden floor in what I assume is a tango move.

"I got those for Emma, idiot," Sarah says. Locke's overwrought teasing face goes blank. He clears his throat and quickly tucks the intimates back into the bag. Sarah cackles. "There are some other things too, Emma," she says. "If Landon can keep his hands off of them. I knew you weren't allowed to go home for clothes. I hope they fit."

The mirth is interrupted when a quick flash of blue cuts through the night. A shiny white pickup—yes, even the police car is a pickup—stops out front, dwarfing Locke's. Mrs. Locke's fingers fly to her lips. She murmurs something I can't decipher.

"It happened like this," Sarah says up close. "When we were told Aaron was gone." She deposits Annabelle into my arms and peers out the window. "It's Chris," she says. "He's got Dad."

Locke gently staves off his mother's attempt for the door, and steps out ahead of her as Aaron's old partner exits the vehicle. "Chris?" he asks.

Instead of answering, Chris shoots him an uncomfortable smile and walks around the truck to open the passenger side. When he catches sight of me, up on the deck, his eyes linger for a moment. There's no warmth in them. He helps a highly intoxicated Mr. Locke to his feet and braces him until he can stand on his own. Ardea bustles to her husband to lead him inside.

I don't quite know what to do with myself. I want to give Mr. and Mrs. Locke their space, so while Locke talks to Chris out by the truck, I just sort of linger. Annabelle and I look out over the vegetable garden to where fireflies are beaming their hellos, and night-blooming flowers are wafting their scent. "I bet there are watermelons in there," I tell her. "What do you think? Have you ever tasted one? They're very good."

The cicadas are roaring tonight, alternately from the left to the right, like a crowd of swaying fanatics at an outdoor concert. I missed stuff like that when I was deaf. But there were other sounds I was grateful not to hear. Maybe Locke is hearing some of them now.

He raises his voice to thank the officer and knocks on the roof of the truck in goodbye. "Make sure to lock the gate," he calls. A hand waves from the driver's window. Then the truck's wheels make the gravel whisper, and Locke watches it go, thumbs in pockets, until it rounds the bend, and his shoulders slump forward. What must he be thinking? He angles his left foot toward the house, then his body to follow it, when he sees me. And our new baby.

Oh yes. We're still here. I feel like I should apologize.

I'm glad he doesn't try to smile. I like it when faces convey what's true.

Once we meet in the middle, Locke says, "Apparently, Chris found my dad at Aaron's grave, where he had been toasting Aaron's memory. So, Chris joined him, though I think Chris may have been secretly pouring his own drinks directly onto the grave." As an afterthought he adds, "I was hoping to get that gravestone fixed before Dad saw it."

"Locke, I feel terrible to intrude upon you and your family right now. If you'll just point me to a room, I'll take Annabelle there, and we can make ourselves scarce."

"No, I don't want you to be scarce," he says. "I'm just sorry you had to—"

I slip my hand into his. I don't even mean to do it. He stops talking to observe it, and a curious expression crosses his face. Maybe the line across his forehead eases. "I don't want you to be scarce," he says again.

I manage a small, "'K," and he squeezes my hand. He holds it all the way back to the door.

Inside, Mr. and Mrs. Locke have retired to their bedroom. Sarah is shaking a bottle of infant formula over the kitchen sink and when we join her, she gives her brother a look of concern.

"Dad was mumbling something about Sheriff Dunn just now," she says. "I don't think Chris is doing anything to quell his animosity. Or you either, for that matter. The good guys didn't get Aaron killed, Landon."

"I know," Locke says. He thumps his long body against the kitchen island and studies his hands.

"Yeah, well, Dad doesn't. He can't let it go. I think he needs help."

Locke nods. "Pastor Ian asked about him last Sunday. He asked about all of us, but I told him basically what you just said. He wants Dad to make an appointment." To me, Locke says, "Ian's a grief counselor at our church. He lost an adult child too, years ago."

"Do you think Dad will go?" Sarah asks.

"I'll get him to go. I'll take care of it."

Sarah is visibly relieved. She tightens the silicone nipple to the bottle and, on the way to reclaim the baby, she kisses her brother on the cheek.

Locke smooths his forehead with the heels of both hands and heaves a sigh. I roost beside him on the island.

"These are the times I miss him," he says. "Aaron and I would have handled this together. Just like we handled Grandaddy's care."

"You must feel halved." Full-on cloud eyes answer me. "I'll help you," I volunteer. "If I can."

With a small smile returning, Locke angles his head down at me. "You just gonna step right into my mess?" he asks.

"Usually, I like to jump both feet for maximum splash." I butt him with my head. "You may have noticed."

"You are oddly comforting," he says.

I breathe out a laugh. "I get that a lot. Mainly just the *oddly* part."

Locke scans the room. "You hungry?" he asks. "Looks like Mom made pasta."

I'm really not, but I follow his lead and make a plate. Neither of us have eaten today. You'd think we'd dive right in, but our motions are slow, and we just sort of push things around.

"You two look beat," Sarah says. "Let me keep the baby tonight, and you can—"

"Yes." Locke accepts his sister's offer before she completes it. Then he looks for me to agree.

"Yes," I say. "Thank you, Sarah."

After a few more quiet minutes of not eating anything, Locke says, "So, you have a choice. There's a guest suite on the far side of the house that would act as your own apartment. Or you can have Aaron's old room, on this side of the house, right across from mine. I might be able to—"

"I want to be with you," I interrupt. "I mean, I'd feel better if you were close by. I just—"

"It's done," he says without making me explain.

We collect the cat, inside of her crate, along with her litter, and all the toiletries and clothing that Sarah has gotten for me, and we haul them upstairs.

"This one's Aaron's," Locke says. He points with the pet crate into the room his brother grew up using. "And I'll be right there." He motions with his head across the hall.

The lamp is on in his room, and I can see swim trophies and ribbons lining two long shelves on the wall. While Locke ducks into Aaron's room to unload all the things, I walk into his.

"It smells like you," I call to him. "The wood scent that hangs about you, and...something else." I close my eyes. When I open them, he's before me.

"Chlorine?" he suggests.

I make a gesture, first to my mouth, and then as if I'm pillowing my head.

"Is that sign language? What does it mean?"

"Home." I reach around to hug him, and he pulls me close with a hum of comfort that acts upon me like medicine.

"Hey, what did you sign earlier?" he asks. "After you left me the voicemail at the cemetery?"

I cast my eyes around in a show of ignorance. "I forgot."

"Liar," he says, but he's still holding me when he says it.

I back out of his arms and change the subject. "That bed looks like one a body could sink into," I say. And it really does. It's already turned back with puffy pillows lying flat and a weighted blanket that I bet is soft as can be.

Locke follows my eyes. "Oh, no way," he says. "That one's mine. Go get your own."

I laugh through a yawn. "OK. Goodnight."

"Goodnight, Em. Come get me if you need me. Or just call out. I'll leave the door open."

5

PLAYING HOUSE

I sleep later than I intend. When I wake up in Aaron Locke's old bedroom, because The Accidental Cat is kneading me with its paws, I can't recall how the space is laid out. I'm lying upon a king-sized bed with a thick oak headboard. The mattress is so high off the ground, that I did actually have to *climb* into it last night. I feel like Goldilocks, but instead of three bears, I'm exploring a home of tall Texas folk.

There's a bookcase built into the wall to my right. The roofline slopes to meet it. It houses mostly knick-knacks and decorative volumes, not what you'd expect, had a teenage boy still occupied the space.

On the far side of the room, next to the door, is a table, really a desk, but for giants, and a high-back leather chair. To my left: a closet, a recessed nook with a mirror, and my own bathroom—which is nice, since I'm residing with a man I met less than twenty-four hours ago. And his whole family.

I wonder if that bonded-for-life thing has run its course for him. I press my stomach because the thought of that makes me sick. I'd allowed myself to kind of imagine playing house with him. Seemed like a great idea yesterday, when I was afraid for my safety and tired to the point of delirium. I shouldn't have hugged him. I recall the sound he exhaled when I did, though, and make a noise of my own just thinking about it.

I creep to the window to open the wooden blinds on a sunny summer pasture full of wildflowers. Two white ponies are playing chase. It's probably already hot out there, but my room is cool and quiet. Closer to the house is a pool with full-length lanes and someone swimming laps. Someone powerful, by the speed of the laps. Only one man I know with a reach that long.

I took a shower last night before bed, and now I quickly dress, thankful for Sarah's sense of style and her eye for what sizes I wear. I pick out a form-fitting, V-neck T-shirt in the perfect shade of blue to make my eyes pop. And shorts—quite *short* shorts—in white denim, that accentuate my legs. It's never a bad thing to make one's legs appear as long as possible when one is as short as I am. Is it wrong to be aware that they're worth showing off?

When I get downstairs, I find Sarah, head and shoulders collapsed upon the dining table, and her hand around a mug of coffee. Ardea is moving about the kitchen with Annabelle on her hip. The whole downstairs smells delicious. Bacon and eggs. Biscuits.

"Good morning," I greet them. "I slept later than I meant to. I'm sorry. How can I help?"

"I do not blame you," Ardea says. She hands over Annabelle to reach into the oven. "You were exhausted. Grab a cup of coffee." Ardea points her head toward the counter. "Mugs are by the coffee maker."

"How have you prepared all this while holding a baby?"

"Oh, you should have seen me with newborn twins! I was a cyclone."

I snort in appreciation, then examine Locke's sister. "Sarah, did you get any sleep at all?"

Sarah grunts without lifting her head.

"I'll take over from here," I assure her.

Hugging Annabelle to myself, I steal a glance outside to where the swimmer has come to sit on the side of the pool. Locke. Breathing hard. Without a shirt. Locke's chest. Locke's shoulders. The muscles that run down the sides of Locke. I become inexplicably cross and concede that it's probably a defense mechanism. He's breathtaking. Disappointment floods in behind the aggravation as I acknowledge the fact that he won't feel the same way about me this morning that he did last night.

With a towel tied around his waist, the fortress that is Locke enters the house before I've forgiven him. My glare does nothing to wilt his large mood. He fixes me with narrow eyes and says, "We're not going to have to review proper greeting etiquette every day, are we?" He comes to stand too close. He has to know how his proximity affects people. Women. Me. I let out an irritated huff that makes him laugh.

Locke extends a hand, which I survey and then begrudgingly accept. He uses it to pull me closer still so that he can bend down and bump my cheekbone with his nose. "Good morning, *Legs*," he says. I can't help the beginning of a smile that cuts through my effort to remain standoffish. He seems to take it as a win.

"Landon, stop dripping on the guests, and go put some clothes on," his mom chides.

After a lovely breakfast, in which, to Locke's remarkable tolerance, I learn more about his boyhood than any man should have to endure, Locke and I sit on the couch to figure out how to approach our schedule. As part of the fostering agreement, we're supposed to take Annabelle to a doctor's appointment, and Locke insists that we both go. He punctuates his insistence by calling me *Legs*.

"Stop," I say curtly.

"What?"

"*Landon* Locke."

"Yes, Legs?"

"Stop it!" I laugh. "I'm serious. I'm not going to co-parent this child with you if you call me that."

"But they're so pretty," he says. He leans over to try to see more of them, though I have them tucked underneath myself. He gives up on that. "Can I call you *Hair*?" When he grabs for a strand, I slap his hand away.

"You're such a doofus," I tell him. "Hey. Have you seen your dad this morning? How is he?"

"Hungover, I imagine. It's not like him to drink that much."

"Grief does funny things to people."

"Maybe." Locke lowers his voice and scans the hall to make sure we're alone. "He hasn't been himself for a long time. Really, since back when Grandaddy was diagnosed. He stopped being around. He's always been an early riser—he has to be—the barns need attention. But he used to come back for lunch and stuff, you know? It's not like he doesn't have other people helping him. He can take breaks, and he used to. Now, even when he *is* around, he's still absent."

I watch Locke brace the back of his head and think of the way he promised Sarah to get their dad to counseling. He's lost as much as any of them, but his family looks to him to hold things together.

"You've had to become the acting patriarch," I note.

Locke's eyes, downcast at first, make the trek to mine and away again. "I guess I have."

"How do you keep moving?" I ask. "How do you stay available to everybody?"

A robust sigh tells me he doesn't know. "How does anybody?" He stands to pace the room.

"Not everybody *does*." I reposition the baby, who has begun to fidget. The image of my dad's orange taillights blazes in my mind. I'd kept hoping that the brake lights would ignite too, that he'd come to his senses and turn the car around. I'd wanted it so hard; I can see the three-point turn in my mind as if it's a memory. I don't know how it can still reduce me to that fifteen-year-old kid and make me feel the dread I felt back then.

Locke has stopped pacing and he's eyeing me. "I'm sorry I'm such a downer," he says. "I didn't used to be."

"Are you kidding me?" I scoff.

He waits for clarification. I'm not sure what else to say. I'm not about to start gushing about how incredibly compelling, and witty, and noble, and attractive I find him. It makes my expression comically hard. "You shine through, Locke," I manage.

Probably because it sounds like I think he's being thick on purpose, he says, "I can't tell if you truly find me annoying or if you kind of dig me."

"Good," I say, brightly. "Can we take this child to the doctor now?"

I stand with Annabelle, but seeing Locke lacking his usual swagger, I soften. "Come here," I beckon. When he's close enough, I stand on tiptoe to lift my face to him, and he bends submissively so that I can kiss his cheek. His response is a dimple where I've kissed.

Seeing that, I press my thumb to it and mutter, "How are you even real? Locke, if you didn't occasionally get sucked into the vacuum of all you've lost, you wouldn't be human. You're not a downer. At all." I resist the urge to roll my eyes. "You're the most charismatic person I know. People rally to you. You make things happen."

Locke seems gratified, if unconvinced. "You know this after one day."

My hand rises and falls to say, *how could I not?* "You had the police taking orders from you yesterday, breaking their own protocol. You inexplicably enabled us to foster this baby. Oh. And let us not forget that after knowing you for—what, like, eight hours?—you convinced me to *move in with you.*" I over-emphasize the last phrase.

My affirmation overtakes Locke's mouth and puckers his lips. Like a pomegranate. Like a ripe, red— I realize I'm biting my own lip, and I raise my eyes to find him staring. I promptly tug my lip out of my teeth and drop my head. But when I feel his fingers under my chin, I allow him to guide me back.

"Thank you," he says.

I've given him something he needed. I'm glad of it. It occurs to me that among all his great losses, maybe he feels lost himself.

"Don't mention it," I say. "Let's get out of here."

"OK." He claps once and searches around. "What all do we need?"

"Yeah, so, diaper bag, there." I point to the bag by the couch. "And the cradle part of the car seat." Locke procures both items. "I think that's it?" I say. We stride to the entryway where I manage to open the door without dropping the baby.

"Does this count as our first date?" Locke asks.

"No. I do truly find you annoying." The quip dies on my lips when Locke knocks the door shut, braces it, and steps up against my back, effectively trapping me between himself and the wall. There's no room to turn.

He gets down to my ear. I can feel his breath on the side of my neck when he says, "I'm not so sure that you do."

You know that feeling you get in your middle when the roller-coaster plummets? That's what's happening to my insides right now. Why do I have such a visceral reaction to this man's proximity? When Locke swings the door open with a casual, "After you," I have to re-train my feet.

At the doctor's office, I feel completely inept. The nurse asks so many questions, rapid-fire, that I must ask her to repeat herself more than once. Can the baby roll over from her stomach to her back, or from her back to her stomach? I don't know. Can the baby raise herself onto her arms? I don't know. Does she look for a dropped object? Maybe? Does she imitate sounds? Not that I've noticed. Does she turn toward a sudden or new sound? Sorry. I keep glancing at Locke for guidance, but he keeps shrugging.

"We'll have to look for those things," he tells the nurse. "We only just now received custody."

The doctor is in less of a hurry than the nurse. He listens to Annabelle's heart and lungs and prods around on her belly. "She seems strong and healthy to me," he concludes. "She's around seven months old?"

"That's my guess," I say. "But we don't know for sure."

He asks about her vaccinations, but of course, we're ignorant about that too.

"Hopefully, the sheriff will be able to tell us more soon."

"Well, while you have custody," the doctor advises, "let her lie on both her tummy and her back, and offer her a variety of baby-safe toys for stimulation. I'd like to see her sitting up on her own, at least for a few moments, and turning herself over. But all babies have their own timing. Do you know how long you'll keep her?"

"We're not just going to give her away," I spout. "She doesn't have anybody." How could he think that?

"No, I'm asking if you've been given any sort of a timeline. Sometimes there are clear parameters set."

"Oh. No. We don't."

My dad used to say it was the orange hair that made me prone to fiery reactions. He was amused by it. Until he wasn't.

"Where to now, Legs?" Locke punches the down button on the elevator. "Want to try to nab some things from your place?"

I listen to Locke's end of the phone conversation enough to know that Sheriff Dunn is going to send officers to assist us at my place. They still don't know the identity of the woman driver, and they have no more information about where the baby will end up.

When we pull up to the apartment, Officer Chris Michaels is coming out the front door.

"That was fast," Locke says.

"Is he allowed to just go into my apartment like that?"

Locke throws the truck into park and nods his head in greeting. When we get out, there's an awkward delay before Chris says, "It's been tossed."

"My *place*?" I say. I push past him to find my belongings scattered all over the floor and hanging out of drawers. Papers are littered beneath the desk. Books are knocked from the shelves. Not even my bathroom toiletries have escaped inspection.

"Is anything missing?" Chris asks.

"I don't know, Chris," I answer testily. "How would I know that yet?" I'm upset to the point that I can hardly investigate. I find my weekend bag and begin to stuff it with essentials and whatever is piled around them. Honestly. My swimsuit? My underwear? Ew. Who had their hands on my stuff?

Chris displays my Social Security card and my passport. I don't know how long he's been holding them. "Where do these belong?" he asks. I rake them out of his grasp and search for my file box, which I find overturned behind the trash can. I replace the documents alongside my diplomas.

"I don't guess anything's missing," I say. "I don't own anything that valuable."

Saying that makes me walk to the dresser where there's a small jewelry box. I lift out a simple silver chain that holds a circular diamond pendant and fasten it around my neck. "It's from the engagement ring my dad gave to my mom," I explain. "It's not that valuable, but, you know, just to me."

"Is your mom dead?" Chris asks.

"No, but the marriage is." I catch a reflection of myself in the mirror. "Anyway," I say, waving it off.

"*Feeling* bonded for life is not the same thing as *being* bonded for life," Locke says. He's bouncing Annabelle to keep her happy, but he's connecting this to what I told him at the cemetery.

"Yeah," I agree.

Having piled the rest of my belongings without putting them neatly away, I frown at the mess. I hate to think about coming back to it, especially when I have a feeling I won't be in a happy frame of mind when I do come back. But what can be done about it? It's going to take hours to straighten it up.

"Don't you have a laptop?" Chris asks. "Or a tablet?"

Instead of answering, I spin around to re-search my office space, but then recall that— "It's in my office on campus. I rode out from there yesterday."

"And your car?"

I stop to consider Chris. "You have put a lot of thought into what I own and where it is," I say.

"It's sort of what I do," he replies. "I'm trying to make sure everything's accounted for."

"I don't have a car."

Another two officers enter the small apartment. "Miss Caine? What happened here? You were supposed to wait for us." Upon seeing Chris, the officers pause.

Chris motions them in.

I peer from officer to officer. "Wow, Sheriff Dunn must be really concerned about me," I say. "Does he always spare so much man power for things like this?"

Both of the new officers seem to be waiting to hear what Chris has to say, but Chris remains quiet.

"Well, do you think whoever did this is done with me now?" I ask.

Then, just like I'd snapped at him earlier, Chris snaps, "I don't know, Emma. How would I know that yet?"

I cross my arms and analyze Chris Michaels for such a long time he finally takes an agitated step in my direction. At the same moment, Locke bumps into me. "Sorry, Legs! The baby's driving the bus. She says it's lunchtime."

I round on him. "Locke, I swear, if you don't stop calling me Legs, you're going to need the police for your own protection." I launch myself toward the door in time to see the other two officers jerk their eyes up from my legs. "Oh, for heaven's sake," I mutter. I stomp out to the pickup under the weight of my enormous weekend bag and slam myself inside.

I guess Locke makes our goodbyes. Once he rejoins me in the truck, I help him clip the baby into her car seat, grumbling. "Chris is obnoxious."

"Yeah, he's never been my favorite person. He and Aaron part-nered well, though." The parking brake thunks as Locke releases it.

"What do you think he had to do with Aaron's death?"

"What? No. I don't—" Both his face and his body are open to me when he answers. I think he believes what he's telling me. Even though it's not true.

"You absolutely do," I say.

Most guys would be put off by such a challenge, but Locke bites his lip in consideration.

"Why's he so police-y with me?" I ask. "I think *he's* the one who tossed my place." Once I've said it, questions arise. Why would Chris do that? What was he looking for? Can he justify breaking into my private residence? "I know," I say, as if we've weighed the ludicrous questions aloud, "but I *do* think it."

Locke surprises me by saying, "I do too."

"Do you really?" I look at him in alarm. "'Because I don't know if I really do. I mean, no. He's a policeman."

Locke shrugs his brow to say, *Who knows?*

Back at home, we're the only two around. We sit at the Lockes' family table to make short work of leftovers for a late lunch. I free a grape from the chicken salad with my fingers and bite into it. "I feel like I should be paying into this little venture," I say. "Chipping in for groceries and diapers or something."

Locke sits on the front of his chair and leans forward on his elbows. "No, I got it. I'm the one who moved you into my parents' house. Anyway, I think the state compensates foster parents a bit, don't they?"

"Yeah, but not enough to foster parent the foster parent." I find another grape.

"Don't think another thing about it," he says, over his fork. "You don't eat enough to."

"Well, let me make your birthday dinner, then. It's coming up, right?" I know it is, because of the birthdate on his twin's gravestone. "Do you already have plans?"

"I hadn't really thought about it. Last year was miserable. Aaron had just died, and it was the first time since we were like—sixteen—that we hadn't wasted the day on a James Bond marathon. I mistakenly allowed some of our buddies to take me out, and it occurred to me, in the middle of a crowd of people, which was *awesome*—" He adds the last with a meaningful glance to emphasize the sarcasm. "That for the first time in my life, I'd turned a year older, but my brother had not. I'd left him behind."

Locke sounds forlorn. I want to reach for him. Instead, I say, "OK, yeah, I'm gonna cook dinner for you, and then we're gonna make out all night." He coughs out a surprised laugh, so I continue. "Or you know…play board games. Whatever you want."

"You don't have to make dinner. Let me take you out."

"You're scared about the making out. Yeah, that can be intimidating. We don't have to do that."

"You talk a big game, little woman," he says.

"I'd *like* to make you dinner. Who do you want to include? Family? Friends?"

"That's a little kinky for me." When it's clear that I'm not tracking Locke says, "To make out with friends and family around."

"Right," I laugh. "Alone, then."

"Yeah, let's just hang out. No friends. No family. No baby." Locke tilts his head to say, "No offense," to the baby. "We can do it at my house. That would be great. Thank you."

"I'm gonna bake you some macarons instead of cake. Is that OK?"

Locke acquiesces with a bow. "Certainly. Though, I'm not sure what they are."

"Oh, they're amazing! Not the horrible coconut kind, you know. The real French kind with fluffy egg whites and buttercream filling. Barely crisp on the outside, and chewy in the middle."

"And you know how to do this, because…?"

"My mom studied at a pastry school in Chicago, before my sister and I were born. She taught us all kinds of delicious tricks. Soufflés and meatier breads with a crunchy crust. Ooo, and the *best* Chicago style pizza, stuffed to bursting with tomatoes and sausage."

"I think I just fell in love with you."

"Took you longer than most," I joke.

I rise from the table and motion for Locke's empty plate, before I realize he's no longer bantering with me. His eyes aren't smiling either, and before I know what's going to come out of my mouth, I'm saying, "I think I'd do about anything in the world to see you smile."

I get to, with that. "Did I say something wrong?" I ask.

"No," he assures me.

"Then, what happened?"

"What do you mean?"

I narrow my eyes at him and take the opportunity to play Gestapo. Drawing myself up, I slam the plates down on the table. Locke starts. "That was harder than I intended," I say, barely breaking from my newly acquired persona. I stalk over to Locke's chair where I seize both its arms and loom over him menacingly—well, as menacingly as a five-foot-four-inch woman with wild orange hair is capable. I narrow my eyes again, up close to his face so that he gets the message. "There are things about me you should know," I say.

Now he has returned to full humor and his eyes land on my lips. "Like what?" he asks.

"I am a natural-born interrogator," I inform him. "A human lie detector."

"I thought you were a professor of sign language."

I smack the arms of his chair and at the same time I spit, "Forget about that! It's a farce. You have one chance—and one chance only— to come clean about—"

I don't get to finish, because a struggle ensues. Well, it's not really that much of a struggle for Locke, to be honest. It takes him about three and a half seconds to wrestle me onto his lap. and then he gloats. "With such a job description, I'd think you'd invest more time in your combat skills."

I throw my head back to laugh, but it stalls out, because—oooh my. He is just...right there. "Shows what you know," I say. "You've played right into my hand. Now I can read the information directly from your eyes."

Locke glares at me like we're competitors about to spar. "Be my guest," he says.

To be so easygoing, the man can get intense. And to be so intense, I am suddenly flustered.

"No, don't go," he says. He grips my thigh to keep me from swinging off his leg, which I've begun to do. "I'll tell you."

With renewed Gestapo hardness, I say, "I knew it!"

He snickers through his next words. "It's nothing. It's stupid. You were joking about people falling in love with you, and I—I just didn't like the idea of there being other men in your life." Embarrassment makes him timid like a boy, and he shrugs.

"There's no one," I say. "I don't even believe in that stuff."

6

THE BALANCING ACT

"Em, hand me the baby, or hand me the key."

The last five days have been a rather clumsy balancing act, typified by the fact that right now I'm fumbling to unlock my office door using one hand and an infant. Locke has been driving me to the college every day and then caring for Annabelle until I can get home. He walks me across campus on the premise that he simply enjoys my company and, while that may be true, I know he's not comfortable leaving me alone outside the farm—not that I'm complaining. The memory of the men in their noisy car still spooks me, and the encounter at my apartment with Officer Chris Michaels has done nothing but make me question who the good guys are.

Only after I finish at school does Locke head to the woodshop to get his own work done. That's when I take over with Annabelle. Hours that I would have devoted to grading. Or biking. Or breathing. And the next thing I know, it's bedtime.

On top of all that, every morning I hold my breath until Locke surprises me by being just as kind, just as involved, just as present as the day before.

"How do people do this without a partner?" I ask. "Single parents are my new heroes." I give Annabelle over to Locke's capable embrace and, once I'm free to use both hands, my door swings open easily. I float those hands outward in a show of accomplishment.

"Before we met," I confide, "I would have said that my days were full to brimming. But now that I'm co-responsible for keeping a baby human alive, I realize that I had all kinds of discretionary time before."

"And sleep," Locke yawns. He rubs his eyes. I swear the dark circles only make the man sexier. I'm lingering. "What thought is behind *that* look?" he asks.

I don't tell him. Instead, I say, "Thank you for this. I know you're having to work late and you're getting behind on your orders. I hope you don't regret it. It won't be for much longer."

"No, I've just had to make the conscious decision to submit to the baby's needs. If I try to get any work done while she's around, it ends in frustration. You know how yesterday I took her with me to present samples to the client?"

"The one who found Annabelle adorable."

"Right. Well, what I didn't tell you is that I lost track of which sample the client chose." Locke pauses for dramatic effect. "Twice."

I laugh. But only because I share his overwhelm. Work and baby are nearly incompatible.

"Maybe I'll post a request for an upperclassman to help us out," I suggest. "That way I could keep Annabelle here with me and you could have your normal work hours back." *And maybe we could see more of each other in the evenings*, I don't add. What I do add is, "You know what? They should offer this in sex ed. A real baby you have to foster. Students would wait till their thirties at the least. I know I'm going to."

Locke cocks his head in question.

"Wait to have kids," I rush to explain. "Not to—you know."

He snorts out a laugh. "Thanks for the clarification."

"Shut up," I say.

His sweet wink and his, "See you after work," stay with me. Now, an hour later, I'm still envisioning His Handsomeness sauntering away when the strobe light above my desk flashes to let me know I have a visitor. A visitor who has chosen to use the light button instead of knocking.

I open the door to find a smartly dressed woman and a young man with strawberry blonde hair. Her son? A parent couldn't already be upset with me about something, could they? The semester just started.

Not much gets past this woman. I can tell that right away. She reminds me of an eagle. Her sharp eyes do not care whether I approve of her or not. She's summing me up the way I'm summing her up. That's when she moves to offer her hand, and I notice the butt of a concealed firearm underneath her blazer, alongside a badge.

"Dr. Caine?" she asks. Before I can answer, the young man signs what the woman has said. He's her interpreter. She thinks I'm deaf.

I sign, *Yes.*

"I'm Detective Wilkins with the Texas State Police."

The interpreter is quick, and he doesn't insert himself into the conversation. Just relays what's being said and then passes my message back verbally.

What can I do for you? I sign.

"I'd like to have a word." Detective Wilkins motions to my office, and I step back to allow her to enter. She peruses every surface of the room in one smooth sweep. The office is small, but there's seating for all of us, and I wave her to an area where the interpreter can sit beside her.

The interpreter signs to clarify whether he actually *should* sit, and I indicate that he should. *Try to take the same position and attitude your client takes*, I sign. *I want to be able to see you both. Makes for a more seamless translation.*

Detective Wilkins looks to the young man to tell her what I've signed.

"You and I can both sit here," he says. "I was making sure that, as an interpreter, I was supposed to do that." The kid's enthusiasm is endearing. He's not really a kid. He's probably not much younger than I am. I wonder how he even came to be the interpreter here, and why they think I need one.

"Dr. Caine, it has come to our attention that you recently moved from Michigan."

I watch the interpreter. He's doing great.

Surely you don't visit every person who moves from out of state, I sign.

"No, ma'am. That's true. You're staying with the Lockes? You know them well?"

Does this have to do with the woman who died at the cemetery?

The interpreter's eyes go a little wide, but he relays my question without comment.

"Sure, we can jump to that," the detective says. "Tell me about your involvement with the woman. Who set up the meeting?"

We weren't meeting. I didn't even know her. Why follow up about this? I've told the county sheriff the same thing.

The detective doesn't answer. The young man thinks she hasn't heard or hasn't understood, because he begins to repeat what I've signed, but then he forgets some of it and has to ask me to re-sign it. I wave him off. I know that the detective has heard every word. I saw the way that, even though her eyes remained on me, her head tilted toward him while he spoke.

She remains silent. I suppose she's hoping the vacuum of interaction will make me uncomfortable enough to start spewing information in a mindless way that will reveal something. But I don't have anything to reveal. Anyway, if she only knew how at home I am with such tactics... I could play this game all day. I enjoy mental chess.

After about twenty seconds go by, the young interpreter begins to fidget. Finally, he blurts out, "Am I supposed to be doing something?!" I work to suppress a smile. The detective is frowning at me now and I'm sure she suspects what is true, that I can hear the interpreter's voice as well as she can. I practically see her jotting my reaction down in a small, Sherlocky notepad. Which is sort of what I'm doing to her too.

At length, she says, "OK, let's say you didn't know her." With a sigh of relief, the interpreter begins to sign again. "But did she give you anything? Anything at all?"

Nothing.

"A message? An envelope?"

I shake my head.

"Then why are you taking care of her baby?"

I throw my hands out before signing, *Because it's the right thing to do?*

The interpreter throws his hands out too and voices my statement as if it's a question.

Good job.

The sheriff doesn't know the woman's identity yet, I continue. *Until he can find next-of-kin, the baby needs someone to care for her.*

A split second. The detective's eyes shift for a split second when she hears that the sheriff doesn't know the woman's identity.

Is that not the case? I ask.

Detective Wilkins ignores that. "The woman was still alive when you found her," she says. "Could she have said something that, pardon me, but that you couldn't hear? Perhaps to Mr. Locke?"

The interpreter uses a sign with which I'm unfamiliar. I ask what it means. He finds another way to make me understand.

"That is not what she said!" I exclaim out loud, and I'm laughing. "Where did you learn to sign that?"

He blushes, but he doesn't have time to respond, because the detective has just confirmed what she must have been mulling over for a few minutes now, and she rounds on him. "Why did you make me think she needed an interpreter?"

He shrugs. "I need the practice. I need it bad. My examination for certification is coming up."

"This is not a game," the detective barks. "This is important police business. It could have overarching ramifications on a huge operation. I could have you arrested."

The young man clamps his mouth shut and stares through round eyes.

"Stop," I say. I feel bad for the guy. "I'll tell you what you want to know. Out loud."

"He has to go," the detective spits. She points to the door. The young man drags his feet out of my office with his head hung and offers me a look of apology from underneath his eyelids.

"Come find me Monday," I tell him. When the door closes, I say to Detective Wilkins, "The only thing I know from my encounter with the woman is that she loved her baby very much. She mostly spoke Spanish and, even with that, she was fighting to stay lucid. It was slurred. She lost control of her mobility within minutes."

I think about how hard the woman tried to communicate with us, more to Locke really than to me. "I do wish I knew what she was trying to tell us. She was desperate. It was sad."

The detective is good at her job. Her line of questioning is straight, and she doesn't display much of her internal reaction. Except that just then, when I spoke about the woman's struggle, she looked pained. I think it was more personal than the natural empathy one woman might have for another.

"Did either of you handle the needle?" she asks.

"There was no needle."

"There is an empty hypodermic needle in evidence."

"Where was it found?"

"Why do you ask?"

"Because we went all through that car, and we didn't see a needle. I'd like to be sure that the woman injected herself. I'd hate to think that someone did it for her and she was desperately trying to escape. She didn't even take her foot off the gas."

Detective Wilkins surely knows where the needle was found. She doesn't tell me, though. She takes a moment to text someone. Then another moment to be silent. I think she's deciding if she should ask the thing she has in mind. She peers at me more intently now and in a lower register she says, "How well did you know Locke?"

"I only met him that day."

"*Aaron* Locke. How well did you know Aaron?"

This is the crux of the matter. I don't know why, but I know that, for her, it is.

"What was he working on?" I ask.

"Please answer the question."

"I never got the chance to meet Aaron," I say. "But you did, didn't you?"

She says, "You say you met his brother for the first time on that day, and yet you've been living with him since then. Do I have that right?"

I want to be a smart-ass. I want to say, "Have you *seen* the man?!" But I don't. I say, "Yes. Well, there was the baby to take care of, and I couldn't do that without his mother's umbrella status as a foster parent."

Detective Wilkins frowns again. She's got a great frown. It's quite expressive without wrinkling her face too much. But it means she doubts the veracity of my statements.

"It *is* weird," I admit. "It's hella weird. But that's how it is. Locke didn't know me, and I didn't know any of the Lockes. And neither of us knew the poor wom—" I gasp. "You knew her! You know her name."

Detective Wilkins says, "I cannot discuss ongoing cases."

"Please. The child needs her family. She needs a home." I feel a sudden pang of loss and I check in with myself. It's going to hurt to give Annabelle up when we find her family. What if her family sucks? What if they're high all the time and abusive?

"Why are you so invested?" the detective wants to know.

"I told you. She needs someone to take care of her."

"Yes, but why *you*?"

Maybe I don't understand the question. "I was there. No one else was around."

"Dr. Caine, why are you passionate about this particular child? What are you trying to find?"

Whatever the detective is pressing me to say, I am sure it is not what I do.

"I know what it's like to be left," I tell her. "I know what it's like to not be able to keep the people you need or make them stay."

Detective Wilkins stares at me for a long time without speaking. This time her scrutiny burns me. I bow my head.

As soon as the detective leaves, I run an internet search on her, on Aaron, on everything I can think of pertaining to this investigation. It's the lack of what I find that interests me. It's like Aaron didn't even exist. The detective mentioned a huge operation, but if it is huge, it is also invisible. Must be fiercely guarded.

"Hey, are you at home?"

I answer Locke's question in the affirmative, phone to my ear, while Annabelle plays on the living room floor. "Yeah, Annabelle and I are doing research on what babies can accomplish at seven months. What's up?"

"Do you mind checking my bedside table to see if I left my wallet? I just ordered fifteen pizzas for the team without having a credit card on me, and they're going to be delivered there. I can't find my wallet anywhere. I'm so tired."

I bound up to his room, and by the time he's finished speaking, I've located it. "It's here."

"Awesome. The guys will be there soon, and I'm scrambling to get myself back. If I don't get there before the pizzas, do you think you could use my bank card to pay for them?"

"Sure. Um…what guys?" A long pause.

"Have I not told you that the team's coming over?"

"No. Um…what team?"

"OK. I guess this is what they call a reality check. Hiii. I'm Locke, the man you've been living with, and I swam for the University of Texas. Now I'm the swim coach at the college where you teach. Every year I invite my guys over to the house for a casual start-of-season practice. And that is today. Iiin"—Locke's voice drifts for a moment, like he's pulled the phone away to check the time—"less than two hours, actually. I'm going to stop making fun of my friend, Ricks, for leaving his wife in the dark about his schedule. It's not as hard as I thought—when life's moving fast and there's a kid to take care of."

"Especially if you've had plans for longer than the five days you've known your wife."

Locke makes a choking sound which I think is him laughing and trying to take a sip of something at the same time. "It's been six," he corrects, once he's recovered.

"Where are you right now?" I ask.

"At a red light. Heading to the grocery to grab some things."

"Without your wallet?"

"I've got some cash in the glove box."

"Do you have enough to grab a few bags of chocolate chips?" I'm downstairs again, rooting through the cabinets.

"What are you thinking?"

"I'll make cookies if you can get the ingredients." I list a few other things to procure.

"Yeah, I can do that. Thanks, Em. Sorry to spring it on you."

"I don't mind. Tomorrow's Saturday, right?" It's a cozy interaction. Homey. I'm glad to have something to contribute.

An hour and a half later, Locke rushes through the door in a flurry of apology, both arms laden with heavy bags of ice and groceries. "Em?" he calls. "I'm sorry! Traffic was stupid. I saw that some of the team were already here. I saw the pizza guy leaving."

I meet him in the kitchen and a comical dance-of-the-bags ensues. I try to help without upsetting the ice. "It's nothing," I assure him. "They're out in the pool." I pilfer cookie ingredients and line them up by the mixing bowl. "The guys. Not the pizzas. Those are on the table." I indicate two stacks of boxes. "It's weird, though," I say. "They only cut that top one into seven pieces."

Locke visibly relaxes. "You ate one," he guesses and lifts the lid to confirm it. "Good." He moves toward me to—what? Hug me? Kiss me hello? He checks himself. "Good," he says again and drops his head. "Thank you."

"I didn't *do* anything, Crazy Pants," I say. "Except open the door twice, but you're welcome." I measure out some flour from its white paper bag. "Go be with your guys. I'll bring out the OOOO—" My sentence ends in a howl because Locke grabs me from behind, by the hips, and whirls me around. About a quarter cup of flour whirls with me and dusts us both. He pays no mind to it. He clasps his hands around my waist, so I rest mine on his biceps and resist the urge to explore the contours there—but *dang*.

"Did you just call me *Crazy Pants*?" he asks. I throw my head back to laugh, and he hugs me closer. There is this moment loaded with potential. He's looking into my eyes. I'm inhaling the scent of him. I break eye contact to brush flour from his shoulder.

"*You're* a Crazy Pants," he says and bumps my head with his head before he backs away.

I turn to the counter to measure the flour for a second time. And to breathe. Then I say, "I hope you don't mind. I bought some other things with your card."

"What kind of things?" Locke's pouring ice into a big cooler he's rolled out from the pantry.

"Oh, you know, things. A month in the Caribbean. Some sandals. A wide-brimmed hat. Four pairs of sunglasses." I roll my head to say, "I tend to lose them. I just want to be prepared."

"I wanna come," he says, now pushing cans into the ice. "Did you get a ticket for me?"

I blow out a breath to tell him it's a dumb question. "Yyyeah," I say. "Somebody has to keep the baby while I go snorkeling and while I lie in the sun drinking frozen, pink yum-yums. Also on your card, by the way. It's all-inclusive."

Locke has finished his chores and, when I glance up, he's leaning against the fridge watching me. "I like the way you joke with me," he says.

The problem with, well, one of the problems with having orange hair is that your skin betrays everything you feel. "I like it too," I say, trying to hide the warmth rising to my cheeks behind the task of cookie making.

"Alright." Locke claps his hands together and points fingers at me. "Thank you for this. I'm gonna change and check on my time-chal-lenged swimmers." He heads for the stairs. As I start the mixer, he pops my cheek with a kiss. Then hesitates. "Hey," he says. I silence the mixer. "If I'm too free with you—I mean—if you want me to back off, just let me know."

My expression is blank. "OK," I say flatly.

Locke nods once, but the conflict on his face tells me that my reaction is not what he'd hoped for. What am I supposed to do? Tell him that *backing off* isn't even...? I lean like a rag doll to the side to answer his inner query. "I *kind* of dig you," I admit.

Cocky Locke returns in force. "I know it," he says with a wink. "I just wanted to hear you say it." I flick a towel at him, which he narrowly dodges in a chortling dash up the stairs.

Between timed intervals of baking cookies, I put Annabelle through her paces. I swing a bright red ball-on-a-string from one side of the child's field of vision to the other, trying to tempt her to flip herself over. Truth be told, the ball and string belong to The Accidental Cat, but Tac has no use for it lately. She is very, very ready to give birth.

I organize other physical tasks for the baby and make ridiculous sounds to see if she will imitate them. Once the gym-and-babble session wears her out, I lay her in a portable playpen that Mrs. Locke has borrowed from a friend.

The rest of the swim team arrives in carloads, each group louder than the next, but Annabelle sleeps on. I worry what that might mean for sleeping through the night.

The boys are in a grand way. They keep asking if Locke's mom is going to make dinner like she did that one time. Honestly, it looks more like an end-of-the-year youth group party than a collegiate swim practice. They splash and taunt each other, with Locke playing as hard as the rest of them. He races them and usually wins. If not, he makes up ridiculous excuses, and the boys pile on to sink him. I enjoy their antics from a lounge chair near the door, where I can keep an eye on the baby.

Soon someone else is drawn to the fun.

Even though Locke's dad has worked on-site every day since I've been here, I've seen very little of him. I wondered if he was avoiding me personally, but Locke assured me his dad was just anti-social right now because he's depressed. He's worried about his parents' relationship. They grieve in vastly different ways. "Well, Dad just doesn't grieve at all," Locke had said. "He hardly even talks to any of us anymore, about anything of consequence."

But now Locke's dad is jawing with the boys by the side of the pool, and I think that he must have enjoyed this part very much, when his own boys were young. And both of them alive.

He's still an impressive figure at fifty-nine. Obviously, the reason for Locke's stature and broad shoulders. He notices me watching and comes over to speak.

"Hello, Emma," he says sheepishly. "I'd like to apologize for only just now getting around to introductions."

"Not at all, Mr. Locke. I'm sorry to intrude at such a sensitive time. I've heard that the first anniversary is the hardest." He nods his head and looks down at his hands.

"You've known Landon for a while?" he asks.

"Yes," I say emphatically. "About..." I raise my eyes in thought. "Six days now."

Mr. Locke reads the humor in my face. "Well, that's about all it takes," he jokes. He considers Locke, who is now tossing a boy out of his lane. "He's a good man," Mr. Locke says. "What you see is what you get." His tone turns dark. His whole demeanor turns dark. "Unlike his brother, apparently."

That statement holds more weight than Locke's dad can carry. He all but shuts down. I don't understand it, and I'm not sure I'm supposed to ask.

"Mr. Locke? Forgive me, but is this normal gut-wrenching grief that you'll get through, or the falling-down-a-hole-in-need-of-help kind?"

He looks up like he's forgotten I'm sitting here. "I'm sorry. It's just that Aaron's story continues to—" He stops himself. "What a time for you to have stepped into the Locke household. I hope you'll stick around for better ones. Six days or not, Landon is quite taken with you." He cuts his eyes to signal me to observe his son. "I can tell by the way he keeps flexing."

Mr. Locke excuses himself, and I doubt that my presence means more posturing by Locke. He enjoys his strength as much as anybody I've ever seen. He should.

I have just concluded that swimmers have the best bodies of all men on Earth when one of them pops out of the pool to shake all over me, like a dog. I squeal and hold out hands to ward him off. When he greets me by my professional name, *Dr. Caine*, I sober. His face is familiar, but he's out of place. And wet. And nearly naked.

It's John Mark, he cues me in sign. *From class. Signing Basics. Also, I was in your office today.*

Oh, right! I sign. *How could I forget? I guess I'm not used to seeing you without...clothes on.*

John Mark grins and sits down on the end of my chair.

Why did you tell the detective I was deaf? I ask.

I didn't! She came into the lobby asking where your office was, and I offered to show her. And to interpret for her. I thought maybe I could impress you.

You certainly did, I sign.

He's not sure that I mean it kindly. He has a pink-cheeked innocence under his dripping blonde shag, and he's searching me for a clue.

I got a kick out of it, I assure him. *And you sign really well. Apart from whatever you were trying to communicate with that one non-sign.*

"That's why I need to practice!" he says, then signs, *My older brother is deaf, so I grew up signing, but I'm afraid a lot of my signs are just things we made up as kids, and aren't really ASL.*

You shouldn't be in Basics, though.

Where should I be? Will you mentor me?

I'll do you way better than that. I begin to concoct a plan to get John Mark out of Basics and into a private practicum, traded for the help that Locke and I so desperately need with Annabelle.

That's when I notice, over John Mark's shoulder, that Locke keeps stealing glances at our animated conversation. John Mark is cute, and he makes me laugh. I certainly don't mind him hanging out, but I'm beginning to think that his coach might.

So, you think there's hope for me? John Mark asks. *I want to sign as smoothly as you do. It's like a native language for you. Like you're deaf.*

I was. For a while.

But you're not anymore?

Locke's voice booms across the water. "John Mark, is your scholarship important to you?" John Mark makes an *uh-oh* face and dives back into the pool.

When it's time for pizza, Locke snaps a few of his swimmers into service before I can make it two steps with the boxes. They rid me of my load and shuttle the pizzas to the outdoor tables, where I am at least allowed to lay down the cookies I've made. You'd think it was a Christmas feast, by the boys' gaiety.

"Dr. Caine!" I'm distributing napkins when John Mark catches up to me and immediately launches into another lively conversation. He's holding a plate heaped with pizza, so he adapts his signs to keep from upsetting it, and he looks so awkward and exuberant that I burst into giggles. He must take it to mean that we're now equals, because when he finds a place at the table, he pats the empty seat beside him and drops the *Dr. Caine.* He says, "Here you go, Emma."

Locke steps forward to glare down at him until his mouth takes on the shape of an O. John Mark points from Locke to me and back again, with the question on his face.

"Yeah, John Mark," Locke says as if it couldn't be more obvious, but then he flicks his eyes in my direction to see if he's overstepped.

"We're raising a child together," I proclaim. I lean into Locke's side. "We'll probably be raising five or six more by the end of the weekend." The imminent kittens.

"Maybe before the end of the night," Locke says, suddenly far more cheerful.

"That's how we roll." I fling my hands like a rapper with a bad attitude.

"That's how we roll!" Locke howls. "You are such a wild card, *Doctor* Caine." It's later now, and the swimmers have all gone. Locke and I climb the stairs. He's hauling the portable playpen, and I have Annabelle. "How do you have your doctorate already?"

"I have no life outside of school?" I say it like it's a question. Locke's raised brow begs for more information, so I explain, a bit guardedly. "I have sort of dual citizenship in the Hearing and Deaf cultures. My profs, one, in particular, insisted that my personal background demanded a thesis, and she wouldn't let it go until I'd earned my doctorate. It's in communications, but it's really more of a psych degree, with emphasis on kinesthetic language. I like to solve problems that involve reading and interpreting what people communicate behind their spoken words."

There's a pause before Locke says, "I don't know what any of that means."

"Yeah. Sorry. Basically, it means I don't trust people. And in order to control my world, I try to interpret what they mean by watching them, instead of listening to what they say."

"But you trusted me. Enough to allow me to bring you to a strange house and foster a baby with you, without too many questions."

I snicker like I've been found out. "Well, your rules of engagement are pretty straightforward. I like that about you."

Up in Aaron's room, it takes Locke a minute to figure out how to set up the playpen, but once he's conquered it, he peers around, hands on hips. His eyes land on my weekend bag.

"You know you can use the drawers, right?" he says. "You don't have to live out of your luggage." He checks to make sure the drawers are empty.

"Oh, I know. Thanks. But how long will I be here? You know? I'll just have to pack again anyway."

"Yeah, that's good thinking," Locke agrees. It's one of the only times I've witnessed his words mismatch his facial expression. It makes me curious.

"You don't think so?" I ask.

"I mean—yeah. If your goal is to make a quick getaway."

"It's not like that. It's been six days. Don't you want your life back?"

"No. I think it's fun. I like you here. I like seeing you first thing in the morning. When I get home and you're already in bed, it makes me sad."

"It does not," I laugh. But I stop when I realize he's not just trying to be nice.

"Seriously," he says. "You don't know how many times I've stood out there wanting to knock."

"You can knock," I say. "Though I may have an alternative to you having to work so late. What do you think about John Mark? He's a good guy?"

Locke takes a seat in the leather chair. "He's a good...kid," he says, demoting John Mark from the rank of peer.

"Well, he needs help in sign, and I bet he would trade childcare for it."

Locke nods that he understands. "Yeah, he's a good guy. I trust him. The whole family's great."

While I'm mulling that over, Locke is looking around the room. "I'm not sure I've really spent any time in here since Aaron died. I helped Mom and Dad clean up his house, but neither one of us has lived in *this* house for years." Something on the bookshelf catches his eye and he goes to take hold of it. A wooden puzzle box. "One of Aaron's crowning achievements from the summer we were fourteen," Locke says. He turns it over, peruses it with a pleasant, albeit wistful expression, and hands it to me, trading box for baby.

I begin to work out the pieces while Locke entertains Annabelle. This one slides away. This one has to be plucked out. This one has to be rotated and then maneuvered before it will succumb, and that reveals others. "It's really well constructed. Did Aaron design it?"

Locke nods. I remove the last piece to reveal a hidden compartment and tip it to Locke in accomplishment. He makes the baby clap her hands like a puppet. "He was good at woodworking, then?" I ask. "Like you are?"

He shrugs. "He could have been, but he didn't have the patience for it. Grandaddy would tell him he acted like a wild goat in the woodshop and should be beaten as such." I take a break from reassembling the box to see how serious Locke is about that. He shakes his head to show that Aaron was never beaten like a wild goat.

"But you couldn't get him out of the shop *that* summer," he adds. "I think he just enjoyed the concept of the puzzle, more than the craft itself. He made one while I was away at swim camp that I never could open, and it gave him way too much joy. I'm not sure it really *did* come open, now that I think of it. That was probably a big joke to him." Locke searches the bookshelf until he finds the one he's referring to, and then tosses it to me. "He'd bring it across the hall every once in a while, to see if I could solve it yet. Said he was going to patent it."

I remove a few pieces but then get stuck. I roll it over in my hands. "There's a seam here with a tiny defect," I say. "A little puncture that makes me think the rest of it is hollow...huh."

Annabelle reaches for the loose pieces, and Locke lays her in the pen with a toy that is less of a choking hazard.

"A detective came by my office today," I tell him. "From the state police, not the sheriff's office. Nobody believes us, Locke, that we met by chance. I'm beginning to think it's because all this involves your brother. What was he working on?"

Locke half sits, half leans against the desk. "There's a lot I don't know. He was undercover for a long time, working in conjunction with the state police. They gave him a new last name. Moved him somewhere. He was gone all the time in the end. When he did come home, he was tense and tight-lipped. But he was disillusioned somehow. I think he'd found out one of the cops was dirty. He was thinking about leaving the force altogether, and he loved his job."

"What happened to him? Was he shot?"

Locke cuts his eyes toward me, before dropping them with a furtive blink. "Heroin," he says. "We were told he'd OD'd. On purpose. It was intimated that he'd been caught stealing and he couldn't face up to it."

"You don't believe it."

"No. Though...he had become more and more distant."

I can almost feel the weight of Locke's shoulders as they sag.

"That hurts as much anything, doesn't it? The widening gap between the two of you."

"Yeah," he admits. "We never kept things from each other. I didn't even think we could. Apparently, a lot of money went missing, but he didn't take it. And if he got caught up *using*...I just can't believe it. Anyway, he didn't kill himself." Locke holds up his hands to stave off what hasn't occurred to me to say. "I know. Nobody can believe it when it happens in their family. But, Em, I know he didn't." His eyes beg me to believe him. "There's more to the story, but it doesn't make him any less gone."

Silence fills the space between us, and I begin to reach for words of comfort. But what is there to say?

Locke speaks instead. "The night we found out, he looked awful." He stalls. He turns his eyes to the ceiling, and the tears I see there make my own eyes pool. "His lips were blue. His skin was grey." His chin quivers. "There is no medicine for that kind of hurt."

I'm useless as well. They were identical twins, so all I can see in my mind is *Locke* in that kind of shape. I practically define him by his vitality. The image of him blue and cold is jarring, to say the least. I approach him, where he sits against the desk, because I want to feel the rise of his breath. He unfolds his arms and allows me to come.

"He was my *brother*," he says as if he needs an excuse. His vocal cords are rigid. The words escape as a whine.

"I know," I say. The way I pull him against me lets loose a flood of tears. He sobs so hard, I begin to internalize how compromised he feels, how vulnerable. The permanence of the amputation is unbearable. I can hardly catch my own breath.

After the worst of it, Locke remains wrapped around me, his head heavy over my shoulder, his breath drawn in staggered puffs. Finally, his breathing smooths out. He rights himself and dislodges his fingers from my shirt, where he's knotted it in the tension of grief. He goes for an apologetic smile, but when he sees the streaks that have run down my face out of empathy for him, he can't manage it. He smudges the tracks my tears have made. His eyelashes are wet. Gah, he's beautiful.

"Thank you," he says.

"I owed you one."

He watches my mouth form the words. His hands are hot on my cheeks. His eyes are cloudy as can be and something in them shifts to demand a new kind of comfort. He parts my lips with his thumb and moves to close the distance between us.

The baby chooses this moment to beat her feet and her fists on the floor of the playpen. She thrashes about noisily to demand our attention. With a breathy laugh, Locke drops his head, his rough cheek raking my smooth one, and then he peers up at me from beneath heavy lids.

"Hold that thought," I tell him. I squeeze his arms to let him know that I'm still with him and step over to the pen to show the baby that I am also with her.

"Locke, she turned herself over! She pushed herself up, and—nope. Back down."

Locke hovers over the pen to observe the proceedings and shrugs his nose at Annabelle, who is lying on her back again, kicking her legs and smiling proudly.

"Why don't we *sleep now—*" I make signs to the baby, and at the same time, speak in a sing-song voice. "And we'll try again tomorrow?"

I feel the back of Locke's hand down my arm. "Why do you know sign language?" he asks.

"*That* is above your pay grade," I tell him.

"It can't possibly be. Not now."

"You sure?"

"Emma."

I eye him in a way that tells him I'm about to divulge something significant. "I was completely deaf from the time I was fifteen until the morning I left for college. Which, ironically, was a college for the Deaf and Hard of Hearing."

"*Why* were you deaf? Were you in an accident? Were you sick?"

"Nope." I use the most flippant tone I can come up with, but inside I'm anything but. "My mom was screaming and crying. My dad caught me listening from the stairs, and it was clear that he blamed me for what she knew. He yelled that he was leaving us and that he was never coming back. I saw him slam the door—I sort of heard it after the fact, like an echo—and then I didn't hear another sound for three and a half years." I gauge his reaction.

"You were *elective* deaf?" he says. "I didn't even know that was a thing."

"Neither did the doctors. Most of them didn't believe me. But, anyway, an amazing family took me in and taught me sign language, and I fell in love with it." I study his face, his posture, the direction in which he is leaning, which is toward me, not away.

"There's an economy to it," I continue. "Unlike all the words that get blathered into existence every time some hearing fool exhales. It's very factual. You have to say what you mean. Though, I did join an interpretive dance club that tended toward the poetic. That was kind of fun."

"I guess your background *did* beg for a thesis. And then you went to college as a *hearing* person? Did they know?" Locke is staring. And examining. And—

"I hid it for a while. I was scared. But then I realized how much I could help. That I could be a bridge. That's why I became an EMT. The Deaf community needed an interpreter in emergency situations."

Locke's face is unusually hard to read, maybe because his eyes are puffy from crying. "What was the first thing you heard?" he asks.

I soften in surprise. "No one's ever asked me that. It was bluebird parents. Their fledglings were testing their wings, hopping and flying in short bursts, and that mom and dad sang their beautiful heads off. Songs of protection, songs of encouragement... I woke up to it, walked outside, sat down, and cried my eyes out."

Locke is still staring.

"Still feel bonded for life?" I ask, as if, I mean, how could he? What kind of person makes themselves unable to hear?

"I do," he says solidly. "I'm in this. I'm not going anywhere. I'm not going to bring you into my parents' house, and—"

"With a *baby*," I interject.

"With a *baby*," Locke agrees.

"And an accidental cat," I suggest.

"And...*that...yes.* And then leave you hanging, wondering if my will is in this. I would never *do* that. And, by the way, when you see me in the mornings, after we've been apart, you can just go ahead and know that. You don't have to guess."

Pause.

"I believe you," I say.

"Good. Then we have an understanding."

"I'll believe you until you tell me that you're done with me."

"No, I'm not going to be done with you. That is the opposite of what I'm telling you."

"I know." I smile. "I was kidding." I sign and say, "Thank you." I make another sign after that.

"I know the *thank you*," Locke says, mimicking the action by placing his fingers on his chin and moving them forward. "Right? What's the rest?"

"It's your name sign."

"It means Landon? Or it means Locke?"

"It means *you*." I gesture to all of him. "We bestow name signs for the whole person. I'm trying to figure out exactly how yours should be."

"I like it. I'm broad."

"Yes. Broad. Sturdy. But it's not enough. I'll work it out."

"Well, you're still Legs."

I accept his joke and show him how to spell out L-E-G-S, and how to indicate *legs* directly. "But you'll want to use an E for Emma when you make the sign."

Once he masters it, he says, "Em, tell me what you signed at the cemetery. The thing you wouldn't say in the voicemail. You had just said that you didn't have much faith in *bonded for life*, and that I'd have to...? If I still wanted to tomorrow...?" Locke leaves the sentences hanging, the way I did on the voicemail.

"How do you remember that?"

"I may have listened to it since."

"I signed the rest so that I wouldn't have to say it," I tell him.

"You must have wanted me to know, or you wouldn't have signed it." Locke coaxes me like he's trying to win over a skittish stray. "Tell me what it was. I'll be careful with it."

With eyes straight ahead, not upon his, I suck my teeth. "To prove that being bonded for life exists." I almost don't say the rest. But I think of how hard he cried just now. How much he trusted me with that. And I add, "For me."

Locke nods that he understands, and he steps forward to hook a strand of my hair behind my ear. He stoops to say, "Do you still want me to?" His warm hands cup my jaw. My head barely nods yes.

"I accept." He kisses my temple. "Do you hear me?"

I nod again. I rarely allow the longing. But his promise is that tempting. I close my eyes. Before he releases me, he kisses me once on the lips. Soft and without demands. Then, with the effect of clouds rolling away from the sun, he changes his tone and brightens the whole room. "Teach me to sign something else," he says.

I teach him *Good morning*, and *How did you sleep*, and *Did you make coffee*. Finally, I fit all my fingers close together, and move them to pillow my head.

"*Home?*" Locke says, asking if it's the same sign I'd made to him on the first night.

"Close. They both have the sign for bed." Locke raises his eyebrows. He points to himself and then to my bed.

"It means *sleep tight*," I laugh. "In your own bed."

"Well, that's no fun," he grumbles. On his way out, he says, "Good-night, Legs. Give a shout if you need me." He grins over his shoulder. "Or if you change your mind."

I shake my head and mouth the word *no*, though the very thought of it...

Once in his own room, Locke leans back into view to say, "Or if the cat goes into labor."

The cat does go into labor. It's not enough that Miss Annabelle has decided to become nocturnal. The Accidental Cat's imminent kittens decide that now is the time to try life on the outside. Around four a.m., Locke stumbles in to help. Really, all either of us do is to sit on the carpet and watch, as the cat has it pretty well covered.

There are five in all. Tiny, wet, hardly-any-hair-there kittens. In white. And one in orange. "Look, Em, this one belongs to your hair." Locke lifts the pathetic beast into the air.

"Rude," I say flatly.

"To the cat," he quips.

"Set it down," I command. As soon as he complies, I launch myself at him with several devastating blows, which he is nonetheless able to block, despite the fact that he's cracking up. He catches and traps both my hands and holds me against himself where he kneels. "You know I think you're gorgeous, right? If you'd let me, I'd kiss every sexy freckle on your fair skin."

"You would?" By the way I ask, I betray my desire for that very thing.

Locke makes a pleased uh-huh sound. "And I'd twist your wild tangles in my fists till they'd submit." He rises further onto his knees to do it, guiding me up to join him with fists full of my hair.

"Anything else?" My question is a breathless wisp of a thing. I don't care.

A slow smile begins to spread over his face but recedes as his lips meet mine—and then the baby begins to wail. We remain suspended in that almost-kiss for a moment before Locke falls back onto the carpet in defeat. "That baby hates me!" he says.

I reach for Annabelle, laughing. "She's just trying to keep your priorities straight."

"My priorities are plenty straight," he mutters.

Towards dawn I fall asleep on the floor, the baby wide awake beside me, and a hand over the fence we've made from boxes and newspapers for the cats.

7

FROM AARON'S TO THE WOODSHOP

When I awake around ten in the morning, I am in the bed. I can't remember putting myself to bed. I can't remember putting the baby to bed. I can't find the baby. I tear downstairs with a yelp, and skid into the kitchen.

Ardea and Sarah, who have spread a blanket on the living room floor, are making silly faces for a safe, and dry, and well-fed Annabelle. They both lift their heads at my sudden appearance. The baby's eyes go from the toy in Ardea's hand to Ardea's face, and then vaguely toward where Ardea is focused on me.

"What's wrong, Emma?" Ardea asks. "Are you ill?"

"No. No, not at all, Mrs. Locke." I rub a hand over my eyes. "I just panicked. I woke up and the baby was gone, and—I'm not thinking clearly. I didn't get much sleep."

"Landon wanted you to be able to rest."

It comes to me why I can't remember putting myself to bed. Locke lifted me up and snugged me in. I smile to myself. I am so out of my depth here.

"Emma, look at this," Sarah says. "I found him asleep on the couch with Annabelle lying on his chest, and her little lips were moving on their own like she was dreaming about her pacifier. I took a video." Sarah presents her phone.

"Please send me that," I say. "That is just—"

"I know, right?"

I look at the way Annabelle is sleeping, with Locke's protective hand covering her back. It's probably not right to be jealous of a baby.

"Landon said you had to be both mama and midwife last night," Ardea says. She rises to get coffee for me.

"Please, don't serve me," I object. "You've already done so much."

"I feel like we owe you, Emma. That boy has smiled more in the little time that you've been here than in the last two years. He left your bike by the pool in case you'd like to get a ride in." Ardea motions that way. "I'd be happy to keep the baby."

"Thank you. I'd love that. You know, you have raised a very thoughtful man." After I say so, I inwardly hope I haven't highlighted the fact that Ardea has actually raised *two*, but only one of them is left for me to know. If I have, she doesn't show it.

"He's down in the woodshop working on an order. I think he'd like for you to see it if your explorations lead that way." Ardea stifles a knowing smile. "I'll draw you a map."

I am grateful for the fresh air, and I feel revived as my muscles propel me around the property. I hold my face up to the morning sun. *Thank you for this. Thank you for*—I'm praying again. I can't remember ever feeling close to God, though I have often envied the genuine faith of others. I also can't remember feeling this happy, this light, this…at home.

But you're not really, I remind myself. *You'll have to go back to your real life eventually. And that's OK.* It doesn't feel OK. *Shut up. Just enjoy this.* I push my pedals harder to get lost in the simple pleasure of exerting myself. I've explored for over two hours when I consult the map that Ardea has drawn for me. I must have left the boundary of it. I backtrack to rejoin the dusty lane that leads down to Locke's woodshop, or so I think. I ride past paddocks and fence lines to a sturdy log cabin.

The cabin is small, but the roofline is high, and I can see that it must be wide open inside, with a large upstairs loft. The steps, which still resemble the logs they were hewn from, lead up to a deck. There are Adirondack chairs on that deck, more than one could possibly need, and a low, round table around which they are gathered. It's all very masculine. Well crafted. Attention to details. Not homey details. That is, there are no cushions or splashes of color, no live things growing. But it's a strong skeleton of a place.

It doesn't occur to me that I'm not at the woodshop. It was described to me as a cabin, and there it sits on Ardea's map. I knock on the solid wooden door. No answer. Though I think I hear movement from inside. Maybe Locke is working with earplugs. I try the door.

Not a woodshop. At least not this part of the house. "Hello?" I call. For the first time, it dawns on me that I am not where I am supposed to be. I might actually be standing in the middle of someone's private home, uninvited. The living area is furnished, and there are some personal effects, but it doesn't feel lived in. It smells...not bad, just...unused.

No dishes in the sink. I can't help myself. Nothing in the fridge. Nothing in the trash. I scan the living room. There's a magazine on the coffee table, but it's over a year old. There's a collectors' edition of photos and facts from the James Bond movies. Everything is neat. Too neat. Perfectly folded throw over the couch. Perfectly placed pillow on the chair.

I stride over to pick up a photograph of Locke from when he had short hair, military short. Whoa. He looks a lot edgier that way. I can't decide which hairstyle I like best. I know I love his easy smile though, and in this picture, he looks just shy of mean. There are other people around him: his sister Sarah, Officer Chris Michaels from the police sta—oh. I'm not staring at a picture of Locke. At least, not *my* Locke. It's Aaron. This is Aaron's house.

The realization makes me sad. I sit down in the middle of the deep couch and survey the room from that perspective. I fall back against the cushions, lifting my eyes to the high ceiling, to windows that let in plenteous light. There is debris floating through the air. Tiny dust particles, illuminated in a diagonal column of sunshine. I wonder how many times Locke has come here to his brother's house to do this exact thing.

Death sucks.

Outside, clouds have covered the sun. The column of light dissipates, and the house grows dark. I stand to go. On my way out, I pass by a workspace. A tidy desk with a corkboard above it. I find another picture pinned there; this one is of all three siblings. Sarah sitting on a railing between her brothers with an arm around each of their necks. I honestly can't say for sure which one is Locke. Both men have their hair cut close, and both are laughing. I unpin the picture to look at it up close and dislodge a small sticky note that was hidden underneath. I retrieve it from the floor.

It reads: *I have a treasure for you, my Love. Come find out.* A tiny heart, and an A.

From somewhere below me, I hear the sound of men's voices and the pound of boots on stairs. I spike with adrenaline. A door creaks open from the back of the room and Mr. Locke appears, holding a small, worn, leather casket and a large plastic bag. Behind him is Chris Michaels. Chris is frustrated. He hasn't found something he'd wanted to find, and he *has* found something that displeases him. The sheriff is riding him harder than the day it happened, "and when you destroy that—"

"Emma?" It's Locke's dad.

"Mr. Locke," I reply, thumping a hand on my chest, "you startled me." I don't need a doctorate in communications to know that I am not welcome in this scene. I hold out Ardea's map. "I'm not sure that cartography is your wife's forte. I was trying to get to the woodshop, but I ended up here. I'm sorry if I disturbed you."

I nod at Chris in greeting, but he barely acknowledges me. "Well, anyway, I'll go." I pin the picture back into place and notice Chris take a special interest in the effort. I know, without a doubt, that he is going to inspect that photo as soon as I'm gone. And gone is where I want to be. I stop at the door when I remember the defective map. "Um. Sorry. Again. Could you point me in the direction of the woodshop?"

It turns out that there is a trail between Aaron's house and Locke's. Somewhere along the way, it opens into a wider lane, and *that* runs to the woodshop. When I come to it, I snort to myself. It is obviously a workspace and not someone's house, though it does have a cabin-y feel to it, more like a camp lodge. There are huge sliding doors on every wall, and Locke has all of them open. I can see him working. Two golden retrievers are lying on the floor at his feet. The floor, by the way, looks like it used to belong to an old ballroom or a dance studio, with wide wooden beams displaying their tree's knots and swirls.

Locke has his hair tied in a short ponytail. He's missed a strand, or it's come loose, and he reaches up to push it behind his ear. His thin white T-shirt stretches across his back when he leans over to inspect something he's done.

"Help me," I murmur. One of the goldens raises his head and thumps his tail twice, but Locke is unaware. He wears earbuds. Now he straightens from his work to pound out the rhythm to whatever he's listening to, with a drummer's snarl wrinkling his nose—and abruptly stops when he catches sight of me. I've propped myself against the shop's open wall to enjoy the show. I raise my brow in greeting while a blush washes over his cheeks. As if he could possibly be more endearing.

Locke removes one of the earbuds and holds it out to me, so I step forward to accept. "Greta Van Fleet," I say. "I knew you were cooler than you looked."

"Hey, that's not nice." Locke's eyes travel the length of me. "You look...salty." He flashes his eyebrows, apparently pleased with his description.

I'm not going to ask you to find out. I'm not going to ask you to find out. I'm not going to— "Yeah, well I've had quite a ride this morning, Locke. Look at this 'map' your mom made for me." I make air quotes with my fingers when I say the word *map* and reach into my pocket to produce it. A stowaway comes out as well. The sticky note I'd found at Aaron's cabin. It attached itself to the back of the map, and I peel it off while Locke considers the paths his mom has penned.

"It's a wonder you didn't end up at—"

"Aaron's?" I offer. "Oh, I did. And guess what? I wasn't the only one there. Your dad and your brother's old partner came up from the basement and nearly gave me a heart attack."

"They did? What were they doing there?"

"I didn't ask, because I was clearly disrupting them." I tell Locke what I heard, that they'd been looking for something they couldn't find and that Sheriff Dunn was mounting on the pressure. "Hey, who was your brother's girlfriend? Were they going out when he died?" I hand over the sticky note.

Though it only holds eleven words and the letter A, Locke stares at it for several long moments. "Where did you get this?" he asks.

"It was on the corkboard over the desk. I unpinned a picture of you and your siblings, and this fell out from underneath." I kneel to stroke one of the lazy dog's fur. "I guess it got stuck to the map when your dad startled me."

"If Aaron had a girlfriend, I didn't know about it. I swear it's like we stopped being twins when he went undercover."

I abandon the dogs to tend to Locke, whose eyes have become fixed on the corner of the room. "I didn't mean to upset you," I say. "I'll let you find out how salty I am. If you want to."

My comment is shocking enough to recharge his mood and smack a look of intrigue onto his face. "Really?"

I shrug a shoulder as if this is a normal allowance. As if I've just offered him a paddle from the cookie dough I've been mixing.

"I want to," he assures me. He takes a decisive step forward, causing my bravado to falter. "Do I get to choose which part of you to...test?" Now that he's close enough to do it, he's searching for a spot. I swallow.

"I guess?" I say.

Locke rakes his hands down the sides of me with enough pressure for me to feel it up my spine, and he bends to my neck, where he pushes my chin upward to gain access to my throat.

"May I just..." He kisses between words. "Sample randomly?" His breath is warmer and wetter than the Texas morning. When he begins to taste and to *pull* on that part of my throat, I let slip the tiniest whimper. His response is to press in and make a slow feast of me in an agonizing trail to my ear.

I turn to kiss his hair, his cheekbone, his—

He's gone. He's standing to full height, having solemnized his features. I feel it like a betrayal. "Oh, please don't just be messing with me," I say through a cringe.

"No, sweetheart," Locke rumbles. His fingers press the inside of my wrist. "We have company."

"I hope I'm not interrupting anything," comes Chris's voice too loudly. The goldens jump up in clumsy haste and bark in garbled *woo-woo-woos* until real barks have time to form. Chris strides in like he owns the place. "What's up Fili? Kili? You haven't forgotten me, have you?" He extends a hand to greet them.

I know my cheeks resemble vine-ripened tomatoes. They are literally radiating heat. I pace away on the pretense of exploring the shop and try to disappear behind counters of organized tools and countless choices of wood stain. I can feel Locke's eyes upon me, though he fields Chris's questions with measured courtesy.

When I come to a section of completed projects, I am mercifully distracted from my mortification by the level of mastery in the man's skill. No wonder he stays busy with orders. His work is as sturdy and as beautiful as he is.

Moving further, I notice that not all of his work is furniture. There's a corner where a four-foot forest grows. Slender, delicate pines boast flexible needles, soft to the touch. They loom over a cabin, a replica of Aaron's, except that there are colorful touches: yellow flowers and whimsical red-headed woodpeckers. Wooden deer forage nearby. One of them, a buck with long antlers, seems to be spying on me warily. There are white-spotted fawns too. And a—what was the word?—a *fez* of armadillos. I smile. Slight variations in the whittling styles make me wonder if I'm enjoying the collective work of several Lockes over time.

I'm feeling better now. And I'm glad not to have to fake my way through the small talk between Chris and Locke, but a change in the tone of their conversation brokers my attention.

"Was Aaron seeing someone when he died?" It's Locke who asks it, and I can tell by his hesitancy that he is loath to reveal his own ignorance.

"Why are you asking that?" comes Chris's sharp reply. "I mean," he gentles his voice, "what reason would you have to ask that...now?"

The silence that follows is notably absent of Locke's usual friendliness. He fixes Chris with a stern expression, and I think that, if he were to turn it upon me, I would wilt.

Finally, he says, "Chris, you keep showing up here, all chummy with my dad. If there's something going on that I need to know, now is the time to tell me."

"You sound just like your brother," Chris sneers.

"Yeah, well, since he can't speak for himself, I—"

"I was his partner, Landon!" Chris breaks in. "Do you think I *allowed* him to die?"

Locke's lips shape a silent, *What?*

Chris says, "I'm here because the sheriff is under all kinds of pressure to account for about seven hundred *thousand* dollars that went missing last year on Aaron's watch. State police are pissed that they lost their foothold and they're grasping at straws. I went to your dad as a courtesy, and he invited me to go through Aaron's place."

"OK, first of all, you come to *me* next time," Locke says. "Stop dragging my dad into it. Secondly, you can't possibly think that Aaron stole that money. Did you not know him any better than that?"

"You'd be surprised," Chris says. "Pretending to be someone else undercover *does* things to you. But it's all bogus. He was stealing from thugs if he was stealing. He was a Robin Hood."

Chris's words seem to hurt my friend. Locke looks wary and defiant at the same time.

"Why else would he have killed himself?" Chris adds. "He knew he was caught."

Locke shakes his head in quick movements. "You know I don't believe that."

"He said he left something for you in his safe. What was it?"

"That's between brothers."

"Yeah, well maybe that's for the police to decide."

"Well, it wasn't seven hundred thousand dollars, Chris! Why are you asking about all this *now?*"

I make my way around the room and return to Locke's side in time to find Chris pointing at me. "Maybe your new girlfriend knows," he says. "She seems to keep showing up at the right places, at the right times. Managed to cozy up to you enough to have free rein of the place."

Locke steps into Chris's personal space. "You are forgetting yourself right now." He uses the dangerous tone he'd used at the police station.

"Do you know where she's from?" Chris asks. "Or have you skipped all the small talk to get on to...other things." He waves a finger between us.

I swear that Locke growls in warning. I try to defuse the situation. I display my right hand and point to the top of my pinky. "Right here," I say.

"Right there," Chris echoes. "A stone's throw from Canada."

"Actually, you have to pass through that tiny part of—"

Chris cuts me off with a jerk of his head, and I shrink back. He does the forearm thing, where he rubs the inside of his elbow for no apparent reason and says, "Aaron, don't you think it's—" He corrects himself. "Landon. Landon, don't you think it's—"

"Dude, are you *high* right now?" Locke asks.

"Think about it," Chris says. "The traffic from Mexico to Canada has a fairly direct route."

"So, you think Emma's a drug mule now? Because she's from Michigan? This is exciting police work, Chris. I'm sure the sheriff will be impressed."

Chris blanches. I am *so* curious about that. Is it just that he doesn't want to appear incompetent? Or is there something he doesn't want the sheriff to know?

In a slightly more respectful tone, Chris asks me, "Where were you from the time you quit school at fifteen until you moved onto the campus of Gallaudet University? It's like you fell off the face of the Earth."

"You don't have to answer that," Locke says.

"It's OK." I shrug. "I mean, it's not a secret. I dropped out of school because I couldn't hear what the teachers were saying. Eventually, I moved in with a family who homeschooled their own children in sign language. They live a few hours from my mom, in Central Michigan. And I can assure you there were no drugs around. Though there were mules. They're Amish."

When I stop speaking, there's a collective pause, after which both Chris and Locke, at the same time, make a *huh* sound.

"Can I confirm that?" Chris asks.

"Sure. If you want to travel to—" It's a snarky gesture. I admit it. But I display my right hand again, this time punching the center of my palm with the tip of my finger. "They don't have video chat. You might want to take an interpreter too. I mean, they can read lips perfectly and can speak almost as well, but they're too proud to admit it."

In an unforeseen shift, Chris says, "You're familiar with interrogations." Locke's sidelong glance says that he'd like to hear the response to that too.

"I've never been on *this* side of one," I tell him.

"But you've been a consultant for the Michigan State Police."

"Yep. ATF even."

"Because of your expertise in body language?"

The *whole* story is less impressive than it sounds. A few years ago, I bumped into a childhood friend at a coffeehouse. He'd gone into law enforcement and had found himself outsmarted by a suspect. When we got to talking about my doctoral dissertation, he asked me to come observe an interview. I enjoyed the work and I turned out to be good at it, so I was invited to consult on other cases.

But Chris doesn't need to know all that. Instead of answering, I nod at his elbow. "What's up with your arm?" He draws it into himself with a frown.

"Why are you asking?"

"Because you're going to rub it raw. Are *you* using? Is *that* where the money went?"

Chris remains silent.

"Is it injured?"

Still nothing, except a surly glare. Finally, he says, "Are you here working for the DOJ?"

"Do you think she's one of the *good* guys now?!" Locke asks. I smile to myself. Locke doesn't have all the information about me that Chris has dug up, and yet, he's defending me as if it doesn't matter.

Chris's posture shrinks, and I feel a wave of pity for him. "He's not sure who the good guys are," I comment.

"Now I *know* you have more information than you're letting on," Chris spits.

"That was telling," Locke says. Chris rolls his eyes. "Look, Chris." Locke tries to appeal to his humanity. "I don't know what's going on here, but you have to leave my dad out of it. Can't you see that he's still too sore? He's not thinking clearly. He needs to move on."

"*Yeah*, Landon?" Chris turns up the heat about four hundred degrees. "He can't move on from his son being tortured by an injection of dirty heroin? Do you have any idea how your brother died? Scared to death and blubbering gibberish like a fool! Your dad and I are so glad that *you* aren't having any trouble moving o—" Before the words are out of his mouth, Locke has knocked him to the ground. "Get up!" he snarls and wrings out the hand he's used to throw the punch.

From where Chris has landed, to my amazement, he starts to laugh. He rolls over onto his back and guffaws until he groans. The skin across his cheekbone is burst wide open, and he fingers the length of it, only to start laughing again when he pulls his fingers away to find blood.

"You have never looked more like Aaron Alexander Locke in your life. How many times did he surprise me with that left hook?" Chris sighs like a steam kettle. "I needed that."

"What you need is help. As much as my dad does." Locke doesn't show any sign of the amusement that has taken Chris. "Don't waste your sanctimonious crap on me. Don't come around here anymore. You're unstable."

Chris pushes himself to sit. "You don't know what all is going on here, Landon. But if you want to keep your family safe, you'd better turn over to me anything Aaron left for you."

"Are you threatening my *family* right now?" Instead of rising in volume, Locke's voice shrinks to fit the laser focus of his anger. Chris is an idiot. Locke's people are his lifeblood. I stay him with a touch. I have no love lost on Chris, but I think he's blustering out of desperation. I just can't figure out whether the desperation is fear of getting caught, or greed for the money, or something else entirely. After a quick glance at my hand on his bicep, Locke says to Chris, "Go. Do not come back."

Back at the house, after we tend to the kittens, and finally manage to settle Annabelle for the night, Locke and I both sit against the headboard of the bed. "What did Aaron leave for you in his safe?" I ask.

Moments pass without him answering. I follow with, "I'm sorry. Am I'm prying?"

"No. You can ask me anything you want to," he says. "Anytime." He's been massaging his left hand where it's swollen from the impact with Chris's eye socket, and now he allows it to drop onto my leg. "There was nothing special in the safe." The bitterness in the answer is obvious. "I just didn't like Chris's attitude. Aaron had written a letter. All the police do. They keep it on the job in case the worst happens, you know? And the last line was something like, 'Tell Landon I left something for him in the lockbox.' But the only things in there were—"

Locke stops speaking. His eyes journey in a slow trek beyond his field of vision. With a lurch, he hauls himself to the bookshelf where he procures Aaron's impossible puzzle box. "He used to call it 'The Locke Box,'" he says. "With an E, like our last name." Locke turns it over in his hands, scrutinizing it as if for the first time. He removes the pieces that he can. He shakes it close to his ear. He stares so intently; I wonder if he's going to speak to it. But then he tosses it onto the bed in a gesture of surrender.

I pick it up to study the interior angles. "How good did it feel to punch Chris in the face?" I ask.

"I'm sorry I did that."

I peer up to see if he really is. "I'm not," I say. "He was outrageously out of line."

One of Locke's cheeks reveals its dimple. "Then I'm not either," he says.

"If I were as strong as you, I would have decked him a long time ago. I would have decked him at my apartment."

"I guess that lack of self-restraint is why God made you small," he muses.

"Have you always wanted to?"

"Punch him? No. He just got to me today."

"You sure? You're guarded around him. You essentially blocked his affectionate, if misdirected greeting at the police station. You inter-rupted him the other day at my apartment when he challenged me."

"I thought I was being subtle," Locke says.

"By crashing into me with a baby?"

He huffs a laugh. "I didn't like how the officers were surprised to see him there. It just didn't sit well. Like it didn't with you. And I've been thinking about what you said. I'm not ready to say that I blame him for Aaron's death. But he's obviously withholding information. I get that he can't speak about an undercover operation. But he could give me *something*. It's so irritating when he acts like he knew Aaron so much better than I did."

"Were he and Aaron actually moving drugs for some cartel? Is that the gist of it?"

"I think so. I know they were in the middle of some pretty bad stuff. When Aaron died, they pulled Chris out. He came back to work for the sheriff. They kept everything quiet. Even the funeral. Even where they'd found the body."

"Do you trust the sheriff or no?" I duck into the bathroom and reemerge, brushing my teeth.

"I guess so," Locke says. He resumes his seat against the headboard. "The only part he played was to loan his officers to the state police."

After a bit, he changes the subject. "Em, what is the Amish family like?" I tap my toothbrush against the sink and from there I say, "They're amazing. They saved my life. They'd already been married for twenty-five years when they took me in, which, I mean..." I make a face to show what an accomplishment that is. "They weren't always happy with each other, but they always made up." I sit down on the bed, facing him, one leg crossed in front of me and one leg hanging over the side. "Why do some couples get to have it for real?" Without waiting for a reply, I brighten. "Guess their names," I implore him.

My change of mood brings out his playfulness. He accepts the challenge by rubbing his hands together. "They both come from Amish families?"

"Yep. The dad was adopted in. He's African American, which is kind of rare in the Amish community."

"Daniel," Locke guesses.

"Nope."

"Jonah."

I mouth *noooo*.

"Hmm. Noah."

"Right!" I laugh. "And the Mrs.?"

"Rebecca."

I shake my head.

"Beelzebub."

"Really, Locke?"

"Ummm...Hannah."

"Yes!" I exclaim. I hold up a hand for a congratulatory high-five, before counting off the names of their six children on my fingers. "Their kids are Ruth, Samuel, Esther, Moses, Levi, aaaaand..." My voice rises in pitch as I draw out the word. "Lysle."

"What?" Locke laughs. "How did *Lysle* slip in there?"

"Right?! Isn't it funny? Hannah and Noah are like Amish American hipsters. They're not really what I'd call *strictly* Amish. And they do totally video chat. I just didn't like Chris's attitude either. They both went to the university I ended up attending. That's why I went there. And then they moved back from DC to the almost Amish lifestyle without any regret. I just love them."

"They sound great." Locke yawns. "I want to meet them."

"I'd like that. We used to take trips to the Upper Peninsula. They have a house there. The water's always cold, and there are rocks to dive from. I've spent whole days in kayaks there. I was the first in our family to—I call them *family*, you know?—I was the first to discover a small red lighthouse that stands on one of the cliffs, and all of us made the climb to explore it. You can go *ice* climbing there in the winter, and, oh you need to see the trees, because—" Locke's eyes have drifted shut. "Because they smell like all the things you love," I say quietly. I shake my head, feeling as tender toward Locke as I can ever remember feeling toward another human being.

He rouses himself. "Sorry." He starts to get up from the bed.

"Will you stay?" I ask.

Locke raises his sleepy eyebrows in question.

"I mean, not to—" I interrupt myself. "Will you just stay?"

"I thought you'd never ask." He scoots down to lie on his side, on top of the covers, his hands between his knees, his eyes falling shut again.

"Are we safe?" I ask.

"Yes." Locke settles in further. "Don't worry. I'm hypervigilant." He falls asleep, almost, before the end of the sentence.

I cover myself with the blankets and watch him until my own eyes grow heavy, which isn't long, and I fall asleep beside him. Sometime in the middle of the night, I wake to find that Locke has turned out the lights, but has come back to lie beside me, still on top of the covers. It makes me happy. I remind myself that it isn't real. It isn't a promise.

I put my head to his. He's sound asleep. Long, deep breaths. "I love you," I whisper, just to try the phrase on to see if it fits. I kiss his soft sleepy mouth.

Locke hums in his sleep like he's answering a question I haven't asked, but his lips won't form the words. I smile. Then tears threaten to fall. "I wish I could have you for real," I say.

I roll away to face the wall, but when I do, Locke pushes himself against my back, spooning me through the bedclothes. He lays an arm around me. "I'm right here, Em," he murmurs against my head.

The darkness makes me bold. "But what about—"

"Emmm," he warns.

"Yes?"

"You're not going to ask whether or not I'll be here tomorrow, are you?"

I find myself snickering, but I deny it. "No. It's already tomorrow, and you're still here."

"Why do you think I'm still here?"

"Because you want to test your virtue, the way Ghandi did?"

He chuckles, and I can feel the deep tones of his voice resonate inside my own rib cage. "Go to sleep," he says. "Before I wake up too much to care about virtue."

8

LET'S JUST LOVE EACH OTHER

When I open my eyes the next morning, Locke is propped on one arm studying me. Golden light is doing its best to create entryways through the blinds behind him, so I can only see him in silhouette.

He draws soft fingers from my shoulder to my wrist. "I think that you told me you loved me in the night," he says. "Yeah, you definitely said that. In a dream, maybe."

I shrug like I have no idea what the man is on about.

He makes an *Ah, well* gesture.

"Happy birthday," I say.

He tilts his head in thanks.

"Is Annabelle still asleep?" I ask.

"Sarah took her a few minutes ago. For my birthday present."

"That. Is. Great." I begin to yawn, but most of it is ejected from my lungs when the cat leaps onto my abdomen. It rubs its head against Locke's chest and plops down between the two of us. "Look," Locke says, "Even the cat needs a break from babies."

"I guess so. Can you imagine feeding five of them from your own body?"

His lower lip tightens along with the skin on his jawline. "I cannot," he says.

A breath of a laugh escapes me, and my eyes close involuntarily.

"Wanna get some more sleep?" Locke asks.

"It's *your* birthday," I say from behind my eyelids. "I want to do whatever yo—"

Locke initiates a series of long kisses that puts an end to any cohesive thought I have going. When he pulls away, I open one eye to find where he's gone and lift my head and shoulders.

"That's really all I want to do," he says.

"What about the macarons?"

He doesn't answer me. He nudges the cat out of the way to lean over me, and I wrap my arms around his neck.

"You're acting like a man in love," I say.

"Well?" Kiss. "There's a reason for that." Kiss. "It's because I'm a man in love. With you."

"But when you're finished being in—"

"Oh my gosh, Emma." Locke raises himself to scold me. "Can we not at least *enjoy* the in-love part before you doom the whole relationship? You may find that I can surprise you. That I work hard to make you happy. It's insulting, really."

"I'm sorry. I wasn't even being that serious. I was just—"

"Just keeping me at arm's length." Locke looks down at my arms, which I'm still using to corral his head. "Metaphorically. You're not a throwaway. I'm not going to toss you out."

I sink my head into the pillow, and my hair halos around me. "Come back and kiss me, then," I tell him. His scolding gives way to a grin.

He follows me down to the pillow. "Fall in love with me back," he says. I stretch to meet his lips, but he withdraws to tease me. "Let yourself," he urges. He kisses my cheek on the way to my ear where he whispers, "It's not bad to feel good." Cheek again. Each. Eye. "Emmaaa..." He draws my name out in a low growl and bites my lip. "Fall in love with me." Kiss. "Today." Kiss. "And every day." Kiss. Kiss. Kiss. Kiss.

By the time we get to the grocery store, I can't stop smiling, and Locke can't stop gloating about it. He pays for all the groceries—even though I've picked up way too much, and I'm doing this for *his* birthday—and he takes me back to his house.

"It's the mirror of Aaron's," I note. Locke parks the truck, and we both stare up at the steep roofline through the windshield.

"Except I got the pond," Locke says. I see what he means. Past the back of the house is a large pond bordered by cattails, conical purple flowers, spreading waterlilies. There's a small dock stretching into the water, along with a shiny wooden canoe that I suspect Locke has fashioned.

"It's from a storybook," I tell him. "How'd you guys settle on the properties? Did you have to fight it out?"

"Did you not see the shooting range behind Aaron's place? With the mounds and barriers? That's all he wanted. Enough room to play paintball and to wreck his ATV. And a few deer stands."

Locke's dogs are waiting for us to emerge with their wild tails swinging. As Locke walks to the truck bed for the grocery bags, he holds up a hand to keep them from advancing and flattens it for them to lie down.

"You use sign language with your dogs," I say.

"Yeah, baby, I was *made* for you." He releases the boys with a flick of his wrist, and the dogs lead the way up the stairs to the front door. "Fili and Kili are twins," he informs me, as we follow. "Fili belonged to Aaron, but Kili and I ended up raising him. Isn't that right, Kili?"

Kili is standing with his nose to the door and when Locke speaks to him, he shuffles sideways to bark a quick reply.

"You think so?" Locke asks. Kili barks again. "He says that *he's* borne the brunt of the burden," Locke interprets.

Since Locke's hands are laden, I step ahead to try the door and let myself in.

Even Locke's furniture is the same as Aaron's. But the feel of the home is different. It's lighter, for one thing. Maybe there are more windows. I can't remember being able to look out the back of Aaron's house, but Locke's is a wall of glass that exposes the pond, bird feeders, a back deck, and living things, like ferns.

Locke sets the bags on the counter and crosses his arms to give attention to the canines, who are sitting expectantly by their bowls. "I'm sorry for the irregular feeding times, boys. We've had some things to deal with." Locke scoops dog food out of a bag inside the pantry door and tells me to rummage around for what I need. "If I'm missing something, I'll see if we can borrow it from Mom."

I find mixing bowls, a strainer, spatulas. It's a tiny kitchen, but it's well stocked. "Do you cook?" I ask.

"That's funny. No, not really. Though, I guess I can grill about anything."

"Including peanut butter sandwiches?" I lift out evidence in the form of an empty jar and tilt it for Locke's perusal. "How were you going to feed me with this?"

"I told you we could stop by the store." Locke trashes the jar.

"Alright. Get out of here." I shoo him away.

"I can help."

"I really don't think you can," I joke. "Go watch your football game, or do some other manly thing."

Locke hoists his upper body over the counter that separates us, and waits for me to step into a kiss, which I do. Like it's just a normal part of my wonderful life.

"Thanks for this," he says. He launches himself over the coffee table to land on the couch. Soon sports announcers are exclaiming about some tremendous play, because...college football in the South. It's a big deal in Michigan too, I guess. I just don't care.

"Hook 'em Horns!" I call. Because I've heard it said locally. Not because I know anything about it.

"It's A&M," Locke remarks. My face is void of comprehension. "Not UT," he adds.

"Aaand the difference is...?"

His face becomes grotesque. "OK, we have to talk," he says. He draws himself to the front of the couch, and while he expounds upon the rivalry between the Longhorns and the Aggies, I mix and measure, chop and dice, bake and sauté.

"And which one are we for?" I ask at length. I look up to find him gaping at me and purse my lips to keep from laughing.

"The *Horns*, Emma. We're for the *Horns*."

"Got it."

"Honestly, woman," he mutters under his breath. Even Kili shows disdain, rolling over with a groan and covering one eye with a paw. Locke strolls to a closet, and I can hear him rooting around. When he reappears, it's to display a burnt-orange baseball cap with a white longhorn stitched to the front. He nestles it onto my head with a nod of satisfaction.

Just then the voices from the TV grow more animated. The announcer calls off distances to the goal line in increments, and Locke positions himself in front of the TV to encourage the runner. Finally, he throws his hands in the air, and both he and the announcer bellow, "Touchdown!" He thunders, "That's what I'm *talking* about!" And turns to find me staring. "Too loud?" he asks. I shake my head. "Then why do you look like you're in pain?"

"It's a good hurt," I assure him.

I'm just going to enjoy this. I'm just going to fall in love with this man. I'm not sure I have any choice about it anyway.

I'm weighing these considerations when we hear a vehicle roll over the gravel drive and stop in front of the house. I'm the closest to the window. "Bright red pickup?" I say.

Locke looks pleased. "It's Ricks." He stomps out onto the deck with the air of a king addressing his subjects. "I'm not available for kidnap this year," he proclaims. "I have a date." The overt friendliness of his voice warms me. It doesn't even matter that it's directed toward someone else. I peek out to see a sandy-haired man with tanned skin leaning back against his truck. He waits for Locke to traverse the stairs. I can hear them bantering but can't decipher what's being said. Before too long, I am summoned. "Emma!" Locke yells up. "Stick your head out to prove you exist!"

I remove the Longhorns cap and smooth my hair, which is a lost cause, but apparently, hope has been rekindled in me. When I step out to stretch over the deck's railing, Locke motions in my direction to present me as proof. He says, "Em, this is one of our oldest friends." I think that *our* must include Aaron. "Richard Hendrick Landsman the

Third." Locke says the name as formally as possible, but follows it with a simple, "Ricks."

"She can come too," Ricks says. He tilts his face up to me. "In fact, she can come *instead* of you." Locke punches him. "Is that a no?" Ricks says, laughing and cradling the shoulder that took the punch. He turns a more sober eye on Locke. "You OK, then?"

"Quite."

Ricks makes fun of Locke's word choice. "*Quite*, huh?" He glances at me and stifles a grin while he nods. "I see. Emma!" Ricks shouts up, "Just so you know, Landon is an absolute nightmare to be seen with in public. He only orders drinks that come with colorful little umbrellas. It's embarrassing. And that's just the beginning. Whatever you've got going on here, you should think it through."

"That's disturbing," I answer. "What else can you tell me?"

Cutting impish eyes at Locke, Ricks makes a dash up the stairs, but Locke is ready for it. He nabs Ricks around the waist and swing-tackles him to the ground from the third step. I yip in surprise. "I have more to share!" Ricks yells. His words are chopped with laughter and the combined effort to wrench himself out of Locke's grip. "Don't you want me to hang out with you guys?!"

"Not even a little bit," Locke answers. It comes out strained as he grapples to maintain the upper hand. The goldens bark and bow in playtime poses before bouncing around to figure out how to join in.

Ricks is able to capsize Locke, and they roll twice before Locke slams him onto his back again and bends Ricks' arm underneath him. "I give up!" Ricks howls, still cackling like it's the most fun he's had in ages. Locke rises to his knees, and then to standing where he takes Rick's outstretched arm, wrist in wrist, and hoists him to his feet.

It's just not something you see women do. I return the baseball cap to my head.

Without releasing his grip on Locke's wrist, Ricks drags him into a hug. "Happy birthday, brother." He raises a two fingered salute to me, which turns into the sign of a longhorn when he notices the cap.

"We're for the Horns," I announce, causing Locke to choke.

"Yeah! Hook 'em!" Ricks agrees. Out of the side of his mouth, he says, "She's not from around here, huh?" Locke shows him, on his right hand, what part of Michigan I'm from, but it's lost on Ricks.

Ricks rounds the side of his truck. "I'm picking you up Saturday, with the boat," he says. "Early. Be ready." To me, he says, "You too, if you can tolerate this guy for that long. My wife and our three-year-old will be at the lake house, so you can fish with us, or hang out by the water and pretend to understand toddler speak. Kid says an awful, awful lot these days. Talks incessantly. No idea what he's saying."

After Ricks pulls away and Locke reenters the house, he inhales with a noisy sniff. "Whoa. This house has never smelled so good. Please marry me."

"I would," I return, "but I don't think I can deal with all those little umbrellas. Hey, I don't mind if you want to call Ricks back for dinner. It's *your* birthday. We have plenty."

"No way. Are you kidding me? This is the first time I've had you all to myself." Locke creeps over to nibble on things, including my ear, because, as he says, he can no longer resist me in his Texas cap. "You want to go with them next Saturday?" he asks.

I slap his hand out of the cookie dough, but he's already successfully gathered a finger full. He sits against the counter to suck it off and says, "It's a nice property. We could kayak. Or paddleboard. No red lighthouses though."

"Would we take Annabelle with us?"

"Oh yeah," Locke says. "We have a baby."

"You go. I need to get some things done anyway, and you can catch up with your friend."

"No, let's just take her. Ricks' son will be there. Come on, Em. I want them to get to know you."

"Why?" I'm partly distracted by the pan I have on the stove.

"What do you mean *why*?" I feel myself being spun into Locke's embrace. "Because Ricks and Natalie are a big part of my life, and I want the people I care about to know each other."

"Oh. That's really nice."

He smiles into a kiss. "And I want to show you off."

Dinner is a sophisticated take on a peasant's meat pie, and the face Locke makes when he tastes it is reward enough for the work. We eat by candlelight, though periodically I jump up to remove loaves of bread from the oven and to pipe buttercream filling between the cookies.

When I carry a plate of them over, Locke refuses to try one until I sing Happy Birthday to him, which I do, rather quickly, and hold a macaron to his mouth.

"Oh my gosh, Em, these are amazing," he says.

I try one too. They really are. "They'll be even better tomorrow," I tell him, but he says, "I'm not sure there will be any left to test that theory."

Locke sits back in his chair with a sigh. "I honestly didn't expect to enjoy another birthday. I sort of thought I'd ignore the rest of them."

"We can watch a James Bond if you want."

"You know what? That would be perfect."

"You find one, and I'll do a quick clean up."

Locke tries to help with the dishes, but I push him out of the kitchen, so he settles on the couch to scan our choices. "Which Bond is your favorite?" he asks.

"Daniel Craig," I tell him. "Hands down."

"The deadliest?"

"The most fun to look at."

"Well now I know which one we're *not* watching," Locke mutters. He picks a Sean Connery and pushes back to make room for me to lie beside him. We snuggle in, shoulders and hips and hands and knees all very happy. My eyes travel the room contentedly. I don't even bring to mind any reasons to stop enjoying it.

"Where is your bedroom?" I ask. "Up in the loft?"

He drops his voice to say, "Why do you want to know?" But he laughs before I can answer. "Yes. It is for now."

Locke pauses the movie, and I roll my head to find him peering at me over my shoulder. "I built this house with the ability to expand the whole footprint," he says. "The wall behind us—" He twists his torso to knock on it. "I can move it back to make more bedrooms or office space or— Really the whole layout can be revamped. The kitchen could be three times its size. If a cook lived here. I'll show you the plans." He brings them up on his phone and takes me on a virtual tour.

"What do you think?" he asks. I'm not sure why he's showing me, other than that he's excited about all he can do with the place.

"I think it's great. You'll have tons more room."

"Yeah, but which one do you like best?" He actually wants to know. He's all into it, which makes me want to get into it for his sake.

"Go back," I say. Instead, he hands me the phone, and I flip to the plan I like best. "This one," I say. "The big kitchen's perfect. I like the high ceilings and how many windows there are. But *here* you need a fireplace." I enlarge the part of the plan I mean. "And this could be a workout room, overlooking the pond. Or a guest room. Or a nursery, I guess."

"No, the nursery's here next to the master," Locke says. "That way you won't have far to go in the middle of the night, and you can just jump back into bed with me."

I can't hide my smile and, believe me, I try. I am that delighted to be so casually thrown into his dreams of the future. I say, "Why do I have to be the one to get up?"

"Because I'll be too tired from having built you the home of your dreams. I mean, look at how many rooms there are. Honestly woman, how many kids do you plan on us having?"

"None for a while!" I laugh.

"Oh, that's right." Locke rolls onto me and braces himself on his elbows. "You're going to wait till your thirties."

"On the kids' part," I remind him.

"On the kids' part," he agrees.

We forget about James Bond. We make out until we hear the TV click itself off, and we're breathless. But now it's eleven, and we promised to relieve Sarah of the baby, so we drag ourselves away.

Back at the big house, I trade Sarah macarons for baby. I leave a few loaves of bread wrapped on the counter and climb the stairs, leaving Locke to speak with his parents, who want to wish him a happy birthday.

When I round the stair rail to Aaron's old bedroom, the door is open wide, which is odd, because I've been leaving it closed to confine the cat. I've only entered the room when I come to a halt. Something is off. The hairs on the back of my neck bristle. Things have been moved. I turn in a circle to try to pinpoint what has been disturbed and hold Annabelle closer to my chest.

I check on the kittens. They're all accounted for, though mewing pathetically. Where's the mama? "Tac?" I call. I shut the bedroom door and check under the bed, then behind the curtains. "Tac? Where are you?" I check in the bathtub.

When the sound of the push of alternating paws comes from behind me, I do an about face. "How did you get locked in there?" I ask. I open the closet, and the cat shrinks back like she's afraid of me. Then she cranes her neck to peer around my leg.

That makes me want to peer around myself, though I know no one else is in the room. When the cat decides all is safe, she limps out of the closet. "Tac, what happened to you?"

A knock on the door makes both of us jump. "Emma, these macarons are out of this world," comes Sarah's muffled voice. "You should go into business!"

I wrench open the door, but instead of accepting Sarah's compliment I say, "Did you come into the room today?"

"Yes," she says, her mouth full of pastry. "Annabelle and I lost, like, three pacifiers. I think they're made with some kind of cosmic homing device that zaps them back to the Land of the Binkies wh—"

"Did you see the cat when you came in?"

"Yes. Why?"

"Did she seem OK?"

"Yeees. Why?"

"Did you go into the closet for any reason?"

Sarah rolls her hand round and round on her wrist. "Information. I need information in order to answer what you're really asking."

"Just now," I explain, "the cat was trapped in the closet, and look.

She's limping."

Sarah goes to study the cat. "She was in the kitten nursery when I came in. I don't get it."

"You don't get what?" Locke asks. He fills up the doorway and deftly snatches the macaron Sarah's about to eat.

"Dude!" Sarah hunches over her stash. "It is not your birthday anymore. Back off."

Locke consults his watch. "It *is* still my birthday. And that is my cake."

"You're gonna get fat," Sarah says, stuffing a whole macaron into her mouth before Locke can make a play for it. "You're gonna get really, really fat." She can barely form her words, but she points at her brother to emphasize each one, then closes her eyes and stops chewing to groan, "I'm gonna get fat too." Locke grabs for the bag, and Sarah tries to jump out of his reach, but his reach is long. He tussles with her and comes up with half a macaron, which he pops into his mouth before she can swipe it.

"Guys!" I grumble. Both siblings lift their heads. "Somebody's been in my room, and now the cat's hurt." As if to prove the point, the cat complains mournfully.

Locke settles, and I describe what I've come back to. He rifles through the hanging clothes and checks the bathroom. "Is anything missing or anything else misplaced?"

I shrug. "Things have been moved."

My clothes are still folded in my weekend bag, and yet they're unstacked from the way I placed them. The bag itself sits, as it has since we got it from my apartment, on the counter beside the bathroom door, but it's facing in a different direction. It's possible that I did that, though, I guess.

"Do you *live* out of that bag?" Sarah asks.

I don't answer because I'm still trying to figure out what has happened here.

"Emma likes to know she's able to make a quick escape," Locke says. "She's got one foot out the door at all times."

"That's not *true*," I snap.

A little bit, Locke mouths, presenting his finger and thumb an inch apart for reference.

"There's plenty of drawer space," Sarah suggests. She steps around me to reach for the clothes in question.

"No, Sarah." I block my bag. "Can we focus on the problem at hand?"

"Yes," Locke says. He walks across the hall to his own room, but is back in no time, to indicate that nothing is out of order there. I go through the pockets of my bag, one by one, first the interior compartments and then the large one on the outside.

"Nothing's missing," I say. I unzip a small pocket-within-a-pocket to make sure my necklace is there, then zip it back.

"I'll go ask Mom and Dad if they've been up here for any reason." Sarah leaves to find out, but doubles back for her pastry bag, throwing a look of suspicion Locke's way, before exiting again.

"It's probably nothing," Locke says. "I mean, Mom stores things in the closet. She probably came up to get something, and the cat was accidentally trapped inside. She's not badly hurt. She's not even really limping." Locke tugs on the windows to make sure they're locked. "You tired? You wanna try to rest?"

I shake my head, frowning. "No. I'm too amped up now."

"You wanna...play charades?"

"You're kidding." I'm being too curt with him. I should probably sequester myself until I cool down.

"I am," he says. "Look, I get that you're unnerved by this, but there's no sign that an *intruder* was here. No damage done." I let out an incredulous pop of breath, and throw an arm out toward the cat. "*Other* than the cat," he cuts in, "which was probably an unwitting accident."

"I'm not trying to be a—I'm just upset that someone rummaged through my personal space. *Again*! And that the stupid cat got hurt. The one *stupid* thing that belongs to me. It needs me. And I let it get hurt."

"You didn't let it get hurt. You weren't even here."

I lift both my hands and make a *pff* sound.

"Em, everything is OK." Locke braces me by the arms and then turns his attention back to my clothes. "Here," he says. "Unpack your bag. I'll help you."

I feel the frustration pinching my face. "Why are you challenging me right now?"

"Come on," he says. "Let's move you in."

"I am not unpacking my bag, Locke! I am not going to *stay* with you! Honestly, it feels like you're pricking my insecurities on purpose."

"Emma, why is this such a point of contention? You're just being stubborn."

"Locke! None of this is real." I wave my hand around. "This is not my room. Your family is not my family. We don't even know each other. We're just playing house here. We're just pretending."

Locke's head kicks back like I've physically struck him. He acknowledges my words with a few small nods, his jaw slightly distended. "Well," he says. "Thanks for pretending all that stuff today."

My heart sinks, but I don't respond. He stares at me pointedly, waiting for me to say something, but I'm stuck. I want to form words, want to pull the brakes on my own runaway tantrum train, and assure him that I wasn't pretending. That this was the best day of my life. But I can't. I can't even sign it.

After a few seconds, he exhales scornfully. "You know Emma, it's hard for a relationship to be real when only one of you believes that's even possible."

Locke stalks to his room and on the way out, his eyes fall on Annabelle. Annabelle, who is happily gnawing on her fist. I can almost hear his inward conflict. *What happens when duty to the baby intersects with the crazy, mean chick across the hall? How in the world did she ruin such a perfect day? How can I get her out of my parents' house? Thank goodness she never unpacked her bag.*

He slaps his door shut, and my shoulders fall with the sound of it. I slump into the leather chair with my head in my hands. The cat circles my ankles. "What is wrong with me?" I ask it.

I'll have to extricate myself, of course, but I can't legally foster

Annabelle away from the Lockes' house. Maybe I can just hole up in the mother-in-law suite on the other side of the house. I'll have to apologize, though. It isn't his fault I have no tolerance for risk. He's been nothing but kind. And generous. And funny. And sexy— I stand up.

He's not going to want you now that you've shown what a lunatic you are, I tell myself.

Myself says back, *You still have to say you're sorry.*

I decide to brush my teeth. No use being doubly offensive. I pull on a T-shirt and some sleep shorts. It's not like I can transition tonight. I wash my face.

When I come out of the bathroom, I take a stabilizing breath. I stop to doubt myself and to roll the hem of my shirt a few times. I resolve to go through with it (again), and so I make my feet move (again). On the way to the door, I recite an apology, but it sounds more like a resignation letter.

About halfway between the bed and the bedroom door, I feel a presence in the room, and spin to find Locke sitting against the headboard, watching me.

Neither of us speaks. I forget about the apology. I kind of want to poke him to make sure he's real. I'm gawking.

"Are you *that* shocked that I came back in here?"

I don't know if I'm supposed to voice my authentic reaction, which is, "I'm not even sure you're corporeal," or if I should give a more appropriate, "No, not shocked, just a bit surprised."

I'm pretty sure he sees the truth.

"I'm sorry I walked out," he says.

"You had every right to walk out. I was being a jerk."

"Yeah, and with a *normal* person," he says. I spare a withering glance. "I might have taken some more time to feel sorry for myself, but I know how you think, and I wanted to make sure you knew I wasn't *leaving*, leaving. I was just…emoting."

"You deserve to emote," I tell him. I can't quite meet his eyes. "I'm sorry."

"I know. I heard you crying. And it made me sad." He pushes

forward. Now he's sitting straighter, and he motions between us. "This is real for me. I know it's happening fast, and it's been intense, but it's still real. And I think it's real for you. But if it's not, or if you're not willing for it to be, I need to know that. I need to know it now."

"It is real," I say. "It just scares me."

Locke nods his acceptance, gets to his feet, brushes past me. I want to stop him, want to grab him up. Want to come to a better understanding before we part for the night. I certainly don't want it to *end* here.

"Please don't go yet," I say.

Locke lifts a blanket from the back of the leather chair and scans the room like he's trying to find out to whom I'm speaking. "I'm not going anywhere," he says. "Except to sleep. Beside you." He scoots past me to lie on 'his side' of the bed, on top of the quilt, and he uses the blanket to cover himself. He stretches waaay over to turn out the light on my bedside table, and then I hear him reposition himself.

After a delay in the dark, in which I stand wondering what has just occurred, Locke says, "Is there any reason you're still hovering over me like a ghost, instead of lying next to me like a woman?"

Well, that is the question, isn't it?

I say, "I don't *want* to be a ghost."

"Emma, get in this bed."

I feel my way around to my side and climb under the covers where I lie facing him, as inert as a corpse. In a minute I say, "We're OK? Just like that? I mean, I don't get put on probation or...lose any points?"

"You really don't get how this relationship thing is supposed to work, do you?" When I don't answer, he says, "Give me your hand."

I hold it out in the dark for him to find. He spreads my fingers and presses my open palm against his chest. "Feel that?"

"I...certainly do."

"It's OK?"

"It's hard as a rock."

I feel him laugh. "I mean my heart," he says.

"Ah. Um, yes. Seems quite well."

"It was doing that for nearly three decades before I met you." He rolls me onto my back, places my hand over *my* heart, and covers it with his own much larger hand. He quickly aborts that maneuver, saying, "OK, well that may have been too awkward and/or incredibly arousing, to prove the point."

Which makes me laugh. "But the point *is?*" I ask.

"I don't need you."

"Oh, that's nice, Locke," I spout.

"Hear me out. You keep coming back to things needing you and you getting to keep them because of what you do for them. But that means that if they quit needing you, or if you quit meeting that need, they can hit the road. I'm not going to hit the road, Emma. As much as it would hurt me to lose you, I'm not dependent on you. I am giving myself to you, and that is why you get to keep me."

"OK, well, it's just hard to trust that you're going to stick around when all the shiny stuff wears off. When the kissing and—stuff—is done."

"You think so little of me," he accuses.

"I think you're amazing. I don't think much of my own...charm."

He rolls back to his side of the bed, taking my hand with him. It's dark. I can't tell more about his body language than what I can feel.

"Is Hannah all that charming?" he asks. "I mean, all the time, every day?"

"Why are you asking that?"

"Because you said that Noah has been faithful, right? It's been like thirty-five years for them at this point? I assume it's because Hannah is enchanting at all times."

"OK. I get it. No. She is a lovely human being, but she is a human being. She is sometimes given to surly bouts in which she is nearly insufferable."

"Huh," Locke says, in mock confusion.

"Aaaaaalright," I say. I reach up to feel his cheek and find that he's smiling. He turns to kiss my fingers, before pressing them back against his chest.

"We don't even know how many beats we get, Em. Let's just love each other."

9

YOU BELONG TO ME

When we pull up to campus on Monday morning, John Mark is waiting at the curb, as his coach has requested. He salutes until after we've both stepped out. "John Mark Hollander! Reporting for duty! Sir!"

Locke rolls his eyes and places Annabelle's carrier at John Mark's feet. "Just don't forget what we talked about," he says.

John Mark solemnly signs that he will adhere to me like a guard dog, and that he will try not to gaze upon my lovely legs too often or steal my affections away from Coach in the process.

Locke peers at him blankly. "What did the kid just say to me? I saw 'legs.'"

"John Mark says that he is more than happy to do *whatever* Coach asks," I interpret. "And that he is well impressed with Coach's massive strength and protective disposition."

"Close," John Mark snickers.

"Mm-hm." Locke signs his own message. That he will be keeping an eye on John Mark. Then he kisses me openly, causing John Mark to whistle like a falling stone and to cover Annabelle's eyes.

As we're walking away from Locke, John Mark says to me, "But for real, when are you going to break the news to him, about us?"

Four days pass this way, John Mark caring for Annabelle with all the boyish enthusiasm he employs in the other areas of his life. He's a godsend. He keeps pretending that he wants to steal us, both Annabelle and me, away from Locke, but in truth, he adores his coach and would go to any length to earn his respect.

Now it's Friday morning, and five-twenty-two comes with Locke pressed to my side, albeit through a sheet and a blanket. The baby is the one who wakes me. How much I long to fall back to sleep against the warm body beside me is difficult to overstate, but Annabelle needs me, and she's going to wake Locke, who has worked round the clock to serve us. I force myself up.

Fifteen minutes later, Locke stumbles down the stairs to find me seated on the living room rug. I've pulled the baby to sitting too, and Annabelle has been able to remain upright, so there she sits. Locke braces himself on the arm of the couch and looks at us through tired eyes. "You left me," he says.

"No. At least, I didn't want to. Go catch another wink."

He shakes his head no. "Can't. I gotta make coffee."

Locke runs his fingers through his hair and plods into the kitchen. While the coffee brews, he joins us on the floor. Annabelle has eaten her cereal and is now sucking on a bottle with gusto. When she sees Locke, she pauses long enough to reach a hand out to him, and he allows her to grip his finger.

"It's hard to have a baby," he says.

"Yeah," I concede. "They try to tell you..."

"Did you steal my toothbrush?" Locke asks.

"Yes," I immediately reply.

He bites back a smile. "Why did you do that?"

"To add to the shrine I'm building. That's how into you I am. I pilfered your shoelaces too. And a sweatshirt. Actually, I *did* swipe a sweatshirt. You seem to think the upstairs should be covered in a layer of frost."

"Yeah. To get you to snuggle up to me. Did I brush my teeth in your room at some point?"

"You're just over-exhausted. You've laid it somewhere odd. It'll turn up."

"It's been gone for days now. I've been using a tiny toothbrush that came from the dentist. I think I must have been about five when I put it in the drawer."

Annabelle finishes her bottle, and I hold her upright to pat her back. "One of my sister's boys had colic," I recall. "She and her husband never got *any* sleep. That child cried any time he wasn't vertical."

"Are you two close?" Locke asks.

I think about that. "We're not *not* close, but she's six years older than I am. I was an accident. I think I'm the reason my dad left. The start of the slow decline. He hadn't signed up for all that."

"He *had* signed up for all that," Locke counters. "The day he married your mom."

"Yeah," I say, in acknowledgment. The thought hadn't bloomed for me that way before. I'd spent too much time trying to figure out *why* Dad left, and not enough on the fact that he wasn't supposed to. "I think I just needed for someone to say it like that."

"So, is that the reason you take care of abandoned things?" Locke's long legs carry him to the coffee pot. "Accidental cats, and babies, and strange men in cemeteries?"

"Maybe," I answer. "Hannah and Noah took *me* in when I had few other options. Family's where you find it."

"Amen to that." Locke hands me my cup and clinks it with his own. Then we lean back against the couch to watch Annabelle play under a stand of swinging toys. "Grandaddy would have loved you, Em," Locke remarks.

"I hope so. I love *him* dearly." He questions my statement with his brow. "For the role he played in making you who you are," I explain. "And because you light up when you talk about him." I put my cup to my lips, but instead of taking a sip, I smile and say, "And because you still call him Grandaddy, like a kid."

Locke doesn't mind. He crouches over Annabelle and tells her that

Grandaddy would have loved her too. Annabelle kicks her feet when she sees his face. He repeats, "Gran-dad-dy, Gran-dad-dy," until Annabelle imitates the movement of his mouth. I still.

"Locke, do that again," I tell him. So, he does. Same results. "Try a different sound. Like *baa baa baa*." I pitch the *baa baas* up high. Locke looks 'round at me, but I nod my head to say, *Just do it*. He does.

"Locke, she's imitating the shape of your mouth."

"That's a good thing, right?"

"Yeah, but she's not vocalizing at all. She's not imitating sounds."

"Not following."

"She's doing all the things she's supposed to be doing for her age. Except imitating sounds. Hang on." I scan the room for something to clang together. I rummage through the cabinets and grab a large stew pot and a wooden spoon. Aborting my initial attempt, I warn, "This is going to be loud." Then I whack the bottom of the pan three times, which rings out in shocking reverberations.

"Ow," Locke says, covering his ears.

"Yeah," I agree. "She should be crying her head off right now. She didn't even look over."

"You think she can't *hear*? Now that would be an even bigger coincidence than we've had yet. For *you* to be fostering a baby who's—"

"What just happened?!" Sarah appears, clutching the chest of her robe.

"Sorry!" I rush to say, suddenly aware of how early it is. I hold both pot and spoon down by my sides with stiff arms and bite my bottom lip.

Both of Locke's parents appear as well.

"I'm so sorry!" I say again. I'm cringing now. "That was dumb. That was just me. I am so sorry."

"Emma thinks the baby can't hear," Locke explains. "It was a test."

"That actually makes a lot of sense," his mom says. "I'm never able to comfort her or distract her with just my voice."

"And she sleeps through loud noises," I say, excited by Ardea's affirmation. "Like when the whole swim team was here."

"We'll make a doctor's appointment," Ardea says.

I open my mouth and close it again. Through my years with Hannah and Noah, and then in my studies at Gallaudet, I've come to accept the idea that being Deaf isn't a disability. It's just another culture, a different approach to language and life. So, when Ardea suggests a doctor, I want to point out that Annabelle isn't sick.

"Em?" Locke questions.

"Yeah, I guess we need to know why she can't hear, in case something's wrong."

"In case something's wrong?" Ardea asks.

"In case the reason she can't hear is troubling. A brain tumor. Or something that could harm her."

"You wouldn't want to take her for the simpler goal of opening up the world of sound for her?" Locke asks. "For the songs of bluebird parents?"

On the morning my hearing returned, Noah had ambled out to enjoy the morning sunshine and then had rushed to me when he found me weeping in the yard. The sound of his coffee mug shattering on the front deck is the second sound I remember. I'd been slow to tell him that I could hear again. Afraid he'd kick me out of his life. I needn't have worried. He'd been happy for me and had asked me to describe the bluebird songs in vivid detail. He'd called me *Little Blue* from then on and had assured me that he'd continue to look after me long after I left for college.

There are other sounds I wouldn't want to live without. Locke's low voice in the dark, for instance. "I'll make the appointment," I say. Then, through an apologetic smile that is more of a grimace, I say, "And may I also pour coffee for everyone?"

"We have to be up anyway." Ardea waves away my embarrassment and moves to the kitchen to fix her own cup. "I have to get to work, and Thomas has to tend to the animals."

"You're still going to talk to Pastor Ian this morning." Locke says it as half question/half statement to his dad, for whom he has scheduled the appointment.

"Yes. Yes," his dad says.

His dad seems more upbeat this morning. Affectionate and kind. Hands on Ardea's shoulders. A kiss for Sarah. He tells Locke how proud he is of him. He even tells him to "hang on to that one," about me. Sarah and Locke exchange a silent *what the heck* sibling communication.

"I took a better look at your proposal, Sarah," Mr. Locke says. "I had it drafted into a contract. When you're ready to take over the farm, it's yours. Just go to the lawyer and sign it."

"You did?" Sarah exclaims. "I didn't know you were considering it. I thought you were—" She doesn't finish. Ardea looks just as surprised as Sarah.

"Dad, that's great," Locke says. "It's been a long time coming. It'll free you up to do more of the tasks you love, and less of the—"

"Ones I'm no longer able to?" his dad says.

"That's not what I was going to say."

His dad claps him on the back. "I'm just giving you a hard time. You've both been right. It's time."

"We should celebrate," Ardea says. "To new beginnings."

Mr. Locke says that he'd like that, and so, even though they have to get to their jobs, the family makes breakfast together.

I have a later schedule this morning, and Sarah declares that the time has come for Annabelle's first swim lesson, so I put on my swimsuit. When I meet Locke back downstairs, I find him staring at the door where a note has been taped. *Heads up.* And an arrow pointing straight ahead.

We both peek through the blinds. Sarah is bouncing the baby in the far lane, and another person, a woman, is swimming laps in the lane closest to us. "Ah," Locke says, and he scratches his head. "So, full disclosure…I went out with the women's swim coach some this summer, Claire, and she is here."

I feel the color drain from my face, but instead of remaining open to the man, who has been incredibly open to me, I shut down. I imagine this horrible Claire cozied up with him on his couch discussing which James Bond is the best, or worse, which house plan is to her liking.

"It's not like we're married," I tell him. I shrug to emphasize how much this does not matter to me. Not one little bit.

"No, listen," Locke says. "It wasn't anything. I thought maybe it could lead to something, and I think she did too, but the more we saw each other, the more it became clear that we were just—"

"Dude," I cut him off. "You don't have to give an account." I grip the door handle. He grips my arm.

"I didn't know you. You understand? I wasn't cheating on you."

"There's nothing to cheat on," I say. "Do whatever you want. It's not like you belong to m—" I swallow down the rest of the word, because everything we'd worked through on the night of his birthday now jumps up from the ground in the form of formidable, if imaginary, Mongol warriors, pointing curved sabres at my throat, and screaming about what a hypocrite I am. In Mongolian. But I'm no fool. I get the gist. Beyond them, the emotion that has hijacked Locke's features is more incredulity than anything else, but there is definitely hurt there too.

I could probably fix things right now. Tell him that I want nothing more than to own him. Show him that I value him enough to deal with whatever comes to light. That I'll fight for this. That I trust him. Instead, I push out the door, past Claire, who is intent on her workout —she doesn't even notice me—and I sit down on the side of the pool next to Sarah, who is bobbing the baby in the water, making goofy faces.

Locke allows the door to close on him. It's another ten seconds before he walks out. Somehow Claire totally notices *him*. "Hey, Coach," she says.

"Hey, Coach," he returns, his voice friendly, but forced. "School's closed this morning?"

"Yeah. Just maintenance. Hope you don't mind." She's wearing a swim cap and lifts her goggles to rest them on her forehead. I can't tell much about the way she looks. Her swimsuit's ugly, so...

"I didn't think anyone would be around," the interloper continues.

"I hope I'm not—" She glances over at me. I am pretending not to know it. Because I am pretending not to care. Because I am an idiot.

"Nope," Locke says. He sits down on the edge of the lane next to Claire's, and submerges his feet. She must take this as an invitation. She crosses under the rope.

"Who's Sarah's friend?" she asks.

Locke hunches over to answer her, his hands on either side of him, the muscles in his back spreading like a cobra's hood. I can't hear much. I catch my own name. Claire asks a question.

"Uhhm, nope," he says. There is plenty of volume this time and some heat. "She's made it clear that there is nothing much between us."

"Oh, good," Claire laughs.

"Oh, *good*," I mock to myself. I toss my shirt with more energy than the shirt deserves and slip into the pool.

"What's *that* all about?" Sarah asks me.

"Oh, that's all about what a total moron I am," I say. "I told your brother, rather brashly, that he didn't need to account for his relationship with Claire, and that he didn't belong to me." I wrap my arms around myself.

"Why did you do that?"

"Because, Sarah, I like to sabotage my chances of happiness whenever possible. I am a total coward. And I am a total *moron*, as I stated before. Honestly. Keep up."

She gasps. "You *do* like him," she says, in some sort of twisted triumph. She gasps harder. "You *love* him. I knew it."

I exhale a frustrated breath and look down my nose at my new friend. It's probably less convincing than I hope since I'm half a foot shorter.

"Anyway," Sarah says, "he's totally into you. I've never seen him fall so hard. He certainly didn't for Claire. That just sort of petered out."

"Then why'd he even bring it up?"

"Because he's Landon. Think about it. If you found out right in front of her, or by accident, wouldn't that feel worse than just knowing upfront? Now you know, and that's that."

118

"If I haven't ruined everything," I say. "I sort of tried to ruin it all on Sunday too."

"What happened?"

I think of the way Locke placed my hand over his heart. He'd let me rest my head there later on. "He forgave me," I sigh. "It's like I get so scared of him being done with me I just try to get it over with. I go into psycho mode. I think I might be a lost cause."

"You're feeling sorry for yourself."

"Yep."

"You're wallowing."

"Shut up," I snicker. "How many strikes do you think I get?"

"I don't think Landon views it that way."

"Everybody has their limits."

I clap my hands half-heartedly and hold them out for Annabelle to 'swim' to. Locke has decided to do laps on his own. Next to Claire.

Despite the aching in my gut, I enjoy watching Annabelle grow accustomed to the water. Locke would have too. A little while later, he appears from under the rope. I cautiously fly the baby to him. He takes her, smiles at her, but not at me. Speaks to her, but not to me. Sarah is conspicuously gone. As is Claire.

"I'm sorry," I say. "Again. I don't know what got into me." Locke still doesn't look at me. I roll my eyes at myself. "Yes, I do," I correct. "I was jealous of whatever you may have done with Claire." That took a lot to admit. Should I keep going? "I got scared I couldn't keep you. So, I pushed you away. Which, now that I think about it, makes no sense." Still nothing. "But I didn't mean it. I'm the one acting like a leaver. Not you." I wait. I glance around, hoping that a solution will present itself. "Locke, will you please look at me?"

"I can't," he says.

"OK. Why?"

"Because of your—because of you in that green bikini."

"What?"

"I haven't been able to think clearly since you took your shirt off."

"Well," I laugh, "will you forgive me?"

"I *do* belong to you," he says. He slowly raises his eyes to meet mine.

All. The. Brooding. He steps closer, dragging Annabelle's legs through the water.

"You do?"

"*You* say it," he says. "*Don't* put a question mark on it." He is very close now. He is not smiling.

I drop my head, but he lifts it. "*You* say it," he says.

I start to sign it, but he shakes his head and snatches my hands, making me tense. "Out loud," he growls. "I want to hear it."

It takes three heartbeats before I can. "You belong to me," I say.

"Say it again," he orders.

"You belong to me."

He looms over me and lowers his voice. "Say it *again*."

"You do," I whisper. "You're mine."

"Stop. Doubting me. I haven't done anything to deserve it."

I close my eyes. "I know."

Then his lips are on mine, soft as a flower, and I draw breath for what feels like the first time since I walked outside. Annabelle starts to squirm in between us. "I love you," Locke says. He backs off, but I reach around to keep him for another moment.

"I love you too. I do."

And then it's like Locke forgets all about the part where I've disowned him, and we play in the water until Annabelle grows cross and tired. Locke lays her in the shade, cradled in towels. I'm wrapping a towel around myself when he tackles me back into the pool and initiates a very different type of play. Now I'm at risk of running late to work.

On the ride to school, the sun is high, and Locke's hand, across the baby, rests on my knee. Have I always been this nourished by physical affection? I feel lighter than I have in years, since before my dad left.

"I'm not going to do that anymore," I declare. "I'm not going to push you away when I'm scared."

Locke glances at me sidelong and back at the road. "Doesn't matter," he says. "Just gives me another chance to convince you I'm sticking around."

"Yeah, but I don't want to wear you down. I'll do it right from now on."

When Locke brakes by the sidewalk, John Mark is already waiting on the curb. Before he gets out, Locke turns to me with a look of concern that surprises me. "I don't want you to muscle through and *do it right*," he says. "I want you to be free."

John Mark taps on my window, and when I open the door, he immediately leans over to release Annabelle's carrier. "Morning, Coach," he says. "I will again guard your ladies with my life. Unless someone scary shows up. But then I will attract attention for them when I scream and flail my arms wildly while running in the opposite direction."

With half a smile, Locke thanks John Mark and shoos him out of the truck. Then he takes my face in his hands. "I love you," he says. He wouldn't have had to say it. The way he's looking at me makes me want to pluck out my heart and hand it to him.

"Just take it," I tell him. I reach down into my shirt and come out with the invisible organ. Locke carefully receives it in both hands.

"No take-backs," he warns.

"No take-backs," I agree.

I really love how he gets me, even when I'm acting like a quirky weirdo. I guess it takes one to know one, because the next thing I know, he's shoving my precious heart into his mouth and gulping it down.

"Did you just eat it?!" I squeal.

"Yes, thank you." He wipes his mouth. "It was delicious."

"Oh my gosh! You ate my heart."

"Get over here," he laughs. He pulls me into a kiss. How he can kiss me and smile at the same time is a mystery I enjoy exploring. This is so good. How did this come to me? I can't wait to be back in his arms tonight.

"You don't mind staying till after practice?" he asks.

"No. It'll be fun to see you in action. We'll meet you at the aquatic center and go from there."

"Hey!" John Mark says. "Are you coming?"

"Yes! Yes-yes-yes." I swing myself out of the truck.

"See you at five, Legs," Locke says.

He does not.

10

AT THE HOSPITAL

When my phone rings, it's several minutes past five. Annabelle and I are sitting on the bleachers next to an Olympic-size indoor pool. Locke hasn't arrived. His assistant coach has begun to drill the team without him. I smile at his name on the caller ID. "Hello, love." Did I just call him *love*? It makes me laugh into my next words. "Where are you?"

"It's Sarah." Her voice is shaky and hoarse.

My tone instantly hardens. "Sarah, what's wrong? Is he OK?" I step out of the pool area to hear above the reverberating noise of the swimmers. Visions of some horrific circular saw accident are playing in my mind.

"It's Dad. We're waiting for an ambulance. Landon's trying to keep him calm. I think he's—" Sarah chokes back a sob. "I think he's been poisoned or something."

"Sarah, no. Where will they take him? What hospital?"

Sarah sounds like she's turned away from the phone, and her voice comes out as more of a squeak. "I don't know."

"I'll figure it out. I'll meet you there."

When she hangs up, I rush to John Mark's lane. He's a little over halfway to where I stand. The assistant coach asks what wrong. He blows a whistle and slaps a hand into the water. The swimmers' heads pop up from their various locations to await the new instruction, and the coach makes a gesture that brings John Mark across the other lanes and out of the pool. When John Mark understands the dilemma, he tells me that he knows where to go, and only halfway towels off in his rush to collect his things.

At the hospital, we find Sarah in the waiting room, hugging herself and pacing between two rows of faded blue chairs. Her eyes are puffy from crying and they seek around the room incessantly.

I leave the baby with John Mark to go to her, and when she sees me, she shakes her head. I fear the worst, but I catch a glimpse of Locke through an opening in one of the examination room curtains. He's standing tall beside a gurney, with one arm around his middle, and the other balanced on top of it, his hand fisted over his mouth. He's listening to someone beyond my view. His mom is seated in a chair next to him.

"It's just like when Aaron died," Sarah says. "Everyone standing around waiting for answers."

In a few minutes, a woman in a white jacket sweeps out from the curtain, and Locke sees me. His face morphs from strong brace to worried kid, and he hangs his head as he walks over. I hurry to him, hug him, ask what in the world is going on.

"I don't know." He speaks crisply. "I was working. Pastor Ian called to express concern about Dad's state of mind. He apologized for breaking confidentiality, and that's when I began to understand that Ian thought my dad was a danger to himself. I challenged him. Told him how happy Dad had seemed lately, happier than he'd been in months, but he said that when people decide to die by suicide, there's often a sense of relief, that the despair will be over soon, and they appear happy."

"Is that what happened?!" I exclaim. I think about how different his dad had been that morning and anticipate Locke's feeling of culpability, his primal need to keep his loved ones safe. "Oh. No. Locke. You could not have known. You can't take responsibility for this, if that's where you're going."

The sweep of his eyes says *It's a little hard not to, but I know,* and he continues. "While I was processing that, Sarah called, scared out of her mind. I could hardly understand her. Dad was screaming in the background. Kept yelling that Sarah was supposed to be at work. She honestly thought he was going to harm her. She'd locked herself in her bedroom to call. I don't even remember driving over."

The surreal sense that I am trapped in a nightmare is exactly what I hear in Locke's voice.

"When I got there, I couldn't find them. I called for them. Jogged all over the house. Finally, I heard Sarah yelling from the front. Dad was lying on the deck clutching his stomach. His lips were blue and he was mumbling something, but no sound was coming out. I tried to reassure him, but all I could think was—" Locke's brow crinkles in pain, and his chin begins to tremble.

I finish the sentence for him. "That's how Aaron went."

Locke nods. "But without me."

Sarah comes over and weaves her arm through Locke's. It seems to stabilize him. He swallows. He sniffs. "He's gonna be OK, Sar," he says, thickly.

"Was it heroin?" Sarah asks. Locke nods. His eyes go to the ceiling and back.

"How? It doesn't make any sense. I mean, Aaron was working the scene. But Dad? *Our* dad?"

Locke glances back toward his father's bed. "Sarah, will you go sit with Mom till I can get back over there?" She goes right away. Locke says, "Mom hasn't articulated a single word. She was still at her school when I called. A co-worker took the phone from her, talked to me, and drove her here."

"Locke, what can I do?"

"You're doing it." He surrounds me and kisses the top of my head.

John Mark paces over with Annabelle in hand, and Locke grips his shoulder around my back. "Thank you, brother," he says. "Do you think you could take them back to my place, and stay with them there?"

John Mark's "Sure," is drowned out by my, "No, I want to be with you!" I lean back to look up at him. "With all of you."

"And I want you to be with me, but they're not allowing many people back there. I need to know you're safe. I'm feeling pretty vulnerable about my people right now."

Of course, he is, and I welcome the fact that he counts me among them, but I'm not going anywhere.

"Anyway," Locke says, "it's no place for a baby. She'll get sick. You're probably already out of diapers."

I shake my head, but John Mark says, "He's right. I used the last diaper before swim practice."

"John Mark, how often have you been changing her?" I ask.

"Every half hour," he answers proudly.

I roll my eyes, and Locke starts laughing. It's a good thing to hear. He laughs harder than the situation warrants.

"Who told you to do that?" I ask, getting the giggles myself.

"I don't know," John Mark says defensively. "She doesn't have any food left either, though."

My incredulous, "What?" is lost in a raucous bustle from the curtained area. Sarah and Ardea have been shown out, and hospital staff infiltrates the space around the gurney. It's like a bad TV show, too dramatic, too surreal. A woman's voice barks the word, "Clear!" And the sound of the electrical current can be heard, along with the thump of Mr. Locke's body. I can actually see the end of his bed jump. I see Locke too, his hands on his mom's shoulders. I hadn't even known he'd made his way back over there.

Everyone holds their breath in anticipation. One shock is all it takes. Mr. Locke's heart rhythm rights into a satisfying pattern of steady beeps. Another two minutes, and the auxiliary workers trickle out of there. "The ICU is open," someone says.

A doctor tells the Lockes, "We're going to move him. With every hour that passes, his chances of survival increase. Once he starts to show improvement, we'll send someone to help you make decisions about rehab."

"Oh, no, my dad's not an addict," Sarah says. I wonder if she said the same thing about Aaron.

The doctor's face holds an overabundance of understanding. "Well, no matter what the case, he's going to need help to straighten back out." That is probably an understatement.

I turn toward the sound of the outside doors sliding open. Officer Chris Michaels stalks into the ER in full uniform, and suddenly I remember what Locke's dad had been holding that day I'd surprised them in Aaron's cabin. The small casket from Aaron's basement. The plastic bag.

I practically lunge at him. "*You're* responsible for this," I accuse him. Chris backs up, shaking his head. "Why can't you just leave this family alone?" I say. "Can't you see they've got enough to deal with?"

Locke hasn't noticed me confronting the officer, a fact for which I am enormously grateful. He follows his dad's gurney out of sight, and Chris watches them go, raising hands to show me he means no harm. "Is he going to be OK?" he asks.

"They don't know yet. Why'd you let him keep it?"

Chris's face hardens. "I don't know what you're talking about," he hisses, "but you'd better *stop* talking about it if you really care for this family."

John Mark places the baby into my arms. "What's going on?" He asks it casually, though his posture says he's ready to intervene.

"Nothing that concerns you," says Chris. "I need to speak to *her*."

"I'm Emma's legal guardian," John Mark says. This earns him a look of warning. Chris grabs my arm under the shoulder and drags me several paces away.

Apart from the gash with which Locke had decorated Chris's eye socket last week, there are other wounds. Three scratches run down his neck, equidistant from one another. When it dawns on me what I'm seeing, I slowly say, "Chris? What happened to your neck?"

His fingers fly to cover the marks.

"You were in my room at the Lockes'! My cat scratched you! And you trapped it in the closet. You *hurt* it, by the way. It was *limping*. It's *lactating* for goodness' sake!" People are watching now. A small crowd begins to gather. Chris observes them darkly.

"If you do not keep your voice down," he says through a clenched jaw, "I am going to arrest you." He waves away the onlookers.

"For what?" I ask. "Calling you out as a cat kicker?" Then I gasp. "You *are* the one who tossed my apartment. I didn't want to believe it." All the passion flees from my face, and I shrink out of my aggressive stance. I go quiet, and it seems to frustrate Chris even more not to know what I'm thinking.

"What?" he demands.

I can literally feel my blood pressure throbbing in my ears. It's not like I can run. I'm holding a baby. I will myself to be calm, but questions are flooding through my mind like adrenaline. Was he working with the men who ran me off the road? What could Annabelle's mother have given me that would wind him up this tightly? And then I get it, or I think I do. That woman worked undercover with him before he was pulled from the operation. Before Aaron died. That would make sense. Detective Wilkins knew the woman personally. I'm almost sure of it. Chris thinks she gave us something that could implicate him in Aaron's death. Or maybe in her own.

"Chris?" My voice shakes. I swallow, then try again, speaking softly. "If you are mixed up in something, I don't know about it. OK? I don't have anything to incriminate or exonerate *any*one. And neither does Locke. We were just in the wrong place at the wrong time. And now we're trying to help this baby and do the right thing. Please just leave us alone." I glance at John Mark and am relieved to see that he is intent upon us. He raises his brow for a cue.

"Emma, there's more going on here than you understand," Chris counters. His tone has changed. He's all of a sudden gentle and imploring. He grips my arm again, but not harshly, just…beseechingly. "If you are working for someone, I need to know it. If you have something, anything, I'll make it easier on you if you just turn it over to me."

I run through the list of general tells as I scrutinize the man, and I try to trust my gut, but my stupid gut is trusting *him*! So, I ignore it.

"OK. Chris? You are freaking me out right now. I don't have *anything*. And you should know it, because you've been breaking and entering. And kicking cats. If I did have something, you'd be the last person I'd turn it over to."

The automatic ER doors slide open with the sound of Darth Vader's breath, and Sheriff Dunn saunters in.

The new vulnerability in Chris's affect switches off, and he takes on an abrupt hardness. He's a merry-go-round.

"Well, I'm sure the state is going to want the baby to be placed with someone more forthcoming," he declares. He reaches for Annabelle, but I twist her away.

"No way! Are you kidding me?!" I practically yell it. "You show me papers, or you get out of here!"

John Mark steps up. "Officer, please," he says, but Sheriff Dunn stiff-arms him to keep him from advancing.

Chris is glaring at me. I've buttressed my side toward him, to shield the baby. Onlookers begin to regroup. Someone is holding up a cell phone, presumably to record the interaction. Sheriff Dunn advises Chris that it's time to leave.

The sheriff moves toward the exit, and Chris's body does two things at once. His shoulders shift to follow his boss, but his head shifts to look me full in the face. In his brow, the same conflict takes place, like two sides of an argument being debated in milliseconds behind his eyes. Chris stoops down, plucks something off the ground, and takes a step toward me. When John Mark tenses, he stays him with a glance and forces whatever he has picked up directly into my palm. "This fell out of your bag," he says. And with that lie, he is gone.

When the police have exited, I open my hand to reveal Annabelle's small bracelet.

Mixed messages much?

For someone who's supposed to be able to map out another human's mental landscape, I am at a total loss when it comes to Chris. I feel like a kid who's been given a roll of toilet paper and asked to build a raft that will save everybody I love. From piranhas. And a volcano. And maybe a giant pterodactyl.

"I can't make a raft out of toilet paper," I whine. "It won't hold people. It will absorb water and rip through. I need popsicle sticks at the very least."

"Right," John Mark says as if that makes any sense. "Well, until we can get to the craft store, we need to figure out what to do next."

John Mark runs a hand through his wet hair. He's still wearing his swim shorts, and there are chill bumps on his arms. I've taken him for granted, and now I feel a huge surge of affection for him.

"Go home, John Mark. You've gone above and beyond. I really appreciate it, friend."

"Oh, yeah," he says. "Like I'm gonna leave you here with an infant among all the sick and worried disenfranchised, and the lunatic cops. Coach would kill me. Let me take you to his house like he said."

"That's not happening."

He draws a breath to challenge me but sees my expression and just blows it out. He holds a hand toward the sitting area, and the two of us sit, looking very deflated in the faded blue waiting room chairs.

"Hanging out with you is exhausting," John Mark says. "And dangerous. Frankly, I don't think things are going to work out between us."

"I could pay you in kittens," I offer.

"No, thank you," he laughs. "What would *really* help is if the cat would take on Annabelle as one of her brood. The way dogs sometimes take in orphaned lion cubs at the zoo." Bantering about that ridiculous statement makes us giddy, and we end up spending far too much time discussing the ramifications of growing up feline.

An emotionally and physically exhausted Locke finds us a few hours later. John Mark is pacing with his hands wrapped around a small cup of hospital coffee, and I'm lying on a row of hard chairs that cut into my backside in inescapable increments. Annabelle is asleep on my chest.

"John Mark, go home," Locke says. "I got 'em. I owe you, man."

"You sure?" He is. So, with a salute and a call-me-if-you-need-me, John Mark leaves for the night.

From my prone position, I say, "We're lucky to have him.

Annabelle's lucky to have him. He signs to her all the time. I think she's beginning to mimic it."

"Come on, Em. Let's go home." Locke picks up the baby with one hand, like a pro, and extends the other to me.

"Your dad?"

"He's stable. Mom's been able to talk through it, finally, and to ask questions. She's asleep now. Sarah's going to stay with her."

"How are *you* holding up?"

We walk out into the steamy night, streetlights throwing gaudy artificial illumination, and black asphalt emanating heat as we cross to the parking garage.

"I'm not sure. I mean, my dad tried to kill himself, so…"

It's a quiet drive home. Once back, Locke takes a long shower, and I give the baby a warm bath. Annabelle finds this invigorating. She flails her arms and tugs away the bath cloth repeatedly.

Even though I long to lie down, I play with Annabelle and lather her hair into a wig of bubbles. Then she looks so adorable that I'm compelled to take pictures, so Annabelle tries to tug the phone away too. "Oh, no, you don't," I say and sign. "We need to talk. Today has been very hard for your fath—" I catch myself, with a thumb to my forehead, making the sign for *father*. I can't believe how naturally the word is escaping from me. "For Locke," I correct. Wow. Just how much is this little fairytale going to cost?

"I am quite attached to you," I tell Annabelle, and make a tickle game out of drying her off. "I'm going to miss you when you go." When we're all through, I say, "You must sleep now, OK, Miss Thang? We're too tired for anything else tonight. Please."

Locke is cleaning up after the kittens and making sure Tac has food and water. I present the baby in a hooded towel that has ears and a mane. The lioness Annabelle reaches for Locke, and he bends to kiss her, holding his dirty cat hands behind himself. While he washes them, I diaper the baby and dress her in a soft onesie and wrap her up in a blanket like a mint green burrito. Patting her padded bottom, I hold her close, kiss her head, and sign, *Goodnight, precious Annabelle. I love you.*

Locke watches us from where he stands in the doorway to the bathroom, drying his hands. The baby lies underneath a motorized mobile, and I click off the overhead so that she can watch the soft lights and stuffed lambs that rotate above her.

"Is it weird to be doing such mundane tasks," I ask, "on such a traumatic day?"

"No. It's the most comforting thing I can think of."

I take a seat on the bed, and motion for Locke to come to me.

"Second most," he amends, obeying my summons.

He lays his head in my lap and wraps an arm around my backside. "I'm sorry about all this," he mumbles into my leg. "Thank you for being here."

"There's nowhere I'd rather be. I mean that." I pull his damp hair off of his neck and comb it through my fingers until his breathing evens out.

"Do you think you'll be able to sleep some?" I ask. In response, Locke tugs me down by the hips to lie next to him and hauls the covers over us. No separation of bedclothes tonight. All three of us mercifully fall asleep.

11

OUT OF THE LOOP

Of course, the baby wakes far too early, but Locke is already up. I hear him on the phone, outside the bedroom door. I can tell that he's pacing the hall, in and out of his bedroom, keeping his voice low for my sake. It's probably Sarah on the phone. The doorknob turns, and Locke reaches down for Annabelle while holding the phone with his shoulder.

"I'm up," I tell him. "I've got her." He mouths a *thank you* and steps out again, away from the crying. I go to the bathroom before tending to the infant. All the while, Annabelle howls. When I return, I sign and say, "You know, grown-ups have to pee-pee too, and we can't just let it go anytime we feel the urge. We have to put the pee-pee in the potty." I hear Locke chuckle from behind me where he places the phone on the desk.

"I guess I'm gonna have to learn to sign, huh?" he says.

I've thought about that, but what's the point? We won't have Annabelle long enough for Locke to use what he learns.

"Was that your sister?" I ask.

"Yeah. Dad feels like crap and he's not making much sense, but the doctor says he's doing better. Mom's a mess. She feels betrayed. And guilty. And angry. All of it. Sarah's going to bring her home, and I'm going to go to the hospital."

"May we come with you?"

"Certainly. But you don't have to."

"We want to." I twirl Annabelle's bracelet around my finger and wonder if I should divulge anything that might add to Locke's burden. I decide that he'd want to know. "Locke, I had an encounter with Chris Michaels at the hospital last night."

So, sometimes I define moods by assigning them colors. The stormy grey of sorrow and longing. The sunbeam yellow of humor and joy. The warm orange glow of comfort and home. Right now, Locke's goes pitch black. His voice drops in tone and volume. His eyes glint. His muscles tense.

"Why are you just now telling me about this?" he demands.

My heart speeds up. "Well, at the time, you were with your family. And later, you had too much on you. Nothing bad happened. John Mark was there."

"*I* should have been there." Black. I can't see through it. I debate how much to reveal. Seems like Locke is already at the breaking point.

"But there was no need," I say.

"Because *John Mark* was there?" Last night Locke had been grateful for our young friend's involvement. Now he speaks like a jealous lover.

"Locke. John Mark is devoted to you. You know that. He worships you. I *was* glad to have him there, but—"

"If he was so devoted to me, he would've taken you home as I asked! What happened? Tell me everything."

I study Locke's posture. Weaponized. Foreboding. His face is uncharacteristically hard. *Just shy of mean.* Like the picture of Aaron I'd found in Aaron's house.

"Can you feel how much of your brother you're channeling right now?"

"Don't do that," he snaps. "Don't try to get inside my head."

"Landon Locke. This is not you. Come back to me."

Locke curses. "Just tell me what happened!" He physically towers over me. The baby starts to cry. Maybe she *can* hear. Or maybe she can just sense the tension. I set her in the pen and get right back into Locke's space.

I'm small next to Locke at any time, but right now I am a child by comparison. Instead of posturing or yelling (or running away), I stand up to him like little David before the giant.

"Locke, my love." I push into the words all the affection and respect that I hold for him. I try to slow the conversation and turn it upside down. "What was the thing that Grandaddy said? The thing you told me when I first arrived, about the table that sits on the front deck."

A battle takes place behind Locke's eyes, not unlike the one I'd witnessed Chris work through last night. He fights to hang on to the black rage that encompasses him. It must feel powerful, like armor. Like vengeance. But I can see that I've brought to mind the exact words his grandaddy used about his *first real achievement*, and they find the chink. The love and pride of his grandaddy are in opposition to the rage and, already, the black is receding.

"I'll bet he never called *you* a wild goat, did he?" I say. "Maybe sometimes you wished he had. Why didn't you follow Aaron into the force? Was it something Grandaddy said?"

A funny thing happens, then, to my perspective. In the next few moments, Locke shrinks from being stretched to height, and I no longer need to tilt my head back to see him. I watch his eyes until he's gazing up at *me*. From his knees.

He answers quietly. "He said that I was an artist, and that wisdom was my weapon, the key to life."

"The key," I repeat.

"Emma." Locke's eyes shift ruefully.

"Shh. We're OK." I marvel at him, kneeling before me. "You listened to me," I say. "You came back." I hold his face in my hands to study him. "I'd follow you anywhere."

Locke blinks up at me as if he can't believe what I've said. "I'm sorry."

"You're wounded. You want to fight back."

"But I don't want to fight you. I'm ashamed I stood over you like that."

"You are the scariest, most threatening monster I have ever met." I look down my nose at him, and he allows me to turn his head from side to side in time with the words. "I mean that as a compliment."

"You challenged me anyway," he says. "You weren't having it."

"I knew you wouldn't hurt me. Well, I was *pretty* sure. If words hadn't worked, I was going to strip." That brings him back to humor.

"You shouldn't have told me that. I'll hold out next time." Locke rolls to a sitting position on the floor and rubs his hands over his face. His next words sound more like a groan. "Oh, I feel like I'm in a pressure cooker."

"Of course, you do." I walk over to check on Annabelle.

"I scared her," he says.

"You did."

Locke hops up to scoop Annabelle out of her pen and he peers into her eyes. "How do I tell her I'm sorry?"

Gah, I love this man.

"Make an A sign, like this." I show him. "And rub your chest in a circle. Your face should match your meaning, but it already does."

Locke signs, *I'm sorry*. He kisses the baby's cheek and hugs her to his chest. He pulls me into the hug too. "I promise to remain calm if you'll tell me what happened with Chris."

We journey downstairs to make coffee and to feed Annabelle while I tell Locke how things went down with Chris. Along the way, Locke notices the thing I have wrapped around my fingers.

"What are you holding?" he asks.

"Yes!" I point at him like he's answered a question correctly. "You *know* what it is. It's Annabelle's bracelet. The one you found in my hair. The one I gave to Sheriff Dunn on crash day. Chris *pretended* that I dropped it last night. He stooped down to pick it up from the ground and placed it directly into my hand."

"But why? Did he sign it out of evidence? I'm confused."

"Right?! Wait till you hear more! He's the one who kicked our cat!"

"He *was* in your room?" Locke repeats that with a different emphasis. "He was in your *room*?! I am gonna kill him. Why was he? What did he say?"

"He didn't cop to it. Ha! Cop to it." I look up expectantly. "'Cause he's a—" Locke deadpans me. "Never mind."

"I'm gonna kill him," he says again. "Also, I like that you called it *our* cat."

I exhale in relief because this is my Locke. Aloud I say, "He's sporting the gash you gave him the other day, which made me happy, and now he has three nice deep scratches from Tac. I know that's what they are."

"Good. Let's give him a few more."

"I'm supposed to be able to read people, right? But he sends so many mixed messages, I end up trying to build rafts out of toilet paper."

Locke all but skips the part about the toilet paper. His eyes squint for half a second before he gives his head a tiny shake, a decision to ignore it. He says, "Yeah, Emma, 'cause he's a liar. He probably can't even remember what to lie about anymore. I think he's psycho. He seemed psycho in the woodshop, didn't you think so?"

"He seemed like he was suffering from post-traumatic shock to me. He keeps rubbing that crease in his elbow, like a nervous tic. He called you by Aaron's name. And remember how he laughed when you decked him?"

"Yeah. Psycho."

"But there's this," I say. "At the end of our talk, he said something about the state wanting to place Annabelle with someone more *forthcoming*. Like he still thinks we have this important piece of information, and he's going to use Annabelle as leverage to get it. Can he do that, do you think?"

"He's the police. If he wants to play rough that way, I'm sure he can."

I don't mention my suspicions that Locke's dad received the heroin the same day he and Chris were scavenging in Aaron's house. I need to be sure before I drag him down that road.

"I'm beginning to hate that guy," Locke says.

"I know. Let's just take care of your dad. There's nothing we can do about Chris. And let's take care of Annabelle so they don't have any reason to doubt us."

We must have passed Sarah and Locke's mom on the drive to the hospital because they're not there when we arrive, but we do hear voices from within Mr. Locke's room. Locke motions us to wait. "It's Pastor Ian," he mouths.

I like the straightforward language Ian uses. He's respectful, but he doesn't beat around the bush. He speaks honestly. He's talking about forgiveness, saying, "No, Thomas. God isn't angry with you. He hasn't been angry with you since the day Jesus died. Be at peace, my friend."

Mr. Locke says, "I did the unforgivable. How will my kids— How will Ardea—"

"Maybe part of restoring the relationships," Ian offers, "will be to give them room to feel what they need to feel. But God is ready for you to run to him right now. He invites you to be at peace in his love, regardless of what you or anyone around you has done."

"I just wanted to be with him, with my son!" Locke's dad erupts into sobbing. "I wanted to go through what he went through. I couldn't think about anything else."

Locke can't stand it. He knocks on the open door, and when his dad sees him, his dad's face screws up with misery. "Landon, my boy. I'm sorry." The words are malformed, but the intent is palpable. Locke falls onto his dad, weeping like a child.

When he's able, he says, "I'm so glad you're still here, Dad. I love you."

Ian is crying too. Not just polite crying. Get-a-tissue-out-and-blow-your-nose crying. I wonder if I could embrace my own dad like that. If he wept. If he sobbed about how sorry he was. If he came back. It's all very unnerving, and I suddenly feel that there isn't enough oxygen in the room. I back into the hall.

When I have counted several sequences of three-white-marble-tiles, two-blue in one direction, I spin around to retrace the pattern, eyes to the ground, and nearly run into Ian.

"Felt like holy ground in there, huh?" he asks.

I nod. He extends a hand. "I'm Ian."

"I know," I say, shaking his hand. "Thanks for being here."

"You're Landon's…friend?"

"Sorry. Emma. Locke and I, *Landon* and I, are fostering a child together." I present Annabelle, who remains calm and observant as she rides upon my hip. "Long story."

"I heard about that. I love long stories. Will you tell it to me over lunch, down in the cafeteria? I think your gentlemen could use some time." Ian offers to carry the diaper bag or Annabelle, either one. I give him the bag.

Downstairs, Annabelle sits in a highchair that takes up one whole side of a square table, and she is very pleased with her situation. She happily munches upon baby cereal, checking out each separate O in her chubby fingers before pushing it into her mouth, because oh-my-goodness, is it possible that *this* one can be the exact facsimile of every other!

"She's perfect. Isn't she?" Ian asks. He has ushered us through the cafeteria line and has paid for our meal. Now he sits across from me where I'm watching Annabelle with satisfaction. I nod in response.

"You're going to miss her."

I swivel my head to observe him. "I really am. I've grown quite fond of her."

"And of Landon?" Ian pops a green bean into his mouth. It's a casual maneuver. Light. Friendly.

I sip my ice water and doubt him. "Very much," I answer at length. "But you already knew that. Why ask?"

"Oh, I'm just wondering how difficult it is to walk the line between stranger and wife?"

I pause for half a beat and then chuckle. Throughout my education, and into my personal forays toward mental health, I've dealt with many clever analysts, many egomaniac doctors, and many, many self-righteous counselors. "How'd you know I'd be able to handle that question?"

Ian doesn't reply. He waits for me to answer it, to the point of being rude. So, I retaliate. "Probably not as difficult as it is to pull off the whole meek-as-Jesus routine," I say.

A slow smile spreads across his face. "It wasn't sexual abuse," he says, eyeing me. "Not long term anyway. I think you'd be more manipulative. You're too open. But you're so vigilant..."

I tilt my head in an invitation for him to guess *what then*.

"Daddy issues," he suggests. I *pff* at him. "I know." Ian swipes away his dumb comment. "It's always daddy issues." He regards me. I'm smug. I enjoy this game. "You're going to do the same thing to me, aren't you?" he asks.

"Oh yeah," I tell him.

"Go ahead," he invites. I'm happy to. I launch into an analysis of what I've surmised so far.

"You were pulled into counseling because you needed a positive outlet for your grief. Locke told me you lost an adult child. You weren't a counselor before that, I bet. I don't think you have a natural penchant for mystery or mess. You were into something more formulaic. Something with social outlets, but something that could be solved. Controlled. Something where you could be the expert. Math? Engineering?"

"Math," he answers. "A professor."

"But when your child died—he was a son. You resonated with that part of Mr. Locke's confession." Ian indicates that I'm correct. "You couldn't solve that. It nearly broke you." I soften my voice. "It presented the same dilemma for you that it did for Mr. Locke. Follow him into death, or humble yourself to a power higher than yourself and hope that there's a purpose to all of it. That's what led you into ministry. And ministry led you into counseling."

Though I do enjoy decoding him, I don't enjoy the grief he's gone through. It hurts me for him, actually.

With the same attitude, Ian says, "I was being gracious before when I waved away the 'daddy issues' comment. He didn't assault you.

He abandoned you. Not as a little girl. Not your basic needs. You're too secure. But as you became a woman. You got to be too much. Too constant. Too emotionally demanding." I can tell by the way Ian keeps saying *too*, that he doesn't believe I was *too* anything. It's my dad he's picking on. "Hang on. Too perceptive," he guesses. "You saw too much."

My mouth rests against my hand. I move it to say, "I heard too much. He was on the phone with—the other woman. I told my mom. He hates me." I exhale a humorless laugh. "She does too. Sometimes. Or she did."

"You were young, but not young enough to be excused. Fourteen?"

"Fifteen."

"He never said he was sorry."

"He never said anything at all. He was gone. He might as well be dead. It's possible that he is."

"Do you hope so?"

My eyes reach beyond him, betraying my false stoicism. "It's the same either way."

"Yeah." Ian picks up his fork to push his green beans around. "Landon received his dad back from the dead," he says. "But that's not what choked you. It was the fact that his dad was so obviously sorry for what he had done."

"Stop," I say. I've met my threshold.

Ian gentles his voice but continues to prod. "You deserve the whole thing. The tears, the contrition, the pleading for forgiveness." I shift in my seat. Ian's words are burning me, but he keeps going. "You deserve for your dad to be present and devoted and for him to delight in the complex woman you've become."

"Why are you doing this?"

"Because you're sacrificing your joy to cover your dad's debt. And my guess is that you're asking Landon to pay it too. What if the apology never happens? What if the debt never gets paid?"

"You want me to cancel my dad's debt?" I ask.

"I want you to let him pay his own debt. And I want you to understand that you're not the collector."

"I'm *not* the collector."

"That's what I said."

"No, I mean—" I'm completely flustered now. "I'm not trying to get him to pay me back anything."

Mister talky Ian goes silent.

"Hello?" I am fairly well perturbed now. Annabelle begins to launch baby-cereal missiles at the table next to us, which is full of medical students who seem to find it hilarious, so after my initial attempts to get her to quit, I just let it happen. *I'm going to be a superb mother someday.*

After a time, I reengage. "You're saying that this is between my dad and God, right? That I'm allowed to step out of the loop. That until I *do* step out and release my dad from what he owes me, personally, I'll find a way to get somebody else to pay for it."

"Whoa. Nicely said. Yeah. I think that's exactly what I'm saying." His eyes roam the room and land back on me. "I'm really smart," he confides, in an obvious attempt to comfort me with humor. My tense forehead relaxes some. "*Really* smart," he says again.

"Oooookay," I croon to quell his effort. "But what if God's not going to take care of me? What if he doesn't stick around?"

"Like your dad didn't?"

"Is it wrong to want proof?"

"Like Landon won't?"

"*Ouch.*"

"You have to practice faith to lay hold of it," Ian says. "The moment you open your hands, you'll find it resting there. Especially when you feel like this. Vulnerable. Hurt. Afraid. Angry. Anyway—" Ian presents Annabelle as proof. "You're a smart woman. Do you think you found this assignment by accident?"

"No, I don't," I concede. "Nor Locke's partnership in it."

My phone vibrates. Locke is texting to ask where I am. I punch in our location, but by the time I push send, he's already found us. I stand to wrap my arms around him and squeeze his neck till he bends with an *ow,* and I loosen my grasp.

"I'm not going to make you pay someone else's debt," I tell him.

"I'm gonna step out of the loop." Locke's bewilderment makes Ian chuckle.

"Would you like to say more about that?" Locke asks.

"Nah." I return to my seat, and Locke considers the baby.

"Do you know that Annabelle is showering the table next to you with her lunch?"

"Yeah. I couldn't get her to stop."

Locke reaches across me to remove the baby's cereal bowl from her tray and sets it in the middle of the table where she can't reach it.

"Oh, that was a good idea," I say. When the quick pinch of Locke's nose calls into question my capacity for logic I add, "Shut up. Ian has me discombobulated. Go get some lunch and come sit with us."

While Locke goes through the lunch line I say to Ian, "I was wrong about you. Math must have been a lazy fallback. You were born to be a counselor."

"Have *you* considered becoming a counselor?" he asks.

"Ian. I think we've already established what a mess I am."

"We're all a mess," he assures me. "You absolutely nailed me before. Jonathan's death sent me seeking my own."

"How can you say that with a smile?"

Ian leans in. "I read the last page," he confides. "Death gets his ass kicked."

CHURCH DAY

Sunday comes. We wake to the sound of Annabelle giggling to herself. If you have to wake up to something, this is a delightful option. Locke raises up over my shoulder to glance at the clock. Six-twenty-three. He quietly plods over to Annabelle saying, "Well, Little. You slept a bunch. Thank you for that." Locke changes the baby (he's good at it by now) and glances up to find me watching them. "Look who it is!" he whisper-says to Annabelle. "It's Emmaaa!" He flies the baby, who thinks it hilarious fun, around my head.

"Good morning," I say. I sign it too and reach to hold her. "Annabelle and I sleep better with you around."

"I'm glad." Locke bends to cup my face and kiss me good morning. The dark circles beneath his eyes are more prominent today.

"Did you sleep at all?" I ask.

"I did fine, considering. Will you come to church with me? You and Annabelle?"

"You feel like going to church?"

"It's the only place I feel like going. But I want you with me."

I think of Ian's words. *You have to practice faith to lay hold of it.*

"Sure. Um. I don't really have any church clothes here."

"Nobody dresses up." Locke searches the counter that has held my weekend bag this whole time, but it's not there. He turns around twice, his head leading the way.

"What are you doing?" I laugh. "You look like a dog who's trying to find a place to lie down."

He regards me with suspicion and opens a drawer. "You unpacked!" he says. "When did you?"

"When we got back from the hospital yesterday."

Locke digs through my clothes and holds up my short white shorts. "Wear these."

"Locke, I'm not wearing those to church."

"Jesus knows you have great legs," he says and nods his head deliberately. "He made them."

I used to go to church with my mom and dad every Sunday, but after they divorced, my dad quit church. Turns out, God frowns upon unfaithfulness, and the pastor told him so. Mom was willing to take him back, but he was in love. Not with her. And by that time, I couldn't hear anything the pastor said anyway. I quit church too.

Then one day, on a trip across Michigan to visit my grandmother, Mom and I stopped at a park to stretch our legs. There was a man there sitting on top of a picnic table, and a woman on one of the benches. They spoke to one another using their hands. Their children were close by, running, tagging, hiding and seeking. If I could have heard their play, I would have been surprised by how conspicuously void of verbal exclamation it was.

Emboldened by my curiosity, I approached the family and openly stared at them. Most people would have thought that I was being rude. But Noah and Hannah are not most people. They waved at me, and I waved back.

When it was time to go, my mom came to touch my shoulder. Hannah saw and signed a question. But it was clear, by the way we shook our heads, we didn't know how to sign. Hannah spoke instead. Mom told me, later, that her words were thick, as often happens when someone learns to speak without being able to hear, though she was completely intelligible. Soon, a conversation took shape. Hannah would ask a question verbally, and Mom would answer while Hannah and Noah read her lips.

The couple's children gathered around me. They made wild gestures to get my attention. Each of them was younger than I. They wanted to show off for me. Cartwheels and somersaults. Handstands.

At first, I didn't question the children's various skin tones and textures of hair, because Hannah was light-skinned, and Noah was dark. But then I noticed that one of them, Lysle, appeared to be of Asian descent.

"Mom!" I cried out, although I couldn't hear myself. I typed into my phone: *Are all of these children adopted?*

Mom relayed the question, and Hannah nodded her hand and her head, *yes.*

Are they all deaf?

Yes.

Over the next weeks, Mom and I kept in touch with Hannah and Noah, and each of us—even I—became convinced that our meeting was an appointment. I was invited to move in to help with the kids, and in return, the family would teach me to sign. They required me to attend their church, where there was an interpreter. It was frustrating at first, but as with any language, immersion was the path to fluency.

"Hey, Em." Locke raps on the bathroom door, and I open with a towel turban on my head. "Your phone's freaking out."

Multiple texts and calls from both Hannah and my mom shoot a jolt of panic through me. I quickly dress and before I can do more, a video call rings in. When Hannah's blonde head appears, she begins to sign immediately. I sign back. Noah comes into view.

Locke leaves his seat on the bed to pace around. Finally, he asks, "Is everything OK?"

I sign and speak, "A policewoman contacted Hannah and Noah

about me. She questioned them without explanation, and that made them worry." I wave Locke around so that Hannah and Noah can see him.

"This is L-O-C-K-E." I sign and say. "I've told you about him." Locke waves.

Hannah signs something, and I laugh as I sign back. Noah gives us away when he says, "The ladies must think I won't let a brother know when they're discussing how hot he is."

"Noah!" I exclaim.

He told him what we signed, didn't he?

I speak Hannah's signs, for Locke's sake, while nodding my hand *yes*.

You two seem to be sharing a bedroom.

I giggle the translation.

"That's not all we're sharing," Locke says. He steps out of the shot and returns with Annabelle. The signing picks up speed then. We explain what all has been going on and why the police are still involved.

As we're wrapping up the call, Hannah looks from Locke to me and signs, *He's the one, isn't he?*

I blush and let a moment escape before I answer. *I hope so.*

Locke holds his hands up to Noah in question, but Noah shakes his head. "You'll have to find that one out for yourself. Take care of our girl. She's precious to us."

Locke says, "She's precious to me too."

A few minutes later, my mom has a similar story to share. A police officer visited her as well, and asked why I left home at age fifteen, and what I am now doing in Texas, and what kind of criminal connections I have. For real? Criminal connections? Mom is understandably concerned. She questions why I am staying with a family whose son died of a drug overdose. I decide not to mention the fact that the dad almost died of one too.

Locke strolls into the frame of our chat, straightening the collar of a hunter green shirt that he has tucked into khaki pants. I think now is a *great* time to introduce my mother to His Handsomeness. His charm is not lost on her. His radiant smile and his obvious affection for me put her at ease. Probably, it doesn't hurt that he mentions he's taking me to church—and it's time to go if we're going to be on time. I tell my mom I'll call her later.

Locke and I are still discussing how ridiculous Chris Michaels is, when Locke parks his big old truck between a Mercedes and a BMW and escorts us, his quasi-family, into the church building. The dark-paneled sanctuary, which could easily seat five hundred people, reverberates with the hushed voices of friends greeting one another. Locke's mom and sister wave at us from a wooden pew somewhere in the middle. We approach on an aisle of rectangular white stones.

"Grandaddy made these pews," Locke says, bracing the back of one as we pass. "Before I was born. And the pulpit, and the baptismal font." He points to the pulpit, which juts out into the air above the congregation. It is intricately carved with ancient symbols of the church.

"They're gorgeous," I answer, but I'm distracted. "Locke, people are very dressed up."

"Are they?" Locke searches around. A few women with earrings that match their necklaces that match their cardigans sit up taller, presumably to catch his eye. I make a mental note to pray for them.

Locke looks the part. He's all buttoned and belted. His hair is pulled into a neat ponytail. My hair is as tame as I could make it, but there's only so much you can do with elflocks. I wear a long skirt better suited for a music festival where you camp out with a bunch of hippies in somebody's field. I'm worried that my thin grey top might be too snug for the Lord's people, and so I position Annabelle for maximum coverage.

"What are you doing?" Locke asks.

"Nothing," I snap. He thinks it's funny.

We reach Locke's family and shimmy into seats beside them. Sarah says, "Emma, that shade of grey plays in your eyes like a smokey witch."

I cast said witch-eyes around for meaning. "Is that a good thing?" I ask.

"Yeeeah," Sarah sings.

"Everyone is all buttoned up," I whisper. "I don't want to embarrass you guys."

"You look lovely. You're a breath of fresh air. Give me the baby." Sarah takes Annabelle and makes faces at her while Annabelle makes a grab for Sarah's bottom lip. "We can put her in the nursery if you want," Sarah says.

I mouth the word *no* and shake my head.

"How is Dad this morning?" Locke asks.

"He's fragile. But he's feeling better, physically anyway, and he's making more sense. Apologizing hopelessly. He asked for Ian to come back."

As if he's heard his name, Ian appears. "Hello, Lockes." Ian squeezes Ardea's shoulder and leans over to shake Locke's hand. "You hanging in there?"

Ian and Ardea exchange more words. He jots down information about a support group on a card and encourages her to attend that very day.

Meanwhile, the family at the other end of the pew angles their legs so that Ricks and his wife, Natalie, can scoot by. When they reach the open seats beside Locke, Ricks says, "I'm not sure I've ever been stood up for a day on the lake before."

Locke kisses Natalie on the cheek and introduces her to me. He apologizes for missing their lake date and gives the short version of what's going on with his dad.

"*Landon,*" Ricks emphasizes his name. "What can we do?"

"I'll let you know. We're all just reeling right now."

As another pastor calls the congregation to order, movement from several rows ahead catches my eye. John Mark. He's sitting across the aisle and has turned nearly backwards to get my attention. I wave, and he signs, *I didn't know you came to church here.*

I came with Locke.

John Mark questions the sign I've used, and when I motion to Locke, he signs, *Got it.*

"What did you tell him?" Locke asks.

"The name sign I settled on for you."

You look amazing, John Mark continues. *Ditch the old man and come sit with me.*

I tell him to shut up and pay attention to what's going on up front.

How is Mr. Locke today?

Doing better. We're going to see him after church.

The service gifts me with an unexpected treasure in the form of song, mostly because when Locke sings out along with everyone else, his deep voice beside me is shockingly sexy. This isn't just a formality for him. He doesn't come to church because of Southern tradition. He is actually worshipping someone he believes in.

I make my lips keep moving to the hymn, but I've stopped singing. I know he's a good man. Know that he holds himself to a strict moral code. But he's wounded right now, and to hear him sing out in stubborn faith, despite those wounds, makes my own heart respond with gratitude. That's the type of man who stays.

When the service is over, several of Locke's peers come to question why he appears to have a wife and child. He slings his arm around my neck, effectively owning me, and says, "Mom went out and got 'em for me. She was sick of me dragging my feet."

He brags on me, which I appreciate—even bask in—until he won't stop. Finally, I cut my eyes and mutter, "That's enough." But that just makes him get ridiculous. I hide behind a signed conversation with John Mark.

Once we've extricated ourselves from the social crowd, we walk through the parking lot joking about what a perfect family we are. Locke swings the baby in her carrier so that Annabelle can see my face, and then he swings her away again till she erupts in the bubbling baby laughter we woke up to. We're nearly to the truck when a large woman steps into view, accompanied by a uniformed officer.

Locke checks me with a touch. "Ms. Vaughn?" he asks.

The woman from Child Services nods that that is who she is.

"Mr. Locke. Dr. Caine. I've been sent to collect the baby."

"Annabelle," I prompt.

"We don't know her name," Ms. Vaughn says, not unkindly.

"Then, you haven't found her family?" Locke asks. Ms. Vaughn shakes her head.

"Why take her if you don't know to whom she belongs?" I say. "She's well-loved and cared for."

"I'm not here to dispute that. It's not my choice."

"Whose choice is it?" Locke asks. When she doesn't answer, he says, "I think I know. What I *don't* know is how a police officer can hold that much sway over something like this. And bring you out on a Sunday. I mean, it couldn't wait till tomorrow?"

"Let us keep her while we contest this," I counter. "She won't benefit from being handed around to different people. She's already been so uprooted."

Ms. Vaughn looks pained. "I agree," she says, surprising both of us, and maybe the accompanying officer as well. "And I'm sorry. She has thrived under your care. I see that you're bonded to her. But I'm obligated." Ms. Vaughn displays official documents.

I knew the time would come, one way or another, but I'm still not prepared for it. Locke's looking to me for the gameplay. I'm not going to fight this now. We'll have to challenge it correctly, or we'll lose Annabelle for good. I kiss the baby, wondering if it will be for the last time, and I hand over the diaper bag to the officer, not before reaching into the pocket to keep a token of her.

"Please take care of her, Ms. Vaughn," I say. "We really do want what's best for her. I think that is to be with us until her family can be found."

Ms. Vaughn frowns.

Locke beats me to the question. "What aren't you telling us?" he asks.

Ms. Vaughn exhales sharply and glances to the side before divulging that, "DNA confirmed that the driver was the mother, but she had no next of kin. No birth certificate can be found. As far as records go, the baby doesn't exist."

"How do we fight this?" I ask. "She has nobody. It doesn't make any sense."

"Call me in the morning, and I'll walk you through the process."

She hands me her card. "I'll make sure she's cared for. I promise."

I'm turning away in defeat when one more thing occurs to me. "I think she's deaf. She needs visual comfort and cues. OK? Please."

Ms. Vaughn pauses. "You're a professor of sign language, right? Maybe you're just seeing what you're prone to see?"

"Maybe. But I don't think so. She's scheduled for a visit to the doctor this week."

Locke retrieves the anchor to the car seat from his truck and places it into the car himself. The police officer rounds the car to help from the other side. When Locke raises himself out of the car, Ms. Vaughn thanks him. He's up close to her now and he quietly says, "Will you please tell us the mother's name?"

I don't think she's going to. I'm sure she's not *supposed* to. But she does.

"Anita," Ms. Vaughn says. "Anita Velasquez." She checks to make sure the officer isn't paying attention. "But you didn't hear it from me."

Ms. Vaughn snaps the baby's carrier in and drives away.

Once inside the truck, I buckle myself and sit silently, staring straight ahead. Locke peers at me from the driver's seat. "I'm sorry, Em."

I shake my head. "It had to happen. She's not mine. I don't get to keep anybody." I know I'm allowing myself to indulge in self-pity. And I know I'm undermining Locke's cardinal rule. But I don't care.

"That's not true," he says. "You know that's not true." It's the gentleness of his voice that tells me he knows I don't mean it.

"I have proof, Locke," I persist like a kid. "I have lots of proof."

"And you have counterproof."

I nod minutely and fix my gaze on the dashboard. "I know," I sigh.

Satisfied with my response Locke says, "You ready?" I nod again, and he turns the ignition with no Annabelle between us.

"Wait," I say. I unbuckle my seatbelt, which zips away from my shoulder, and Locke shuts off the engine to await my next move. It is to occupy the middle seat, clip the lap belt around myself, and lay my head on his shoulder. "OK," I say.

He kisses the top of my head and reaches around me to tug my hip against his own. "You know how to make a Texas boy feel right," he says. With that, he re-cranks the engine and pulls us onto the road.

I stare at my empty arms. "What do you have there?" Locke asks.

I open my fist to reveal Annabelle's tiny bracelet. "Is it wrong to steal from a baby?" I ask.

"She meant for you to have it."

A few moments of silence ensue, until— "Locke?"

"Yes?"

"Can I stay one more night?"

"What?"

"Can I wait till tomorrow to go back to my apartment?"

"Your question is ridiculous. Stay tonight. Stay all nights."

Silence again. It's a nice answer, but I can't reside at the Lockes' indefinitely, with no baby for an excuse. Anyway, right now we're headed to the hospital to visit Locke's dad. I change the subject.

"Nobody calls you Locke."

"I've noticed that." He sounds disgruntled. "I wasn't the only one people called Locke, you know. Aaron got it too. Sarah thought it was because no one could tell us apart, but we didn't care. Ever since he died it's like everyone knows it was *Landon* who got left behind, so they're finally able to be confident enough to call me by name. But it feels wrong. We were Locke men."

"You didn't stop being a Locke man because Aaron died, or because people call you Landon. If anything, you're more of a Locke man now. Honestly, you're everything I've ever defined as a man."

Locke squeezes my knee in response.

"Grandaddy used to have a ballot box by the door," he says. "I have it by mine now. Did you see it? It has compartments that contain notecards and those short yellow pencils." Locke displays the length of the pencils between his thumb and finger. "Anyway, you had to choose from a list of three options, whose man you would be, but you could only choose two, and you had to put them in order of rank. Grandaddy made us vote every time we went out the door. Said we had to if we wanted to live right."

"And the candidates?"

"God. Locke. Self." He makes a halfhearted attempt at a smile but drops the farce. "I hate my first name now."

"I understand," I say. "You're Locke. You're everything that means. From your grandaddy's wisdom to the way your soul still reaches for its twin. There's a whole plot of you in the graveyard and a whole history yet to be made. That's why you've been built so broad. That's what your name sign means." I show him. "Sturdy. Steadfast. Enduring. This is you." I hear myself gushing, but it's true, and I think he needs to know. "I believe in you more than I believe in anything else in the world," I confess.

Locke pulls the truck to the side of the highway and comes to a full stop. His rusty door screeches as he shoves it open. He stomps around the hood and right on up the hillside that flanks the road. At the top, he stops with his back to me, his hands on top of his head. I watch his back expand as he draws a huge breath. I step out of my door. Did I say something wrong? Is he having a breakdown?

I breathe a sigh of relief when he begins to walk back down to me, and when he gets within earshot, I say, "Locke, what can I do? Is there—"

But he crashes into me and kisses me so hard I forget the dilemma. To be the focus of that man's passion is bliss.

He breaks away to stare at me with the same intensity he used to kiss me. "How do you do that?" he asks. "How do you always say what I need to hear? How do you fill me up the way you do?"

I glance around in mock confusion. "If you liked what I said, then why did you take the kissing away?"

I think I'll get a smile with that, but I do not.

"Don't go back to your place," he says. "I don't want you to go."

"Locke, what other options do I have?"

I'm not joking this time, but this is when Locke smiles. He gives the kissing back. Two different semi-trucks honk in short bursts as they speed by, presumably to congratulate us on our intimate participation.

13

THE LETTER

"Anita Velasquez. Come on, lady."

We're home from the hospital now and crammed around my laptop, which is stationed on the kitchen counter. Sarah searches her own phone and glances over my shoulder every few seconds. Locke moves back and forth between the laptop and the stovetop. He's pressing sandwiches for us. We search through news sites and social apps. Everything we can think of.

"Stop there," Locke says, "That could be her." He points to a picture of a striking Latina in a pressed white blouse tucked into navy slacks. "Where'd you find that one?"

"It's a news column from several years ago about the rise of immigrant women who have gone missing. She was causing a fuss about it, trying to raise awareness."

"Let me see." Locke moves to study her face. "Are there any more?"

I click through the organization's website.

"There are other pictures of the movement, but not of this woman. Not that I can find."

"Go back," Locke says. "That's her. She's younger there, but I remember her face. Her eyes." I guess he does. They'd stared into his so adoringly as she passed.

"Landon," Sarah cuts in, "that woman was at the station the morning of the wreck. I'm sure of it. She's the one who died? She was not on drugs when I talked to her. She was very focused. Maybe a little nervous, but definitely sober." Sarah gasps and squirms out of the barstool. "Landon, I think she *was* trying to find you! When she checked in at the desk, she kept staring at Aaron's picture, the one up on the wall of fallen officers, and I told her he was my brother and that it had been a year since he died. I told her I was going to meet you at the cemetery."

"I bet she and Aaron worked together," I say. "Detective Wilkins knew her and the more I think about it—" My eyes go wide. "Locke, she was the girlfriend."

"Whaaaaat?!" Sarah squeals.

"That's quite a leap," Locke says.

"It's not," I counter. "The sticky note from your brother's house was signed with an A."

"She *did* have a message for you!" Sarah says. "Or something to give to you. Isn't that what the police have been saying this whole time?"

"Maybe she just went to the cemetery to see you," I offer. "If you were gone, I'd look at your twin every chance I got. It makes sense, Locke. The way she looked into your eyes at the end."

"Why now?" Locke asks. "Why would she wait a whole year?"

"If Aaron was murdered—" I begin.

"He was," both Locke and Sarah interrupt.

"Then she could have been really scared for herself. And, oh my gosh! For her baby!"

Sarah runs the number of months on her fingers and confirms that, "She would have been around five months pregnant at the time Aaron died."

Sarah and I both raise our eyebrows at each other.

"Hang on," Locke says. "Let's stick to what we know."

We do not. We are many steps ahead.

"Did she speak to Chris?' Locke asks darkly.

"Yeah," Sarah says. "She and Chris exchanged words. I remember thinking he'd probably insulted her—you know how Chris is— because she rushed past on the way out like she was ready to get the heck out of there."

"Do you guys have Aaron's phone?" I ask. "Could we look through his photos or his social apps to see if they were connected?"

"It's still in evidence," Locke says. "I have his laptop at my house. I'll get that. He worked undercover, though. He wasn't active on social media. At least not that I know of. And certainly not under his real name."

"Right!" I say. "She would have had an alias too if she was undercover."

"They've wiped her off the internet on purpose!" Sarah says.

"Y'all just hang on," comes Locke's more reasonable admonishment. "Let's do a little more investigating."

Sarah and I take care of the sandwiches while Locke retrieves the laptop. Mainly, I take care of the sandwiches. Sarah twitters about undercover love affairs. When Locke returns and opens the computer, the sandwiches get forgotten.

"You know his password?" I ask.

"Turned out to be the same as mine."

"That's nuts. Really?"

A few more clicks and Locke is browsing the files.

"Yep. Hook 'em Horns."

"Hook 'em," Sarah agrees.

"Are you two just congratulating yourselves right now, or are you telling me that 'Hook 'em Horns' is the password?"

"Both," Locke says.

"And here I was reveling in your mystical twin powers."

"Well, they have hit a snag." Locke is now trying to figure out Aaron's Instagram password.

"Wait," I volunteer. "Can't you just use your fingerprint to call it up?"

"They're not identical."

"Why not?"

Locke is typing away. "Something about fingerprints being influenced by fluid in the womb. They're not strictly genetic."

"Figure it out, Landon," Sarah commands. "You can—"

"Got it."

Whoa. "I am sorry I missed the chance to see the two of you interact," I say.

"Together they were something *more*," Sarah agrees.

"I feel like we still are," Locke says. "I don't feel like our bond was severed. Sounds weird, but—" Locke stills and in a flat-sounding voice he says, "He followed her. On Instagram. She's the *only* person he followed."

He clicks.

"That's Annabelle!" I exclaim. "She looks like her mom."

"None of Aaron?" Sarah asks.

"Stop! That one. That picture of her baby bump." I point, and Locke clicks to enlarge a photo of a woman's naked torso. Her arms are covering her breasts, and a man's hands are cradling her pregnant belly. "Locke, those are your hands!"

Locke shakes his head uncertainly. "Landon Locke! Those are your hands and fingers," I insist. "I've been studying them for weeks. I —*think* about them." The stutter in my words makes Locke angle an intrigued smile my way. I shrug. Sarah laughs.

"Wow. Thank you for that way-too-close-to-visual," she says. She studies the picture. "She's right, Landon. Those are long Locke fingers. That's Aaron." Sarah covers her mouth. "He was a *daddy*," she says. Then gasps, "He was *Annabelle's* daddy."

"That picture was posted the day before he died," I note.

"I'm an aunt!" Sarah screams.

Locke falls back against his chair. "How could he not have *told* me?" He rubs the stubble of his beard. His eyes rove in thought. "There's no way. We're missing something."

"There are other pictures in that post," I say and point. "Click there."

The second picture is nearly the same, only the man's hands hold a tiny silver chain around the woman's navel. A small, familiar charm hangs from it. A key. My heart begins to race. The tiny bracelet. Annabelle's one tie to her parents.

Locke sits as still as his brother's gravestone, glaring at the picture as if it's scolding him. He touches the screen. Finally, he says, "It really is a key."

"You mean, like, figuratively?" Sarah asks.

"I mean, like, literally."

"To The Locke Box, like you thought," I say. "Locke, that hole isn't a defect."

"It's a keyhole." Locke raises his eyes to me. I've never seen them as round. "Oh, my *gah*," he says. "I can *hear* him laughing at me right now. You've got it, right? You grabbed it out of the bag today."

"It's right here, love." I pull it from my pocket, thinking how I'd snatched it on a whim, just to have a souvenir. I'm beginning to doubt that coincidences exist.

"This is GREAT!" Sarah yells. She has only one volume for now: loud. "What's a Locke Box?! Those stupid wooden puzzles you guys used to make?"

There's a moment's hesitation before all three of us lunge for the stairs. Up in Aaron's room, Locke procures the impossible puzzle box and removes the pieces to reveal the hole.

"Please be what we think," I beg it. I hand the bracelet to Locke.

After a pause, ripe with anticipation, he rolls the key around the lock. It was made in such a way that it must be laid down horizontally and swiveled. He turns. Nothing at first. He shifts it and turns again. It takes several fittings, but finally, the smallest click sounds, and the Locke Box breaks apart. Inside is a thumb drive and a folded piece of paper addressed to Landon. Sarah snatches the paper, then seems to think better of it, and offers it to Locke.

"You can read it, Sar. If you want to."

She grabs it back with relish, unfolds it, and reads aloud.

Landon, I'm not really sure how to begin this letter. It's one of those: If you're reading this, then I must be dead, so...I'm sorry about that, Bro.

Sarah's voice fades as she reads. She raises her eyes to Locke, whose lips tighten in understanding. He nods to give her permission to continue.

I need you to do two things for me.

One. Take care of Anita and the baby. She doesn't have anyone, and for her safety, nobody knows about us. Nobody. We're in too dangerous a place. I've never kept anything from you in my entire life. I hope you understand how that tears me up. Everything's happening so fast.

I have big plans, though. The first of which is to get out of this mess and marry that woman. I know. If you're reading this, then I'm not off to a great start. Take care of her, Landon. She's everything to me.

The paper shows evidence of emotion in the form of small water-marks and a smudge of ink.

Right. On to the second thing. All the undercover work to break up drug traffic has led to some larger connections into a tandem network of human traffic. You don't even want to know. Makes me happy that I like to fight so much. As wild goats do.

The thing standing in my way, ironically, is that there's an officer undercover with us. His real name is Conrad. He's using his power to extort money and take advantage of women, using the border as a hiding place.

Anita's a tiger, man. She stands right up to him. She's been working to end this shit since she was a teenager, and now she's working for us as an informant. But Conrad has no scruples. He tried to— Well, let's just say, I'm going to put an end to his involvement now.

Someone's directing him, though, behind the scenes, and that's why I haven't been able to move on it. He let something slip the other day that makes me think it's someone connected to our police department. I just can't be sure who it is.

"It's Chris," Locke says. And the next line of the letter is:

I know that you just said, out loud, that it's Chris.

My jaw drops, and Sarah cackles, "He just busted you from the afterlife!" Locke sniffs out a breathy acceptance of his brother's familiarity.

But it's not. Chris is half insane, but he's solid. Still...watch your back. I can't tell you how much I hope it's just some greedy slob higher up the chain and no one connected to the force. This place is making me paranoid.

It hurts me to drag you into this. I certainly don't want to put you in any danger, but you're the only person in this whole world who I can trust absolutely. I've been recording some of our operations LIVE to an encrypted webpage. Nobody else knows about it. The information for locating that page is on the drive.

Hand-deliver it to Dunn for me. You'll have to stick around to help him access it. You're the only one who'll be able to. He'll have to take it to the state police after that, but I think it will give him all the leverage he needs to yank Conrad out of the loop.

Yesterday I met with him to divulge my suspicions, but he doesn't want to interfere with an operation that belongs to state. Says the operation is more important than the smaller crimes that may happen in the meantime. He's probably right.

On a happier note, UNCLE Landon, we found out that the baby's a girl. We're naming her Annabelle.

Sarah gapes over the top of the letter. She mirrors my own astonishment. Locke just smiles.

Don't you think Grandaddy would've liked that?
  Give Mom and Dad my love. And Sarah. Take plenty for yourself.
  And Landon?

More watermarks around Locke's name.

All the things that can't be said, Brother.
  SeeYouOnTheFlipSide
  Aaron

Locke reads the letter again to himself. The tears that flow over it must be a tremendous relief. He wasn't abandoned. Wasn't forgotten or substituted. The earliest and most precious bond of his life remains intact.

Locke sniffles. "Um...OK," he says, and slaps his thighs with his hands. "I guess I'm going to see the sheriff tomorrow. Sarah, is there a Conrad working there?"

"His picture hangs next to Aaron's."

"He's dead," Locke confirms.

"Yeah. Same day. Hey, you haven't forgotten we have to move Dad to the rehab place, right?"

"Right," Locke says, in a way that means he *has* forgotten. "That's tomorrow too. OK. We'll figure it out. I'll be there."

"And then I'll go with you to see the sheriff," Sarah volunteers, but Locke shakes his head.

"No way. You stay with Mom."

"Well, I'm going," I say.

"No, Em. I want to go by myself."

"I still have to make a raft."

"What?" Sarah asks. My cheek twitches in *never mind* and at the same time, Ardea's voice travels up from the bottom of the stairs. "Roll call!"

Locke rolls his head toward Sarah and both of them croon, "Rooooll call."

"Time for Emma's initiation," Sarah says.

"Time to tell Mom she's a grandmother," says Locke.

"Oh-my-gosh-Landon-oh-my-gosh-oh-my-gosh!" Sarah runs out the door.

The siblings appear before Ardea on the upstairs landing. I follow them, curious, but hesitant to join, for fear of intruding. Ardea waves them down. When they join her in the living room, she says, "How are you, my little ducks?" like they're five years old. She commands them to sit.

Sarah collapses beside her mother on the couch. If she'd sat any closer, she would have been sitting on her lap. Locke obeys too, taking the big leather chair across from them. A pang of longing shoots through me. They have such a loving family dynamic. It isn't fair that they've had to suffer this much.

Ardea's round eyes search their faces. She says, "Where's the other one?" And for a horrifying moment, I think she's asking about Aaron. But then she spies me hanging back in the kitchen and motions for me to come in.

She means me.

"Here!" I say and plop down between Locke's feet, criss-cross-applesauce. What is it about a mother's love that can make you feel as warm and safe as you did when you were a kid? Even in the middle of...all this.

"Hang on," I say, slyly. "Have you been reading the last page?"

"*You've* been talking to Pastor Ian," Ardea deduces. "That man should come with a spoiler alert."

In a caricature of Ian's voice, Sarah trills, "It's a happy ending! Love wins! We can forgive and serve one another boldly."

"Is that what he tells *you*?" I ask. "He told me that Death gets his ass kicked."

After we manage the eruption that that statement provokes, Ardea directs us, each one, in turn, to talk about how we're processing things. She takes it upon herself to begin, having just returned from the support group that Pastor Ian had suggested. It was made up of men and women whose spouses fight addiction and mental illness. She hadn't contributed much to their meeting, but she had felt comforted that she wasn't alone. At the end, they had all prayed for one another.

The next turn in the family check-in belongs to Sarah, and I can hardly keep from spewing every bit of our newfound information before she can. I have to bite my lips, and squeeze Locke's ankles, and rock a little bit to keep quiet.

Sarah must feel the same way. She yells, "You're a grandmother!"

"That was abrupt," Locke mutters. Then, in anticipation of his mother's confusion, or maybe because of the way she's eyeing the two of us, he says, "Not by me."

His mother then pivots toward Sarah, and her puzzled eyes fall on Sarah's belly. "No, not *me!*" Sarah says. "*Aaron!* He left a letter for us!"

This devolves into a free-for-all. The whole story bursts wide open from all three of us like popcorn because none of us can control our excitement. The buzz of Aaron Alexander Locke having loved someone whom none of us had known, nor *could* now know, hums about us like a busy beehive. And the queen is Annabelle.

"Aaron. *My* Aaron. Had a *child?*" Ardea asks. "Are you sure? Landon?" Locke's mom searches for answers from the one man on Earth who would have known the truth if anyone had.

"He'd been afraid for them. He had to keep it under wraps."

"And she's our own Annabelle? It's all so— Where *is* Annabelle?"

"Oh." My *oh* is a small, vulnerable thing, and Locke leans down to put his arms around my neck. He pulls me back against his seat and squeezes my shoulders between his knees.

"They took her away today," he says. "Child Services."

"But she's ours," comes Ardea's defensive reply. "I mean, she is actually ours, isn't she?"

"We're gonna fight it," Locke says. "We'll go see Ms. Vaughn after we give Aaron's information to the sheriff, and then we'll figure out how to proceed."

"I might be reading the last page quite a bit till you get home," Ardea says. "Will you just drop off the drive and get out of there? Let the police handle it. You don't know what manner of thing will be exposed."

"I'll be careful," Locke assures her. "In and out."

I hope he's not wrong about that. But for now, Locke shares the pictures on Anita's Instagram, so that his mom can see, and he downloads a few of Annabelle as a baby, and of Anita so that Annabelle can have them someday.

"Not all roll calls are that exciting," Locke announces. He's been swimming, then showering, and now he enters my room in soft black sweatpants that ride his hips in the effortless masculinity of Locke. He has yet to put on a shirt, because, apparently, his information is so significant, he needs to swagger into my bedroom before he can manage one. I do not mind.

While he was out swimming, I went biking, and I played with the little cats. All but one of them have opened their eyes. They'll need homes soon. I got sidetracked, more than once, by Annabelle's empty playpen. I considered breaking it down, but I couldn't bring myself to do it. Instead, I took extra care of myself, bathing and painting my nails with polish Sarah let me borrow.

Now, as Locke bursts into the room with his urgent treatise on roll call, I'm standing at the mirror, managing my hair. I'm wearing a blue nightgown that hits several inches above the knee and is held in place by long, thin straps, between which *my ladies* are cradled in lace. Upon sight of me, he stalls.

"I—" He nods once and fixes his eyes on the ground, fighting a smile. "Should have knocked." I reach for my matching robe.

"What are you looking for down there?" I ask.

"Nothing. I am trying not to— Is this what you wear when there's no baby to take care of?" He allows his eyes to roam up past my knee, and then closes them altogether, with a whimper of a laugh.

"You know that makes me *want* you to look at me, right?"

"That makes two of us."

"And you're not because…"

"I'm just trying to do right by you. I don't want you to have any reason to doubt me. And I'm pretty sure I don't have enough restraint to keep from—" He opens one eye. "Yeah. I can't even begin to recount for you the flood of ideas."

"You have to now."

Locke shakes his head quickly from side to side, both eyes shut tight again.

"Well, then I'm going to come tease them out of you one by one."

Locke chuckles like my words are welcomed torture. He allows himself to take me in, and his voice acquires the rumble. "I would love nothing more. Believe me. But I got plans."

"Really?"

"Yeah, really. What do you think? I just want to agonize for you indefinitely?"

"I didn't know you were agonizing that much."

Locke puckers his lips. "It's unsettling to me that that hasn't been very...obvious to you."

"Don't worry," I laugh. "There are times I've been aware."

"You're not...agonizing?" he asks.

Generally, this is the part where I shine. A quick comeback full of cutting, though not ill-intended, wit. I got nothing. The truth is that I've been looking everywhere else, myself, except for the long line I'd like to trace from Locke's collar bone to where I could get cut on those hips. My eyes betray me with the thought, and I take an inadvertent step forward.

One of my straps falls from my shoulder.

"You did that on purpose," Locke says, staring at the shoulder.

"I did not," I laugh. I move to slide the strap into place, but Locke catches my hand before it can finish its task. He overshadows me, eyes roaming from where he's trapped my hand, across the lace, and up to my face. He seeks out my lips and kisses me until I can feel the pull of his breath. He stares at me like I've hurt him.

It's an eternity of longing, teetering on the point of concession before Locke replaces the strap and playfully bites into the skin there. Next, he snatches my robe and makes a show of tossing it across the room, but I grab it, so he opens it for me to slip into, and wraps it around me from behind. His beard is tantalizingly rough when he frees my hair from the robe's collar to kiss the back of my neck, but I manage to tie the belt and then to present myself to him with a swish of my hands to say *There. All done.* Locke steps back to peruse me.

"Yeah," he says, but shakes his head no. "That doesn't help."

The robe is just as short as the gown and, though it does cover my arms and chest, it's fitted against all my curves. Locke drives over them with his hands down the sides of me.

"I will soldier through," he declares. He spins me around and tugs me to his chest, swaying, like there's music playing.

We dance like that, in silence, for some time. I think I'll cherish it forever.

"Are you missing the baby?" I ask.

"Not at the moment."

"She's your niece."

Locke doesn't reply. Just keeps moving us around.

In a minute I say, "You're scheming."

He stops to look down at me. "There's no reason for you to come to the station tomorrow." And there it is.

"Let's talk about it." I motion to the bed, where we both take a seat.

"You have to teach," Locke says. "I'll deliver the drive to the sheriff while you're in class."

"You have to be with your family at the same time, to help your dad. I'll just meet you at the station. I'll borrow John Mark's car."

"That's not the issue. You can take Aaron's Jeep if that's all you need."

"Ooo, that Army-green Wrangler under his house?"

Locke acknowledges my enthusiasm, but says, "I don't want you anywhere near that lunatic Chris. I don't trust him."

"I understand, but I'd actually like to talk to him. Somewhere safe like that. If we could find some common ground—"

"Em, you're talking like he's a sane and decent person. What if he's just...not? What if he's dangerous?"

"Your brother trusted him."

"Is that how you took it? I thought he left a lot of room for doubt."

"Sheriff Dunn will be there." Locke is unconvinced. "We'll be at a police station," I press. "What could possibly happen there?"

14

WHAT COULD POSSIBLY HAPPEN THERE, INDEED

I was bold last night when I argued my case with Locke, and he finally acquiesced, though he was not happy about it. Now that I'm at the station, I feel nervous and exposed. Turns out, Sheriff Dunn is not even here. He's out on a call. And guess who else isn't here? Locke. A few minutes ago, he texted to say that getting his dad discharged was taking much longer than expected. So, here I sit in the lobby waiting. Alone. Like last time. Feeling the minutes drag by and wishing that everyone would hop back up on that *right away* schedule.

Folded in my pocket is Aaron's letter, which I finger on the outside of my pants. I found it this morning lying between where Locke and I had slept. I think he must have fallen asleep holding it. Now it feels conspicuous against my leg like it makes me the target of some unknown bad guy's sinister attention.

I stand up to pace and am drawn to the portraits on the memorial wall, where I study Aaron's handsome face. His jawline, strong over the starched navy collar of his uniform, is intimately familiar, and yet I never knew this man. This man who occupies my lover's heart as its twin. My eyes roam the other pictures in the row, making me wonder how many other brothers and sisters are gone from this town. Next to Aaron is Charles. Charles Conrad. Charles Dunn Conrad.

A jarring bang from a metal door makes me go rigid, and when the side entrance reveals Chris Michaels, I want to sink through the floor. He hasn't noticed me. He's consulting his phone and takes an immediate left into an open room to answer a call. I return to my seat as invisibly as possible, though I can see him through the windows that border the walls. He's pacing back and forth across the room while he speaks and ruffing the hair on the back of his head.

When I spot something written on his forearm, I lurch forward in my seat. Since the cuffs of Chris's shirt are rolled, a design comes into focus. A design in the exact spot that he's always worrying with the other hand. I haul myself over to get a better look. I stalk right through the door. When Chris realizes who I am, his head springs back in surprise, but I don't take time to explain myself. I tug at his sleeve.

"What the—" He jerks his arm away.

"Let me see it," I plead. "I need to know."

We face off. The way Chris is staring me down reminds me of a pitcher at a baseball game I went to one summer. The teams shared a rough history, and the pitcher's next throw broke the batter's nose.

I flinch. "Please don't hit me," I blurt out.

"What are you talking about? Why are you here?" Chris realizes he's still on the call and tells the person on the phone he has to go.

"I need to know, Chris. Show it to me."

Finally, with a relenting shake of his head, Chris pushes the sleeve over his elbow. At the bend, is a tattoo. A skeleton key, the handle of which is a skull. Written into the design are Aaron's initials, AAL, and the words *Brother in Arms*.

"You loved him," I say. "Or else you feel guilty." Chris jerks his sleeve back down and wraps his arms around himself.

"Or both," he says. "I wish we'd never gone undercover."

"Did you kill him?"

"Of course, not," he spits. "He was my *partner*." The mournful emphasis on the word *partner* makes it sound like, for Chris, there is no more sacred bond. "But I do believe he was killed," he adds.

"Then why did you keep acting like it was suicide?"

"That's what it was ruled. I wasn't there."

It's not Chris. It's not Chris. My mind spins through the interactions I've had with him in light of his commitment to Aaron. He'd been such a jerk. But that didn't make him a murderer. He'd given me back the bracelet.

"Was it Conrad?"

"How do you—" Chris takes a chance, and I can see that he's risking something. "I thought so at first. He was dirty. No doubt. He shot Aaron, and I thought he'd killed him. I didn't—I *couldn't*—" Chris looks haunted, but he shakes it off to say, "Anyway, Conrad didn't kill him."

"How do you know?"

"Turns out that Aaron hadn't even been shot. And Conrad was already dead when Aaron took the needle."

"How did Conrad die?"

"He *shot* Aaron," Chris reasserts—as if that's Conrad's official cause of death.

"Oh," I say, and if I'm correct, Chris means that he took care of Conrad himself. I don't dig any further into that part. But the way Chris goes back and forth between saying Aaron was shot and also that he wasn't? It must have been the traumatic event that's affected him so much.

"Was anyone else working undercover with you?" I ask.

Chris shakes his head. "It's hard to get a foothold in that sort of thing. We had too many men in there as it was. The state police recruited Aaron, and then he recruited me. I think the sheriff finagled it so that Conrad, who was a real disappointment, but also his own nephew, could try to make something of himself. The whole thing took on a life of its own. Everyone paranoid of everyone else. You lose your ability to see in straight lines, if you know what I mean."

"Who else knew you were cops?"

"*Outside* of the cops?" Chris casts about for the answer. "Aaron's informant."

"Anita," I say. "The woman who died at the cemetery."

"How do you know all this?" Chris appraises me with a new curiosity.

"Chris, I have to know. Did you supply their dad with the heroin?"

"That is just asinine!" Glancing around furtively, Chris closes the door. "We found it in Aaron's basement."

"But Locke had been through the house."

"I don't know what to tell you, Emma. That's where it was. Either Aaron held it back or somebody planted it. Why do you think I've suspected *you*?" Chris huffs in frustration. "I should have taken it that day and destroyed it myself. I didn't want to take it into evidence and throw *more* dirt onto Aaron's reputation. I didn't know his dad was that sick." He pinches the bridge of his nose. "How's he doing?"

"He's OK. They're letting him out of the hospital today and moving him into rehab to get his thinking straight."

Chris nods without meeting my eyes.

"What made you trust me with the key?" I ask.

"Was it really a key?!" he says, leaning in. "I knew it had something to do with Aaron as soon as I saw it, but it was so small."

"That's why you were at Aaron's. And why you were in my room at the Lockes'. You were trying to find out if it fits anything."

Chris braces himself on the back of a chair. "Anita came to the station that day, though she'd been in hiding. It was the anniversary of Aaron's death, and she wanted me to come with her to the cemetery. I thought she just wanted closure."

"What did you tell her?"

"I told her closure was overrated and that she best get the hell back underground. But now I think somebody smarter than me figured out she was going to the cemetery to meet with you. Or Landon. Whatever. And stuck her before she could do it."

"Do you think it was the same person who killed Aaron?"

Chris sighs. "If I had to guess. They died the same way. Aaron's hit was ordered by whomever Conrad was listening to—I'm sure of it—but I was yanked from the operation, and I haven't been able to find out any more on my own."

The tortured look in Chris's eyes helps me make the decision.

From my pocket, I withdraw Aaron's letter and present it to him. "Locke figured it out. That's why I'm here. He's on his way."

It's like the letter slaps life back into the man. Chris snatches it from me and reads it through. His eyes roam the room like he can see options for how to proceed written on different surfaces of the walls.

"Is there really money missing that the police can't account for?" I ask.

"Yeah, there really is." Chris says it with the energy he'd use to swat away a bug. He's too busy digesting the letter. "But it's not police money. It's Del Valle's, the boss-man we were trying to nail for trafficking. It went missing on Aaron's watch."

"Well, doesn't that make *him* the real suspect for Aaron's murder?"

"I know that seems like the obvious conclusion, but he and Aaron had a special relationship, if that makes any sense. Aaron had wormed his way in deep, had even grown to love the man. Not as Aaron Locke, you know, but as his undercover self. Though I'm not sure there was always a clear distinction between the two."

Chris looks up at me and flicks the letter with a snarl that I think is also a smile. "I knew that son-of-a—" He tapers his description. "I knew he and Anita were together. He denied it. Said he'd never let a woman risk an operation." Chris relishes the knowledge with a shake of his head.

Through the windows on the other side of the room, I see that Sheriff Dunn has returned and is headed for his office. Chris follows my gaze and lifts a hand to my back. "Let's go tell him!"

Before we even break the plane of the sheriff's doorway, Chris is calling to him. "Sheriff, Emma Caine has something urgent to share with us."

We enter in time to find the sheriff suspended halfway between sitting and standing. I'm already saying, "Well, it's more Locke's to—" But when I observe the sheriff's rigidity, the wary set of his jaw, the descent of his brow, I promptly shut my mouth. I could understand if my presence made him expectant, maybe even excited, given the way Chris announced me. But not locked up. Not poised like a panther. The sheriff rolls his shoulders and then his back against the chair, one vertebra at a time like he must will his muscles to comply. He steeples his fingers and nods me into the metal chair, but I do not move to take it.

"What is it?" he asks, quietly. Calmly. Because in quicksand, you're not supposed to flail.

My mind works overtime. The sheriff had been one of the last people to see Anita alive. What if the young mother had divulged something about the information Aaron left behind? Or about her intention to find Locke? Her mere return could have worried him, if he had something to hide. I blink several times before I catch myself, and my cheeks flush hot with knowing. The only thing I can think to do is to steer him away from the truth by going on the offensive.

Chris begins to speak from the doorway behind me, but I cut over the top of him. "I stopped by on my way to an appointment with Ms. Vaughn," I say. "I'm arguing that the baby was taken from me as a result of the irresponsible behavior of this department. I wanted to tell you, as a courtesy, in case Child Services has questions for you. And I wanted to ask you to encourage your officers—" Here I shoot a look at Chris. "Not to use babies as leverage to gain *nonexistent information*." I emphasize the last and turn full round to glare at Chris. I glance at the letter, still in his hand. He must feel me urging him to put it away because he casually folds it and sticks it into his back pocket.

Sheriff Dunn's eyes follow the action.

"I know what you're doing," Chris says to me. Does he? He pauses, and I think he's sending me a message. Maybe that's just wishful thinking. "You're trying to shame me for the tactics I used, but I'll do whatever it takes."

The sheriff regards both of us with a frown. "Is that all, Ms. Caine?" he asks.

"Yes."

"I'll see her out," Chris says. It sounds like he's going to toss a drowned rat.

Before we can exit, the office phone on Dunn's desk lights up and a female voice says, "Sheriff, Landon Locke is on his way in."

My heart falls like a stone. How can I intercept Locke and make him aware of my suspicions before he presents Aaron's information to the sheriff? We have to go higher up. The knowledge of all that the sheriff could be guilty of swirls through my brain. Aaron had confided to him that Conrad was dirty—Conrad, who was his nephew—and that there was someone else behind the scenes. If that someone was the sheriff...

In saunters Locke, his shoulders relaxed like he's already crossed into the end zone. Until he sees Chris, and he comes to a halt.

"It's OK, Locke," I say. "I've already wasted enough of the sheriff's time. Chris and I have come to an understanding, I think."

Locke stares at me blankly. His hand is clenched around what I assume to be the drive he's come to deliver.

"Yeah, we're good," Chris says too slowly. I fight the desire to grimace at him or to pierce him with something sharp. He seems to have heard himself too slowly too, though. He continues at a more typical pace. "Ms. Vaughn had me written up, so...no more baby as football. And I trust I won't have any reason to visit with your little girlfriend in the future." He flashes me a quick, unfriendly smile that makes Locke lean in with his head and chest before the rest of himself.

"Chris, if you ever come near her again, I wi—"

"I'm OK, Locke," I interrupt. "Let's just get out of here. We'll be late for Ms. Vaughn."

Locke allows me to guide him from the office, but not without a nasty sneer at Chris.

Chris trails us to the parking lot.

If one could scan our awkward grouping, to map out the emotional and mental quagmire that emanates from us, a lurid and confusing picture would surely emerge. As soon as we're outside, Locke pivots. "I feel a few steps behind," he barks.

"We can't talk here," Chris says. He pushes Aaron's letter against my chest and receives a quick check from Locke's palm, which he ignores. "Drive to the state police headquarters," he tells me. "Ask for

Commander Zendejas. I'll try to tell him you're on the way. I'll come if I can."

"Got it," I say. I start to make a beeline for the truck when I hear the sheriff summon Chris through the front door.

"Officer Michaels?"

Chris's countenance falls.

"A word?"

Chris visibly steels himself and says to Locke, who has yet to move, "For the love of Aaron. Go."

Forty-five minutes later, an officer at the Texas State Police headquarters gestures us into a parking spot near a side door. When Locke steps out, the officer stops gesturing and ends up gawking instead. Locke looks like he is consciously working to keep his eyes from rolling. He holds out his right hand. "Landon," he says. "*Landon* Locke. This is Emma Caine."

"Wow," the man says. "Well, let's get you inside." He directs us to a side door, and along the way he does—not just a double—but a triple take at Locke.

"I take it you knew my brother," Locke says, pausing to allow me to enter the building before he does.

"I'll let Commander Zendejas field that question," the officer says. "I'm not sure I'm at liberty."

We follow the man down a wide hallway. This venue makes the sheriff's office look sloppy. Crisp white walls, stainless steel accents, immaculate windows. The officer raps on the open door of a large conference room. "They're here, Commander."

We're motioned in by a dark-skinned and darker-eyed man who is standing before an enormous TV monitor. The grey that salts his hair is becoming and lends the effect of wisdom hard-earned. No nonsense, though not unfriendly, Commander Zendejas calls out our first and last names as we approach. *Practiced*, I think. *A show of control.* But then I decide that it isn't a show, that he is actually just in control here, keeping close tabs on everything under his jurisdiction. At any rate, there's no doubt who's in charge.

The other officers in the room stand at attention, except for a woman with whom the commander has been consulting. In neat business clothes, she seems higher ranking than anyone else, save the commander. I know her, though I haven't seen her since the day she questioned me in my office—with the devious help of John Mark.

Detective Wilkins greets Locke first, then turns toward me. I wonder if I should sign *Hello*. Not really. I'm hoping against hope that she's forgotten how complicit I was in John Mark's trickery.

"Dr. Caine," she says. "No need for an interpreter today?" She smiles slyly and offers her hand.

"No, not today, Detective." Do I seem penitent, or do I seem like I'm about to laugh? Thank goodness she has a sense of humor.

Commander Zendejas instructs us not to waste time, and Locke looks down at the drive in his hand—a last doubt that he's doing the right thing, maybe—before he hands it over.

As if they are of one mind, Zendejas gives and Wilkins receives the drive. Both of them turn in unison toward a parapet that is stationed in the center of the room. Wilkins climbs a step to insert the drive into a rack that looks to contain inputs for every type of recorded information in existence, whether obsolete or not. She clicks on a computer screen and, without looking around, she says, "It's password-protected." The large screen on the front wall mirrors what the laptop shows.

"Of course, it is," Locke complains. "OK. Let me think." He squeezes the bridge of his nose. "Em, do you have the letter?"

"You think it's hidden in here?" I ask.

"Yeah, remember how he ran some things together? He didn't do cute things like that. He meant for me to see it." Locke scans the letter. "SeeYouOnTheFlipSide," he calls. "One word. Capitalize each word within it." The detective types. The drive opens.

She clicks on the URL that appears and— "It's password protected," she says again, which Locke can see. "Should I try the same one?"

"Sure," Locke says. But the page does not open. In fact, it gives a warning that two more unsuccessful attempts will corrupt the site permanently. A timer appears, but it's not counting down.

"OK." Locke nods his head, his eyes roaming the air above him. "Try 'TheLockeBox.' Spell Locke with an E. Capitalize all the words."

Another notice. One chance remaining.

"Hang on," Zendejas says. "Let's put a team on it before we lose the whole thing."

Detective Wilkins shakes her head. "I've seen this kind of thing before. It could be a hoax, in which case we have all the time in the world, but my guess is that we've already set the self-destruct into play. We've got maybe thirty seconds."

The timer confirms her words. It begins to count down from thirty with obnoxious, digital chimes that announce each number.

"It's all very James Bond of you," Locke mutters. Then he exhales a surprise laugh. "It's Double O Seven," he says. "Zero. Zero. Seven. Numerals only. No spaces. Honestly."

"Are you sure?" Zendejas demands.

Locke nods his head, his eyebrows raised in the withering smirk I bet he'd like to fix upon his brother.

Wilkins watches the commander for permission, and they consult one another silently before she says, "Aaron chose him for a reason." Zendejas makes a tiny movement, an allowance. The detective keys in the numerals. The page opens. Multiple dates and hours of listed recordings appear. Locke defers to Zendejas with open hands and a backward step.

"Let's hit that last entry," the commander says. "August twenty-five."

The day Aaron died.

I move toward Locke. "Do you—"

"I'm staying," he says.

"OK. Me too." We lift our eyes to the screen.

At first, the picture is dark. Then a parking lot can be seen, and, within thirty yards, some kind of delivery platform fixed to a ware-house. In this context, it looks like a stage. There is a large garage door in the background, open wide but dark inside. The camera that shot this scene was near ground level, angled upward, and maybe hidden, because objects like small leaves wave into view from time to time, but so far out of focus they appear translucent.

Locke's face overtakes the frame. Only it's Aaron. You can see that he's repositioning the camera from the camera's point of view. The concentration on his face gives way to an impish grin. He looks directly into the lens and winks.

Beside me, *my* Locke's lips press into a smile even as his eyes fill with tears. His brother's face disappears, and there's no action at all. Nothing in the scene for several minutes. The detective asks for permission to advance the footage.

Further into the video, two men sit on the loading dock with their legs dangling over the side. One of them is Chris. He opens a wooden crate and extracts a small leather casket and a plastic bag. He hands them to a man who stands on the ground below him. After the merchandise is inspected, that man hands it back to Chris, and Chris repositions the lid on the crate. He trades the crate for money, most of which he adds to a zippered cash bag, some of which he hands to the man seated next to him, and the rest of which he pockets.

"Was Chris on the take?" Locke asks.

Zendejas answers, "No. He's just doing his job. The guy with him is the one. Conrad. He'd been extorting money from that little show and getting his kicks with women who had no recourse because they'd sold themselves to get across the border. Chris pretended to be complicit. Here comes your brother."

In the video, Aaron's green Jeep rolls up beside the delivery dock. "It was your brother's job to keep track of the sales and collect the money. He'd come in about seven hundred thousand dollars short a few days before, and the fact that he lived as long as he did shows how far into the game he'd wormed himself."

At that moment, not in the video, but in real life, Chris Michaels strolls through the conference room door. Locke scowls, but Zendejas waves him in.

"This is what we've been waiting for," Detective Wilkins tells him.

"Does it show Conrad?" he asks. "Crooked son-of-a—" Chris positions himself for a better view. "Noooo. He was rolling the day he—" A long exhale punctuates the sentence. "Well, hell, where's the popcorn?" Chris crosses his arms and clamps his jaw shut.

The video reveals a short-haired Locke stepping from the driver's side. Suddenly there is sound as well. At her computer, Wilkins adjusts the volume. "He must have had a mic on his person," she says. "It just connected to the camera."

From the passenger seat, a gorgeous Latina exits. Anita. About five months pregnant. Beautiful brown skin. Thick black hair. Large round sunglasses. She gets shoved aside by one of the men who paid for the crate. She stumbles into Chris's legs. Aaron glowers at the man but otherwise doesn't react.

Conrad grins like a rat. He jumps down from the dock to poke Anita in the belly. "Looks like somebody's already had a turn," he says. "When do I get mine?"

"She's not the merchandise," Aaron says. "She belongs to Del Valle." His voice is as unyielding as a frozen lake. He overshadows Conrad, who bunches his cheek in a disgruntled way, but backs off. The buyers slam their trunk and drive away.

"We're closing up," Aaron tells his fellow policemen. "The boss wants an accounting of everything. Money's missing. He is not real happy about that. The whole operation's about to blow up, and when he finds out who's on the take, God help him. Whatever you've done —whatever you know—now is the time."

"I think you're more loyal to *the boss* than you are to us," Conrad says. "Maybe you're the one who needs to speak up."

Before Aaron can reply, his attention is drawn to something past the camera. "Who are you expecting?" he asks.

Chris frowns in that direction and shakes his head.

"Don't worry about it," Conrad says. "It's a new buyer."

"New buyers get vetted," Aaron says. "And scheduled. Through me."

"Yeah, well you're not the only one with skin in the game."

A large car pulls to a stop in the foreground, taking up much of the lower-left frame. Two men get out of the front and Conrad jogs to meet them. They speak with their heads in a huddle.

They're far enough away from Aaron that the microphone can't pick up what they're saying, but Aaron can be heard speaking to Chris. "What do you know?" he asks.

"Not much. He keeps bragging about someone making him rich."

"I think this is our guy," Aaron says. He glances at Anita, at the open garage door, at his Jeep. He's trying to figure out how best to shield her.

One of Conrad's cohorts is pointing him toward the car, and now Conrad is moving straight toward the camera before he veers off to lean over a slightly open window in the back. His face is suddenly full of concern.

The car windows are tinted so that no one can identify who it is that remains inside. There is only a vague silhouette. I recognize him, not for what he does, but for what he doesn't do. He doesn't enter the action. He watches from the outskirts. He doesn't posture or preen. He sits back and steeples his fingers.

"That's Sheriff Dunn," I say. Every person in the room turns to see who I mean. "Sitting in the car," I explain.

"I don't think so," Chris says. "It was—" Chris's face goes ashen. He rounds on me. "Are you sure? He had the audacity to show up there?"

In the video, Conrad speaks to the passenger and then walks back to the loading dock.

"If she's right"—Chris pivots from me to Locke—"he just gave orders to have your brother executed."

"Why would he do that?" Detective Wilkins asks.

It's Locke who answers. "Because Aaron went to him the day before with suspicions that Conrad wasn't acting alone."

Commander Zendejas furrows his brow, and for the first time, he shows a hint of uncertainty, the way one might if they'd made a misstep.

"Skip it back," I tell them. "To where Conrad spoke into the car." I step inside Detective Wilkins' booth to study Conrad's mouth on her computer screen. Conrad had balked at something that had been told to him. I read his lips. "He said, 'How am I supposed to know where the seven brick—' Ugh, I can't make it out. Where the seven brick somethings went?"

"Seven *bricks*," Zendejas says, emphasizing *bricks* as a noun, not an adjective. "He's referring to the missing money."

"Well, I don't think the sheriff has it," I say.

"The sheriff shouldn't even know about it." Zendejas's tone takes on a silky hunger. "Not at that point. If we can prove that that's who you say it is in there— What was that last thing Conrad just said?"

Chris, in the video, far behind Conrad, exchanges a wary glance with Aaron. As I read Conrad's lips, the real Chris, in the room beside me, looks like he's going to be sick. Locke looks much the same. Commander Zendejas's eyes roam back and forth across the screen.

Wilkins replays it. I speak what I see. "You're the sheriff. You can come back, and—oh." I frown at Locke and begrudgingly reveal what's been said. "Rule it suicide."

Just then, in real-time, the intercom announces that Sheriff Dunn has arrived.

"Keep him in the office," Zendejas calls out. "I'll be right there."

"Uh—let me get him back."

There's a commotion down the hall. Sheriff Dunn's voice is saying that he knows the way. Someone else is saying that things are different today.

"We're about to have company," the commander says. Upon that matter-of-fact notification, officers take places at the two separate entrances to the room. Locke moves toward me where I stand beside Detective Wilkins on the parapet. There are a few moments of anticipation when I can only hear the blood pulsing in my ears. And then the sound of stomping boots accompanies it. A red-faced Sheriff Dunn appears. No steepling of his fingers now.

"Sheriff," the commander greets him. "Come in. We'd like to review some new evidence with you. Your firearm?" As if it is just a matter of professional protocol, though I suspect the sheriff has never been asked to relinquish it before, an officer steps forward to collect his weapon. The sheriff does not comply.

"What's going on here?" Dunn demands. An officer moves to bar the door by which Dunn has entered. Dunn rotates his back to the wall. "What's going on here?" he says again. Louder this time. He surveys the "special feature," and his eyes bulge with recognition. His right hand twitches.

"Where did you get that?" Dunn asks. He scans the room until he finds Locke. I stiffen.

In the video, Aaron draws Anita to the right side of the frame and positions himself between her and Conrad. Conrad tells him to drop to his knees.

"Don't be a fool," Aaron says. His eyes flicker to Chris and back, quick as a blink, but Conrad sees it.

"He's not going to help you, Locke." Aaron's jaw clenches in aggravation. "He's making too much. And yeah. They know who you are, *Officer* Locke." Conrad indicates the other two men.

Aaron looks from Conrad to the car, and I wonder if, in that instant, he puts it all together. If Chris is just acting because he is undercover, then the cover is very deep. Why isn't he helping? I don't know what he's supposed to be doing, but something.

Anita stands behind Aaron with her head bowed like she's praying. She's composed. She isn't trembling or crying. I think she may be readying herself for action.

Aaron feels for her, his other hand raised in surrender. Then, more quickly than I would have thought possible, Aaron does two things. With his right arm, he forces Anita to the ground, and with his left, he throws a hook against Conrad's eye socket that sends him sprawling. *That* is what Chris is waiting for. He frees his firearm and sprints across the loading dock.

The other two men spring forward too, brandishing weapons of their own. It may be Aaron's concern for Anita that keeps him from doing the same. He kneels before her.

Bolstered by the presence of the other two men and furious that he's been dropped, Conrad scrambles up and pounds the butt of his gun against the side of Aaron's head. Aaron falls to the ground, and a shot rings out, causing the video's noise to break up for the time it takes. It isn't apparent where the bullet lands, but it is apparent that it emanates from Conrad's gun, which he is pointing at Aaron's prone figure. Chris screams something unintelligible. He unloads three rapid rounds into Conrad's chest. The other two men take cover behind the car.

The image of Conrad's jerking body, even in the video, makes me turn my head, but not before I register the look of shock on Conrad's face. He thought Chris was on his side. I glance back in time to see Chris diving on top of Anita, rolling her out of the picture. Conrad is lying beside Aaron on the ground. Both are smeared in blood.

Chris and Anita flee behind the building. Mere moments later, a car can be seen hurtling away.

And still, the lone silhouette in the car does not deign to make an appearance.

In the conference room, Sheriff Dunn calmly unsnaps his holster but relaxes his hand down by his side. Chris unsnaps his own, along with several other officers, so that the *snap-snap-snaps*, for just those few seconds, mimic the sound of sleet against a window. Commands are issued from several directions. Everything goes silent.

Chris advances on the sheriff, one arm outstretched in a gesture for him to stand down. The sheriff shakes his head. It crosses my mind that he's trying to get himself killed.

"Was it worth it?" Chris asks.

"*You* took it," Dunn says.

"Sheriff, this is your final warning," Commander Zendejas intervenes. "Drop your firearm and raise your hands into the air."

The sheriff ignores him. He is taut with concentration, and that is fixed upon Chris. When he lurches into motion, it is to force his gun in Locke's direction.

I hiss in a breath and whirl toward my love, but I'm encapsulated by the raised walls of the parapet and Detective Wilkins is shoving me to the ground. We miss the ground of the booth and bump down its one stair at the same time the ear-splitting crack rips through the air. I claw at the carpet to get to Locke.

From all around the room, the concussive bang of every officer's firearm reverberates in what seems like a never-ending cacophony. I cover my ears and tuck my head until all is quiet, and when I uncurl, the sheriff is lying motionless on the ground. The room smells like the 4th of July. The smoke around us is just as thick. I dislodge myself from Detective Wilkins and crawl toward Chris, who is clutching his side, blood seeping between his fingers. He is foolishly trying to get to his knees, but Locke is bracing him, telling him to lie down.

My EMT training kicks in and I use my hands to put pressure on Chris's wound. "I need a towel," I say. My voice is raspy. Locke uses both hands to jerk his own shirt over his head and forces it under the pressure I'm exerting.

"Are you OK?" I bark. I can hardly bear to look, for fear he's been shot too. "Locke?"

"I'm fine, Em. It's Chris."

I feel around Chris's side to his back. "Chris?" I say. "You're gonna be fine, OK? It's to your side, out the back. There's nothing there that can't be fixed. Do you understand? You're gonna be fine."

He doesn't seem to hear me. "Aaron?!" he yells and searches around until Locke stoops right in front of his face. "Aaron?"

Locke nods without correcting Chris for calling him by Aaron's name.

"I thought you died," he says. "I thought I let him kill you."

"You didn't let him kill me, brother. You saved me. You took the bullet yourself."

Chris peers around wildly. No one is helping Sheriff Dunn. A few people are speaking into radios they have perched upon their shoulders.

The video is still playing, but nothing is happening. Then, at long last, the someone who has remained in the car steps out. At first, all you can see is the back of his legs, but as he advances toward the loading dock, Dunn's whole body comes into view. He walks over to the merchandise and pockets several small bags of white powder. He's wearing rubber gloves. He prepares a dose.

Aaron begins to stir. He may have regained consciousness, but

Dunn injects the needle into the crease at Aaron's elbow. In a few moments, Aaron relaxes onto the grass.

Chris, in the conference room, is watching this unfold on the video. He tries to speak, but his throat is tight with emotion. He swallows and manages, "I thought he was already dead. God, forgive me. I thought he was dead, and then I saw him that night after the heroin had taken him and not a bullet hole to be found." He clutches Locke's hand. "Dunn questioned me so hard, I thought he suspected me of killing him. He was just trying to find out what I knew."

"Where were you?" Locke chokes out. "Where was Anita?"

"I drove her away. I was afraid they were going to kill her. I scared her to death. Gave her the take from the day and said if she wanted to live long enough for the baby to be born, she'd better disappear. Maybe the one smart thing I did." Chris's voice is weaker. He begins to slur his words.

"Where's the ambulance?" I yell to the room at large.

"What made her come back?" Locke asks. "Chris?"

Chris has closed his eyes, but he opens them again, halfway. "Here," he says. "I ran this for you on a—on a hunch. Maybe I did *two* smart things." Chris's lips make a small smile like he's dreaming something pleasant. His body goes limp.

"No-no-no! Chris?" I feel for a pulse.

"You ran *what* for me, bro?" Locke says. But he doesn't get an answer.

The EMTs show up. Once they've strapped Chris to a stretcher and hauled him away, a different officer cleans up. He lifts a folded envelope off the ground, looks it over, hands it to Locke.

Locke shakes his head to indicate that it isn't his, but the officer points to the name typed on the front. "Landon Thomas Locke. Right there."

Locke doesn't waste time with it. He accepts the envelope, stuffs it into his pocket, and faces me. Neither of us speaks. In the video, Dunn orders his two men to place both Conrad's and Aaron's bodies into the car. They drive away leaving the scene empty. And silent.

The next few hours are a blur. An officer shoves a navy T-shirt into Locke's bare chest. It boasts a red Texas Rangers logo like a badge over the left pocket, and Locke drags it on without acknowledging the man. The same officer escorts us to a small breakroom where he motions us to a table and thumps down some nasty, sugary snacks and sodas. After that, he asks for our statements.

Commander Zendejas knocks on the breakroom door, enters, and stands by while we finish up. Then he sits across from us and asks how we're doing. These are niceties. I don't believe the commander has time for niceties, not for niceties' sake. And I'm correct. He folds his hands on the table in front of him and stares at Locke from under his brow.

"The videos incriminate more than the sheriff," he says.

Locke's shoulders slump with fatigue. "If you're here to tell me that my brother—" he begins, but Zendejas shakes his head.

"No. Your brother came to me the morning he died." The commander's rueful tone brokers Locke's attention. "His gut told him to, I guess. He was less than thrilled with the way Dunn had handled the news about Conrad's criminal behavior. He confided in me that if anything should happen to him, he had someone in place to deliver information to Dunn. He asked if I thought he should have it sent here instead, but I told him to keep Dunn in the loop. It didn't occur to me that your brother was trying to suss out whether or not I had my own suspicions."

Zendejas produces two pictures, apparently printed from stills of the video. One is of Aaron speaking to a man in a cowboy hat beside a wooden fence. The other is of that same man watching while three young women are herded into the back of a van.

"This man is responsible for the trafficking of human beings. Your brother established a connection with him. Directly with him. Which is..." Zendejas thins his lips to show what a rarity that is. "I know that you lost a brother. But we lost an invaluable asset."

I study the commander. He's setting us up for something. He's positioning us to— "No," I say. And more loudly, "No! Are you out of your mind? Build your own infrastructure. You can't possibly mean to use Locke in his brother's place. Do you have any idea what this family has already sacrificed?!"

Zendejas has the good sense to back off. He frowns in under-standing.

"Let him talk, Emma," Locke says.

I gape at him. "No. Locke? Please, no. Please." I am pleading with him, though Zendejas hasn't yet made the request. I hold Locke's gaze and I know he grasps, even internalizes my fear. Even so, Locke says, "What do you want, Commander? Speak plainly."

"It's not just the heroin." Zendejas is quick to pick up where he'd left off. "Though, as you well know, that's reason enough to put the lives of my officers on the line."

"He's not your officer," I grumble.

Zendejas continues as if he hasn't heard. "Women—*children*—are disappearing. They're being sold. Literally sold into slavery. Made to do deplorable things. Most of them are forced to use drugs so that they'll comply. Or they willingly partake just to get through it. They end up becoming addicted. Even when they can be rescued, it is unlikely that they can be rehabilitated. It became your brother's personal mission."

Zendejas thumps his middle finger down onto the photo. "This man. Carols Del Valle, with whom Aaron had gained trust, runs the whole operation. A roving market across the state. Plain houses on the outside. Something like a rave on the inside. Somewhere different each time and so sporadic we often don't get news of it until it's over, if we get news of it at all. We have intel that one is in operation right now, but not the location."

By the way he peruses the pictures, I know that Locke is being roped in. Which is just what the commander means to happen. I can see as well as Locke can that they're just girls. They don't look terri-fied so much as strung out.

"We have people in place to disrupt the chain. All we need is the address—which we can procure." He performs a pause. "With your help."

Oh, he's good. The timing. The delivery. First class. I don't know whether to smack him or applaud. I shove my chair back to get to my feet.

"We can't let you leave yet," Zendejas says.

"You don't need me for this," I snap. "I'm going outside."

An officer stands in front of the door, but Zendejas waves him away and tells him to help me find the courtyard. On our way out, I overhear him say that they only need for Locke to be seen, and then everyone in the agency will recognize Aaron for the hero he was.

"If you get yourself killed," I mutter, even though Locke can't hear me. "You will be gone as surely as if you never belonged to me at all."

It's another thirty-five minutes before Locke finds me sitting in the small courtyard on a white stone bench, under a red leaf maple tree. A fountain bubbles in the center. Locke takes a place beside me and sits forward with his elbows on his knees.

"I have to do it," he says, his eyes straight ahead.

"What happened to being an artist with wisdom as your weapon?" I feel as defeated as I sound.

"Grandaddy never meant for me not to be a man of action, Em. If I can help give those girls back to their families? If I can make it possible to free them from that kind of torture? Not to mention to be able to finish what Aaron started, what he gave his life for— I wouldn't be able to live with myself, Emma, if I chose to avoid the risk. I have to do it."

I feel too heavy to move any of my body parts. "I know," I manage. "I saw your decision before you made it."

"I'd like to have your blessing."

I lean against his shoulder. "Of course, you have it. And I'm proud of you. But I'm scared too. These aren't just guys who smash out windows and grab purses." Locke repositions himself to lay an arm around me.

"I know. They'll guard me. They just need my pretty face."

"I need your pretty face. When do you have to do it?"

Locke doesn't answer right away. I pull back to question him. "Locke?"

He smiles unconvincingly. "Tomorrow. I'm supposed to go transform into Aaron, which shouldn't be difficult. You know, wear some of his clothes and stuff, and then somebody's going to come to fill me in on the things I need to know. We'll leave them the keys to the Jeep so that somebody can drive it over. You and I are free to go. We can sleep at my place tonight."

IDENTICAL BUT DIFFERENT

It's two a.m. I'm lying on my back in Locke's bed. Every time I doze off, my mind churns out demented fragments of yesterday's violence. This time, I wake smelling blood. Several seconds tick by before I realize it's just in my head.

"You awake?" I whisper. I turn on my side to find out for myself.

It's too dark to see my love. I listen. Soon he becomes aware of me and guides my head and shoulders onto his chest. It's become my favorite place in this whole world to be, but I'm too anxious to take comfort, too scared about what this day will bring. Anyway, he's not fully awake. His arm around me goes slack, and he drifts away from me.

After I'm sure he's settled, I extricate myself and sneak down the stairs to the kitchen. I make a cup of tea by the small light the stove affords, and while it's brewing, I lean against the counter to scan what part of the room I can see. Grandaddy's ballot box stands near the door next to Locke's desk. Upon the desk is a stack of sketches, a pencil, a tape measure. And Locke's laptop. It occurs to me that I may be able to put my sleeplessness to good use. Hook 'em Horns, right?

I take the laptop and the tea to the couch, where I pull my legs underneath myself and get to work. I'm able to gain access to Aaron's videos. Most of them are the same view of the warehouse we'd seen at the state police headquarters, but the subject matter is mundane. You know, mundane for drug dealing. I fast-forward through a number of days. The dates are never consecutive. I can't decipher any pattern for it. It's the same players, usually Chris and Conrad without much action. Aaron occasionally shows up, sometimes with Anita, sometimes with another woman. The other woman is a strong character. Nobody pushes her around. Not even Conrad.

Aaron takes a subordinate role when he's with her. It's different from the way he acts with Anita. This woman is higher ranking, I think. Why would this woman be treated with respect, while others are sold as slaves? I bet she's related by blood somehow to the boss, Del Valle.

In one video, Aaron says something to the woman. I can't see what. I have it muted, partly to keep from waking Locke, and partly because I just don't want to hear the words. I want to see what's happening underneath them. But after Aaron speaks, the woman rounds on him in anger. He bows up defiantly. Suddenly, she's kissing him. Aaron holds up his arms to push her away, but she forces them down—well, who are we kidding, he *allows* her to—and then he responds to her demands. Thoroughly.

Chris walks out of the warehouse, sees what's going on and walks right back in again. Aaron is smiling into the kisses now, and the woman pulls away in some kind of smug triumph, leaving him panting.

"Lupita," I see Aaron say. He's trying to convince her of something. I can't tell what. I pause the video to search for the word Lupita and find that it's a pet name. Sometimes a shortened form of Guadalupe. The way we get Betty from Elizabeth. But I don't find either name in connection with Del Valle.

Aaron opens the passenger door of his Jeep to allow Lupita to enter. He checks to make sure she's inside and slams the door with a sly smile. Then he rounds the back of the Jeep wiping his mouth. He's not smiling at the moment. He looks a bit nauseated.

I'm two hours into this video fest when Locke calls down from the loft. I lift my head to find him at the railing. "You working?" he asks. "Bring it up here."

"You should sleep."

"No, I can't sleep without you anymore. And Kili doesn't like to snuggle."

When I make my way back to his bed, Locke pushes the dog out of my spot, and I prop up the pillows to take a seat. I guess he assumes I'm grading student videos. He doesn't ask. Just scoots up close with a pillow over his eyes.

I'm not sure what I'm looking for. Some sense of control. Some way to give Locke the knowledge he needs to play the part without raising suspicion.

The next videos are much the same. Anita shows up less. Lupita shows up more. She seems to consider Aaron her personal boy-toy, and he doesn't seem to mind, though occasionally I catch glimpses of disdain.

Several months later, by the date on the video, there is a different scene altogether. Open paddock, green grass, wooden fence. A gorgeous farmhouse stands in the background. Anita is brushing a shiny black horse. She knows what she's doing. The horse is huge, but her strokes are sure. Aaron sidles into view. He looks around and then, maybe using the horse as a shield, he entwines his fingers with Anita's. She glances about nervously, but allows him to tug her to himself. He's got this hungry half-smile that makes my own heart skip. It's not one I've seen him use with the other woman. He kisses Anita soundly. It's strange to watch, since he looks just like Locke, and Anita looks nothing like me. But it is quite compelling. They do not lack for passion. So much so, that I hardly notice when the horse steps forward to graze, and in his place stands the man called Carlos Del Valle.

Del Valle raises his eyebrows, but otherwise his face remains neutral. When Anita catches sight of him, she starts. She quickly leads the horse away by the bridle. Aaron stands to height. I've see his exact expression before, on Locke, when Chris interrupted us in the wood-shop. Solemn. Unsure what to expect. Maybe a little pissed off.

Del Valle gestures an invitation to walk, and now the two are moving slowly toward the camera.

"You remind me of someone," Del Valle says. His accent makes me question my translation, but I think I'm right.

"Don't tell me it's your son," Aaron says. "I hate that kid."

I choke back a laugh and go back to make sure I've read his lips correctly. Guy's got nerve. His mouth curls in a snarl when he says it.

Del Valle snickers to himself. "No. You remind me of myself."

Aaron seems genuinely gratified. His face softens.

"I too followed my heart," Del Valle says.

"When it would have been wiser to stick to business?" Aaron asks.

Del Valle shrugs. "When she died it cost me everything. I no longer taste. No longer smell." He waves into the air. "See how the sun throws its net of golden light this evening? It no longer comforts me." He observes Aaron with his head to one side. "Do you love her?" he asks.

Aaron stops. I think he's weighing his answer. He wears pain on his face, and he nods his head.

"Does Lupita know? My daughter is very...focused."

"Nobody knows. But you. Now."

"Keep it this way."

Aaron nods to the ground, and I see a conflict taking shape. Del Valle does too. "What is it, mijo?"

I pause the video to search out the word for the sound he just mouthed. Mehoe. Miho. *Mijo. My son.* I slump back to let that sink in.

When I un-pause, Aaron takes a moment. Without facing Del Valle, he says, "There's a baby." He raises his eyes, and there is so much real concern in them, I find tears in my own.

I think Aaron genuinely trusted this man. This sensitive, poetic man who has apparently known loss, and who is also a drug lord who sells children as sex slaves.

I can see Del Valle's chest expand as he draws a breath through his nose and shrink as he releases it. He nods without smiling and casts his eyes around in consideration.

Aaron awaits his response with growing agitation and finally, in a small, and sad, and desperate plea, he simply asks, "Papá?"

Del Valle looks like he wants to cry. "You will have to go."

"Locke, you have to watch this!" I say. I rouse him. "I'm sorry. You have to watch this."

The sun is just coming up when we hear Aaron's Jeep roll into the driveway. We had watched that video, had discussed its ramifications, had lain together in silence. Now Locke rises to push the sheers away from the open window. "You're not going to believe who's driving it," he says. Out of the Jeep limps Chris Michaels, clutching his side.

Locke throws on a shirt and heads down the loft stairs. I look down at myself. I'm wearing one of Locke's T-shirts, which on me is more like a dress. I pull on the shortest athletic shorts I can find. Now I just look like a clown.

Locke greets Chris with, "Are you kidding me?"

They meet halfway up the deck stair. "Hush," Chris instructs. He uses the hand not clutching his side to brace himself on railing. "The doctors don't know I'm gone yet." Chris has a bag thrown around his neck, and he looks about a hundred times happier than I have yet to see him.

Once he makes it to the door, I'm starting a pot of coffee, and he bids me a cheerful good morning—which I nearly fail to return, shocked as I am by the overt friendliness of it. He wouldn't have noticed. He's halfway across the living room. "Come on," he says to Locke. "We gotta get you ready. And there are things you need to know."

He considers the stairs to the loft and then says, "You'll just have to dress right here."

Clearly, Chris has already been to Aaron's house and has rummaged through his drawers, or else he just keeps Aaron's clothes on hand for such an occasion. From his bag, he withdraws a long-sleeved Henley with three buttons at the neck and the image of crossed rifles on top of a green grenade. Holding it out, Chris urges Locke to "Go *ahead*," and shakes it to emphasize the point. Locke complies, throwing down the T-shirt he's been wearing to snatch up the one Chris insists upon, but Chris is frowning.

"What's the problem?" Locke asks.

"You don't have the tattoo."

"Did Aaron go around without a shirt a lot, in front of these people?"

"One of them," Chris mutters. "But you won't." He stretches the shirt where it clings to Locke's back. "If you're identical, why're you so much broader?"

"I'm a competitive swimmer," Locke says. "Aaron was a competitive shooter."

"It'll work," Chris replies. "I mean, who's to say you haven't been working out for the whole year you've been in hiding?"

Chris reveals some blue jeans and a pair of military boots, then stands back to observe Locke once he's dressed.

"Are we done?" Locke asks. He's tucking his shirt the way Aaron must have done, with more material hanging out at the hips than in the middle.

"Not yet. Come with me." Chris ambles to the bathroom. "And step into character," he snaps.

"You're very bossy," Locke grumbles. "I can't imagine Aaron took well to that."

"Why do you think I'm so familiar with his left hook?"

Chris beckons Locke inside, bouncing on the balls of his feet with barely contained anticipation. I can hear him schooling Locke from where I cobble breakfast together. Cooking, like cycling, helps me manage stress. I am vaguely aware of a faint buzzing sound coming from Locke's bathroom, but I busy myself with coffee and pancakes. And ham and eggs and biscuits and— "Wow. Are we planning to run a marathon today?" I smile at the sound of Locke's voice and lift my head to—gasp.

Chris laughs and leans against the door jam, pressing a hand into his side to keep it from splitting wide open. An incongruous expression of pure delight shines upon his face.

I continue to stare as Locke composes his features and crosses his arms. He's Locke. No doubt. But he's the Locke I spied on in the videos last night. The way he carries himself, standing rigid with equal weight on both legs. The way he flexes his chest. The slight scowl that communicates how lucky everyone is that he's still in the room with them. But mostly— "Your *hair!*"

I cover my mouth with both hands for several seconds, before shaking them out in front of myself like a kid who's caught sight of a puppy. "I wanna feel it!" Then my Locke is back. His quick laughter. His easy smile. He strides to me and bows his head so that I can rub my palms against the buzzcut. The top is slightly longer than the rest, pushed forward at an angle.

"It's OK?" he asks, clearly pleased by my reaction.

"Yyyeah. It's hot."

"Gaaaaaah," bellows Chris. "I'm gonna need more pain meds for this." He passes us by to grab a biscuit.

"Here, Chris, do it right." I take back the biscuit, steal another glance at Locke, and then add ham to it, along with a plate of everything else.

"Are you really going to eat all that?" Locke asks. "With your side the way it is?"

"I'm going to attempt to," Chris says. "I didn't know Emma could cook. Why haven't you two invited me to dinner?"

Locke and I share a silent exchange that leaves us struggling to keep our faces straight. I recover first. "You get him back to me today," I say. "And you can come to dinner anytime you want. I'll let you create a lifetime of menus."

"Deal," Chris says, around a mouthful of pancakes. "How can your pancakes be this much better than anybody else's? Aren't they all basically flour and milk?"

"Yeah, but you gotta stir only so much, and let the batter set. And the temp—"

"Stop," Chris says, pointing a fork. "I don't care. Just...they're good."

Locke and I make plates too but neither of us eats much.

Afterward, Chris pushes back, wipes his mouth on a napkin, and says, "Alright, bro." He draws Aaron's cell phone from a side pockets in his tactical pants. "Time to make a call."

Locke recognizes the phone case that belonged to his brother. "That's Aaron's. You got it out of evidence?"

"Never put it in. I've been paying the bill all year hoping for a lead."

Locke says, "You just kind of do whatever you want to, huh?"

Chris shrugs and brings up a number. He places Aaron's phone on the table. "Now, you hit send and, no matter who answers or what language they use, even if they're silent, tell them you have the demand. And hang up." Chris lifts both hands to say, *that's all. No more, no less.*

I exhale through pursed lips. This is it. They're about to set something in motion they have no real control over.

Locke makes the call. Within two rings a friendly sounding man's voice says, "Bueno."

Chris nods expectantly for Locke to say his line. I see Locke transform once again, and when he says, "I have the demand," I could swear that the familiar voice belongs to someone I've never met. He ends the call.

"Nice," Chris says. "In about five minutes, you're going to receive a text with an address. Then we'll see how Zendejas wants to proceed."

Locke stands up to pace the five minutes out, but instead of five, it's less than one. And instead of a text, it's a call. Chris curses. "Alright. Just let it go to voicemail. I think the jig is up. They're breaking their own protocol." Third ring.

"You mean, that's it?" Locke says. "We've already lost our shot?"

"'Fraid so." Fifth ring. Chris raises his chair a few inches off the ground and slams it in frustration. Then grunts in pain. But Locke suddenly grabs the phone and answers with a surly sounding, "What?"

Chris sucks in a breath, his eyes wide and round.

Silence meets us from the other end of the call. Then a woman's soft Spanish accent can be heard. "No es posible. Is you?"

"Why are you speaking to me? Send me the address."

"You are alive?" At this point a male voice can be heard in the background, but it's hard to make out what's being said, and the call goes dead.

Chris makes *sure* the call is dead, then exclaims, "You sounded just like him, with that bothered *what!*" He huffs a laugh that morphs into another grunt.

A text comes in. "An address?" Chris asks. When Locke confirms it, Chris closes his eyes in relief. He takes hold of the phone as another text arrives.

If you are not in the open, you will not see me. Come alone. Come now.

The smile dies on his lips.

I remain quiet and feel, in my head, that sound is having a hard time cutting through. Locke's face is inscrutable. "Let's go," he says to Chris.

Chris shakes his head. "It's not the address to the market." His voice is loaded. "It's the address to the warehouse in the video. The place your brother died. They could be sending us a message."

"I thought Del Valle was told that Aaron was in hiding," I say.

"Well," Chris says, hesitantly. "*Del Valle* was. I went to him myself. Told him Aaron had killed Dennis—that's Conrad's alias—because he had enabled the money to be stolen, and that Aaron and I dumped the body. Told him Aaron wanted to chase down the others to get the money back, and that he and Anita had taken off together. I didn't even know they *were* together. Looking back, it was like Del Valle did. Like he'd ordered them to go."

"He had," Locke says. "He knew about Anita. He may have been the only one."

"Damn. I can't believe he didn't kill Aaron himself. Especially with the money missing. But Aaron was that close to him. Spent night after night with him playing cards, telling stories, drinking. After I told Del Valle Aaron had run, he grabbed me by both shoulders and said, 'No. He is dead.' Said it just like that. But he meant that that's the story I was supposed to spread. Probably didn't want to deal with all his daughter's drama. She had a thing for Aaron. It was more of a power play against her dad, I think."

"Do they know Aaron's true identity?" Locke says.

"No. There's no way. Nor mine."

"And Del Valle himself has already received the amount of the money that went missing? Along with the news that Anita is dead?"

"Zendejas had it couriered directly to Del Valle as soon as you agreed to this. He included the information, as if it were written from you, that when you caught up to the man, he killed Anita. And you killed him. Detective Wilkins developed a backstory, so that if Del Valle looks into it, he'll find all the connections he needs. It's as foolproof as it can be. But, yeah, Del Valle has the money, with interest, along with your apologies that it took a year to recover."

"Then let him see me and he can judge for himself whether he can trust me with the information or not. *He* didn't kill me—Aaron," Locke corrects. "He didn't kill Aaron."

"No," Chris agrees. "He treated you like family."

Chris dials a number from his own phone and walks out onto the deck. Before the door closes behind him, we hear, "Commander, Landon Locke is prepared to show himself."

Locke speaks to me, but I can't comprehend his words. My forehead sinks into furrows. He puts his hands on my cheeks and gets down to my eye level. "I need to know what you think," he says. The sound comes rushing back to my ears. "Seems like they've covered the bases, right? Starting way back when Aaron died."

"Lupita is the wild card," I say. "She'll have questions. She'll be angry."

"Maybe she won't even know."

"Locke, that is who you just talked to!"

"You don't know that."

"What if it was? What if the address came directly from her? She challenges her father. She plays by different rules. He may not even know you called."

"Well, I'm only supposed to be seen, right? The police won't let her get that close."

I don't have as much faith in the police as Locke does. My wheels are spinning. "The commander knew Lupita could be an issue," I say. "He should have prepared you. When she finds out her dad knew Aaron was alive…"

"You don't know it was her on the phone."

I bite my thumb nail in thought. "You're just going to have to kiss her."

"Oh, OK," Locke says, meaning that it's not. "After nearly getting disowned by you for things I didn't even do with Claire, I don't think that's probably the best—"

"If it comes to that, then you do it. Do it as your brother. Do it to come back to me."

"Sweetheart. Emma. I'm not going to be anywhere near the woman. Don't borrow trouble."

"OK," I give in. "I know." I say this for his benefit.

"I'm coming back to you. Today. In a matter of hours."

"I know," I say again. "I'll have dinner ready. It will probably be large."

Chris reappears from the deck. "Let's roll," he says. He sees me and feigns a look of apology.

"A *lifetime* of menus," I remind him. "Any. Time. You want." Chris grins and gives me a big wink. He enjoys this part way too much, but something about that gives me courage. I walk out to see them off and watch from the deck as Locke ducks into the driver's seat of his brother's green Jeep. And then they're gone. I sit down in one of the outdoor chairs and pray.

The first hour goes by, and I'm OK. I clean up the kitchen, scrubbing the counters perhaps harder than necessary. I straighten up the already straight house and when I pick up the jeans Locke was wearing yesterday, I realize how much of Chris's blood is soaked into them. It's a wonder the man is walking around. I wash the jeans along with my clothes, followed by all of Locke's sheets and towels even though, who knows if they're really dirty or not? It gives me something to do instead of worrying.

I fill the bird feeders, and I march the dogs around the pond. In reality, the boys swim most of it and then generously share with me, in vigorous twists, all of the water their fur can expel. It's a beautiful, bright day, clear and cooler than it has been since I moved here.

The second hour, I consider visiting the big house to check on the cats, but I don't want to risk running into Locke's family, who have no idea what is taking place, other than that we delivered Aaron's information and returned safely, deciding to bunk at his place.

I check my phone twenty times or so. The only texts are from John Mark. I've missed our appointment. I'll apologize later. I move the clean clothes from the washer to the dryer, and now my eyes land on the folded envelope that Locke had pocketed, and that I had un-pocketed in order to wash his bloody jeans. What had been so important that Chris would have remembered it while he was faint from loss of blood? Tempting. I am not above snooping, but it's sealed rather formally. I can wait another few hours, right? Maybe?

The third hour fills me with dread. I consider sneaking to the big house to seize my bike, but (see hour number two). I put on my clean clothes, and when I go to check my reflection in the downstairs bathroom, I find a pile of Locke's beautiful hair in the floor. I sweep it up.

Is it weird that I instantly regret throwing it away?

The fourth hour comes with a knock on the door. I jump. A pain shoots through my chest. "Anybody home?" a friendly voice calls. "It's John Mark!" I restart my heart and rush to let him in.

"Where've you been?" he demands. "Nobody's answering the phone. I was worried about you and your telenovela life." He pokes his head in. "Where's Coach?"

I'm glad for the company. I bring him up to speed as I reanimate breakfast and feed him more than even a collegiate athlete can ingest.

The fifth hour brings a text from a number I don't recognize. *On my way home. Nothing happened except a bunch of waiting.* Another text follows on the heels of that one. *Chris wants to know what's for dinner. We may have created a monster.*

I squeal and nearly squeeze John Mark's head off, but when the sixth hour comes and goes, and still no sign of Locke, my anxiety begins to spike again. Sickening worry roils in my stomach and aches in my chest. John Mark starts a movie and beckons me to join him on the couch.

Finally, I receive: *Chris passed out in the Jeep. I brought him to the hospital. They're working on him now. I don't know why he had to take on so much so soon. I mean, I do, but I shouldn't have let him.*

I'm coming to you, I reply.

I'd welcome that. You know where the truck keys are?

They're already in my hand, that's where they are. I slap off the stove, check the oven, and with a quick goodbye to John Mark, I speed to the hospital—as much as I *can* speed in the ancient, orange truck. We are so getting a Lamborghini. I physically rock toward the steering wheel in an effort to make the truck move faster. I look like a child driving. I can barely reach the pedals, and that is after sliding the seat forward until I'm smooshed against the wheel. I do a sloppy job of parking, but there's no help for it. I'm practically driving blind. The general public should be grateful to remain unscathed.

When the automatic doors to the ER slide open, I spot Locke and hear the mechanical sigh as if it is my own relief. He's standing with his back to the wall on the far side of the room. I'm surprised by his haircut all over again. I'm digging it.

With both legs supporting him in a strong stance and arms crossed in front of his chest, Locke's eyes sweep across me in a subtle arc that doesn't land. I stall with the idea that my relief is premature. He isn't acting like Locke. He makes the slightest movement of his head to one side and back. *No.*

My gaze shifts to a man leaning against the wall beside him. He wears a cowboy hat that shades his eyes, and he *may* be looking at me from underneath? I can't tell. There's also a woman there, with her back to me. I now see that she and Locke have been engaged in a conversation. The woman hasn't missed the slight transfer of his attention. Her black braid swings as she turns her head. Lupita.

Instead of going to him, I force my feet to the reception desk and ask about a made-up friend who'd been brought in by ambulance. The woman at the desk searches her computer records, while I scan the room. I recognize at least two officers from the state police headquarters. They're sitting well apart from one another and wearing plain clothes. They must have followed Locke from the first address to the hospital. One of them has eyes on me. I suppose the recognition is mutual.

That's when Detective Wilkins exits the ladies' room to take a seat beside one of them. Just a normal couple waiting for news about their loved one. Nothing to see here.

The man leans in to speak to Wilkins, and she nods with what looks like a mixture of boredom and impatience. She stretches, as if she's stiff from time spent in the chair, and twists her spine, making brief eye contact with me.

I wonder why the pressure in the room isn't causing people to implode.

As if things can grow any more convoluted, John Mark strides in. He smiles at me from the door, and on his way over he signs, *I think we should broaden the scope of our romantic involvement. The ER as a date venue is highly overrated.* Even through his goofy joke, John Mark pierces me with his eyes and offers me my phone. "You forgot this." He hits the button that lights up the last text I'd received.

Don't come, it reads. I bite the inside of my cheek and will myself to remain calm.

Excusing us from the desk, I take John Mark's arm and lead him to the door. He signs, *Why does Coach look like a misplaced Navy Seal?*

Later, I answer.

Why aren't we talking to him?

Later, John Mark.

He's in trouble, isn't he?

Before we can make our escape, a man wearing blue scrubs and a hospital badge steps out in front of us. He doesn't say anything. Just blocks our path. He isn't nearly as tall or as broad as John Mark, but his very presence is unyielding, whereas John Mark is still a boy, skinny and...sweet.

Please don't let me get John Mark killed.

"Excuse us," I say, attempting to circumvent the man.

"I have news about your friend," the man says. He gestures with his hand. "Let's speak somewhere more private."

"You have news about..."

"Landon," he says.

OK. Good guy/bad guy? I weigh the evidence. He's not forcing me to go. But I'm not resisting him. He knows Locke's first name. That probably means he's a good guy. If he's a bad guy and he knows Locke's name, then Locke's been found out, and that is not acceptable. The guy's wearing scrubs, but the picture on his badge does not match his face.

Detective Wilkins is standing now, facing her partner, holding his hands like they're lovers, but focusing on me over his shoulder. She nods her head in a message to me, and laughs, like her partner has said something funny.

To John Mark I sign, *You have to leave. I'll call you later.*

John Mark's eyes flicker to Locke, and I grip his arm as hard as I dare, for fear of attracting attention. *No.* I snap my fingers together. *Go home. Please.*

The man—who may or may not have killed somebody to use his hospital badge—holds out a hand to indicate the direction he'd like for us to take. "This way," he says. I go with him. John Mark disobediently trails behind. It's all I can do not look back at Locke.

We round a corner, where the man uses a key card to summon an elevator marked "Staff Only," and gestures for us to board it. Then he oh-so-casually surveils the area before stepping in behind us. He spans the doorway until it closes and pushes a round button printed with the number three.

All elevator rides seem to take longer than they actually do, and being trapped in one with a stranger, even at the best of times, can be awkward. But being trapped in one with a stranger who has possibly been sent to silence you is more awkward still. Especially when the stranger himself remains silent, and the only sound you hear is the jarring buzz that indicates which floor you've passed on your ascent.

After four years and twenty-five days, by my count, the elevator opens on the third floor, and the murmur of voices outside in the hallway falls to a hush. "I'm breaking up with you," John Mark mutters.

"Over here," a voice calls.

"Commander," I say and trot to him. "What are you doing up *here*? You have to go get him. He's being held hostage. There are—"

The commander doesn't seem all that interested in what I have to say. He's hovering over an officer who is seated at a table in front of several TV monitors. He's pointing to one of them, asking about sound. The officer relays his question to a hospital employee in more technical language, and after the employee answers, the officer speaks into a headset.

This part of the hospital must have already been set up as a security point. The video monitors show views of several key areas—the hospital entrances and other public spaces—including the ER's waiting room.

"Copy that," the officer says into the headset. To the commander he says, "We can't get a short-range mic close enough. Long-range is twenty minutes out."

Someone close by is making a plan to evacuate the ER. Someone else is arguing that evacuation would cause unnecessary alarm and get people killed. A woman, a sniper, is positioned in front of an interior opening that looks down onto the waiting room below. She's holding a rifle.

"He's not trained for this," I interject. "He was only supposed to be *seen!*"

Commander Zendejas sizes me up.

I imagine that he didn't make his way to the rank of commander without being able to utilize every asset available, even people, whether they're trained or not. "Right," he says to me, or to himself. I'm not sure. "He needs to be seen."

The commander leans down with his hands on the table and stares into a monitor with a feed of the waiting room. "Put a camera on every player's face," he says. The officer hurries to comply. To me the commander says, "I need you to tell me what they're saying."

"You don't think they know you're here?" I ask.

"I don't think they do," he replies. "Wilkins continued to track Aaron's phone after the operation was a bust. She didn't follow openly."

The officer who is changing camera angles asks what works best for me. There are now two opposing views of the waiting room where Locke continues to stand beside the man in the cowboy hat. It looks like Lupita is giving him a piece of her mind. Possibly in Spanish. At any rate, it's too fast for me to read. Locke is listening to her with a slight smirk. I wish I hadn't told him to kiss her.

"Commander, there's a development." Another monitor shows the underpass outside the entrance to the ER. It is upon that which the officer is trained. Three men exit a large black truck.

Zendejas speaks into his wrist, and I can only assume that the officers below are the recipients of his message, through earpieces. "Be advised. Del Valle is entering the building."

He snaps open a folding chair and thrusts it in front of the monitors. "Dr. Caine," he says.

I take a seat.

The tech guy works knobs that are producing a tighter image of Del Valle's face as he approaches Locke.

A wave of cold rolls over my skin. The scene unfolds from different points of view, and I feel as powerless to influence the outcome as if I'm watching a movie. They need to know what's being said, though, and I can help with that.

The men saunter in, more relaxed than I would have believed possible. The general public has no clue who walks among them.

Zendejas instructs his people to remain where they are, except he nods to the sniper. She aims her weapon through the opening. I suppose if anyone were to glance up from the ER floor, they would see the barrel of a rifle jutting into the room from two and half stories above.

Into his officers' earpieces, Zendejas says, "Under no circumstance does Landon Locke leave with them."

The men are nearly there. Lupita turns her anger on her father. I can't make out anything she's saying, but suddenly a headset is being crammed around my ear, and I hear Wilkins translating from downstairs. I find her on the screen with her chin resting on her hand.

"She wants to know how long her father has known that Aaron is alive," Wilkins says. Her words, in my earpiece, are quiet but clear. "She's furious that she was kept from speaking to him at the warehouse. She texted the address herself, I think, outside of Del Valle's knowledge. Del Valle must have foiled her plan to meet with Aaron alone."

Lupita jabs a finger at the man who has been with her all along. Wilkins says, "The cowboy against the wall may be more jailer than bodyguard."

Del Valle and his men have come to a stop directly in front of Locke without speaking. One of them gawks openly, and Locke surprises me by propelling himself into the man's personal space until he shrinks back. He's doing well. He possesses that same reckless nerve his brother showed.

From underneath his hat, Carlos Del Valle steps through his guard and lifts his head to Locke, but I think he's speaking to Lupita. It's all in Spanish. I should really learn Spanish.

"I can't hear him," Wilkins breathes.

"Caine?" the commander prompts.

"Hang on," I say. "I don't know Spanish."

Lupita is speaking again. She's gesturing toward Locke. No idea what she's saying. But she is enraged.

"Can you hear her?" Zendejas asks.

"Loud and clear," Wilkins sings without moving her mouth. "She's demanding to have Aaron work for her personally. She wants to keep him. Like a *león* at the zoo."

Del Valle silences Lupita with a chop of his hand, and dismisses her much the same way. The cowboy beside Locke takes her arm, but she jerks it away. Del Valle says, "Lupita, *Spanish, Spanish, Spanish.*"

Then he says to Locke, "I was sorry to hear about your woman." I repeat that part for the Commander.

Lupita storms off in a huff, the cowboy on her heels. Detective Wilkins was right. He's her jailer. Del Valle has his thumb on her. No wonder she bucks.

I see that one of the police officers also rises to follow Lupita. Locke ignores all of it, except for Del Valle's words to him. He dips his head in acknowledgement of the sympathy.

"What of the child?" Del Valle asks.

When Locke raises his eyes, they look inconsolable. I imagine that real emotion is extremely close to the surface. He swallows hard and clears his throat. He schools his features. "Gone," he says. "You got your money?"

In answer, Del Valle says, "Are you still standing alive before me?"

Locke, through his harder new expression, accepts the answer with a quick lift of his brow. "I don't expect it to be like it was before," he says. "I just want back in the game."

I can tell that he's preparing each statement before it leaves his mouth.

"Why would I allow that, after all that went down without a word from you?"

Locke nods, like he knows he doesn't have an answer that will suffice. "I thought you required my silence," he says. "Still, I chased your money down for you. And now she's gone. And our baby. Gone." He ends with the words that Del Valle himself had used when he had confided in Aaron. "I am even more like you now than before. I no longer taste. No longer smell...Papá"

Del Valle gives him a sad half smile and takes time to consider what he's said. It must be time that feels like an eternity to Locke. Just as Aaron had, Locke waits for his response with growing agitation.

Finally, Del Valle says, "If Lupita will have you, you must belong to her."

Locke doesn't hesitate. "Yes."

"You must belong to her for as long as she wants. And she will be the boss of you. It's the only way."

"Yes," Locke says again. "I will do it. For you."

Del Valle nods. "This could help things. And you will remain loyal to me. If I find you to be false, you will die. There is no other way."

"I understand."

Del Valle offers his right hand, but instead of taking it, Locke holds his own hand in the shape of a gun to his eye, aimed at Del Valle's chest, a seemingly antagonistic and very un-Locke thing to do. I worry that it's going to earn him a slap—or worse—but Del Valle grins. Apparently, he has been holding a scrap of paper to pass along during the handshake. Now he sticks the paper inside Locke's curled trigger fingers and pats Locke's cheek in a fatherly way. He says something close to Locke's ear. Well, as close to Locke's ear as he can reach. Locke's shoulder obscures his lips. I can't make it out.

Del Valle takes a step back, flanked by the other men. Then all of them, as if they've just finished a nice meal at the local taqueria, saunter back across the lobby, out the sliding doors, and into their waiting truck, which is still idling in the ambulance lane like it's their private parking space.

I breathe out a long exhale. John Mark squeezes my shoulders from behind. "Good job, Em," he whispers. I hold both his hands tight, there on my shoulders, and we continue to watch the monitor.

Wilkins subtly gestures for Locke to remain where he is and leaves the waiting room through a different door. I can see, on one of the monitors, that she is met by others who have been biding their time in the stairwell. I make for the stairwell too, but am ordered back upon threat of detainment. So, I watch Locke on the screen. He waits in character with his eyes on the door. Then he sits down in one of the hard plastic chairs, elbows on knees, hands over face, and heaves a magnificent sigh.

"Wait till I say so," the commander tells me. He skips down the stairs and appears in front of Locke, who quickly stands to meet him. I see his mouth shape my name in question and whatever the commander responds puts him at ease.

Zendejas points at the camera. Locke lifts his face. I take that as my cue to escape my benevolent captors. I tear downstairs where I quietly open the stairwell door into the waiting room, and tiptoe to where Locke and the commander are talking, though not near enough to interrupt. I conceal myself behind a pillar.

Zendejas tells Locke, "Your bad attitude saved the day."

"It wasn't *my* bad attitude," Locke counters. He reveals the paper that he's been given, flicking it into view between his first two fingers.

Zendejas plucks the paper, reads it, and barks some more orders into his wrist. To Locke he says, "What did he tell you at the end?"

"Said they'd be moving again before dawn. Whatever my buyer wants must be bought before then. He won't be around again until he is, whatever that means. He can disappear *like I can*. He'll be in touch." Locke pauses and then says, "He offered to take care of everyone related to the man who killed Anita, as a favor to me. As a *favor*, he was going to kill somebody's entire family. And he was absolutely sincere."

"What did you tell him?"

"I told him it had been dealt with." Locke sounds weary. "Anita must have been courageous. I bet she and Aaron were a good match. You do believe it was Dunn, don't you, who drugged her?"

Zendejas nods emphatically. "After Detective Wilkins questioned Emma, she began to ask a lot of questions about where the needle had been found and who had logged it into evidence. There were some conflicting statements, not to mention an impossible timeline, that raised suspicion about Dunn's involvement. More will come to light." Zendejas brightens. "So, you ready to join the force? I can fast-track you. I haven't worked with many people capable of exhibiting that kind of composure."

Instead of answering, Locke says, "Do you have a wife, Commander? Children?"

Zendejas shrugs. "If you change your mind," he says. The commander leaves to run the rest of the operation from the third floor. I have shrunk myself on the other side of the pole, but as he passes, Zendejas says, "You can go downstairs now." He doesn't seem to mind that I'm already here. Before the stairwell door closes, he calls back, "That was good work, Caine." It feels good.

When Locke lays eyes on me, instead of showing delight, his countenance falls.

I rush to him. "Are you alright?" I ask.

"I am now," he says. But he isn't. Worry creases his forehead and he presses his thumb into the palm of his other hand.

"I'm so relieved," I gush. I move to embrace him, but he stiffens. "What is it?"

"If you touch me, I'll fall apart."

I drop my arms and swallow my disappointment.

"I think Chris is—" Locke begins. I give him time to finish the thought, but then I get what he's trying to say.

"Dead?!" I ask. "You don't know?"

He shakes his head and speaks quietly. "This nurse kept jogging back and forth with new bags of blood. I don't think they could pump it into him fast enough. But I couldn't find out, because someone across the room called out Aaron's name. Fortunately, I'm conditioned to answer to it. It's like a switch flipped for me. By the time I turned, Lupita had covered the ground between us and slapped me across the face."

"Locke! What did you do?"

"I asked her if it made her feel better, and she began spouting off in Spanish. That's when I caught sight of Wilkins." Locke jumps subjects. "They walk a dangerous line, don't they? All the running into fire? And the allure of power? How do they keep from playing God?"

"A lot of them don't," I comment. "But hopefully some of them have grandaddies who make them vote every day before they leave the house." This earns me a little smile. "Come here," I plead. He sinks his head and allows me to pull him close.

"When I saw you come through that door, I about lost my mind," he says.

"You were brilliant. You were—" I have no other words to spare. "I'm glad you're OK."

"I don't feel OK. I feel messed up."

John Mark is skulking some distance away, and I motion him over.

"Will you stay with Locke?" I ask. "While I find out about—" I consider how to identify Chris. "About our friend?"

In the ridiculous amount of time it takes to procure any information about Chris's well-being, Commander Zendejas comes back to let us know that Del Valle has been captured. "The other officers are setting up to raid the address he gave you."

A hospital administrator approaches to say that she's sorry, but that she can't divulge any information about Officer Michaels to anyone except for his family. Commander Zendejas pulls the police card. "He's one of my men," he booms and circles a finger among our small group. "*We* are his family. We've been through a lot here today, as you know, since it took up most of your third floor, and we need to know how our brother is doing."

"I see," the administrator says. "I wasn't aware the two incidents were connected. Officer Michaels was checked in yesterday afternoon. I must be missing pieces of the puzzle." She hesitates. I know what's next. I want to shove my hands against her mouth to stop the words from coming. "I'm sorry, Commander," she says. "Our surgeons did everything they could, but they couldn't stop the internal bleeding. Christian Michaels died on the operating table about forty-five minutes ago. I'm terribly sorry. Perhaps you can help us locate his next of kin."

"I'll go tell them," the commander says.

THE GENIE'S BOTTLE

The ride home is silent, and the outside is growing dark. Locke is lost in sorrow, burrowing inward, away from me. Not on purpose. I'm sure. But still, it leaves me feeling raw and needy. I long to be connected to him.

I begin to imagine what it must be like for Locke's mom to bear the loss of a child without being able to share that burden with her husband. How is she supposed to give him the solitude and space he needs to process his grief, without imploding from the depth of her own? It seems like there should be a way to grow more intimate through the shared loss. And yet I know that too often it only tears families apart.

Locke had volunteered to accompany the commander to deliver the news of Chris's death to his parents, but the commander told him to keep his head down for a few days.

"Anyway, they knew Aaron," the commander had said. "It will be shocking enough for them to hear the news without it being delivered by a ghost. Take your woman home and let her comfort you."

Locke isn't able to seek comfort. When he parks the truck in front of the big house, he excuses himself to go swim. Over an hour and a half, in only what light the pool provides, lap after lap, back and forth relentlessly. Every now and then, I watch from my bedroom window, feeling helpless. I understand. I could've pedaled the whole country if it were light out. I imagine that the allure of swimming for him right now is that he has to concentrate mightily on one thing only. When to take the next breath.

I spend the time tidying up and watching the little cats pounce on top of one another. They're starting to exhibit their own personalities. I give special care to the mama, who is woefully in need of human companionship. Or maybe I'm projecting. "I had a hard few days too, Tac," I hear myself saying. "Do you wanna hear about it?"

Tac purrs and stretches one paw impressively. I take it as a yes and reiterate the story of the last two days, with Tac acting as my therapist. Even while I'm telling it, I can't believe I've actually lived it. Tac licks her own belly in response. "No offense," I tell her, "but I'd really rather rehash this with someone who isn't grooming their nether regions with their tongue."

I consider seeking solace in John Mark, but I'd better not. Could be a dangerous path to tread. I'm sure that he would respond with whatever attention I required. But right now, the attention I require is Locke's. I don't want to conflate the two relationships or end up leading my young friend on. I can sit in the ache a while longer. It's not going to kill me to feel bad. It just...feels bad.

Outside, Locke has finally stopped swimming and is sitting on the side of the pool. I debate whether to join him but find myself beside him before I've decided. The poolside is lit by shifting underwater lights and now by the overspill of lamps from within the house as well.

"Feel any better?" I ask.

Instead of answering, Locke says, "I was sure he was dirty. This whole time he just blamed himself for what happened to Aaron." While he speaks, he watches something in the distance, and the water in the pool still laps from his strength. "What made you trust him?" he asks. "He was so mean to you."

"You know the elbow he kept bothering?" I say. "He had a tattoo." I press the spot on Locke's arm. "A skeleton key, whose head was a skull, like you said Aaron had. The design held Aaron's initials. They were *partners*." I emphasize the word as Chris had done. "I don't know what Chris knew about love or friendship, but he was singly devoted to your brother as his brother-in-arms."

"Yeah, I finally got that. Anyone who enjoys being hit as hard as I hit him, because it reminds him of somebody else, really, really misses that person." Locke shakes his left hand like he can still feel the punch. "In the car, on the way back, he told me stories. Funny things I could just see Aaron doing. A few things I didn't even know about him. He was in the middle of one when he passed out. At first, I thought he was mimicking something stupid Aaron had done. Now I'll never know." Locke lifts his eyes to let them roam the night sky. "I'd started looking forward to sharing that bond with him, you know? It was like receiving a little bit of my brother back, only to have him ripped away again."

"Did he tell you something that made you pretend to shoot Del Valle instead of shaking his hand?"

"Yeah. He told me Del Valle and Aaron had this thing where, if anyone offered a hand, you offered a gun."

"Wow. You did your brother proud, no doubt."

"I swear I felt him there with me. Like when he'd come cheer for me at the swim meets."

A few minutes pass. I vaguely hear sounds of movement from inside the house.

"What was in the envelope Chris gave you?" I ask.

"I think we're about to find out." Locke nods to the door where his mom is stepping out with a visitor. He wrestles a shirt over his still dripping chest and walks over to shake hands with Ms. Vaughn, who immediately places Baby Annabelle into his arms. He hugs the baby to himself and kisses her face till she grabs his chin with her pudgy fingers. He holds her out to inspect her with such tenderness, I think his heart is being healed from the inside out. The baby squeals when he looks into her face and there is something very familiar about the shape of those smiling eyes.

Ms. Vaughn spreads a few papers onto the table and speaks words too soft for me to make out. She points to three different areas with a pen, before handing the pen over to Locke rather ceremoniously. He signs where she has indicated. Ardea says something that makes them all laugh.

I watch this with the growing awareness that I've become an outsider. And I guess I've chosen to be. I've walked this path for years. Choosing to live outside of the realm of sound where I couldn't be reached. And then outside of my own family, inside another where I couldn't be permanent. And now caring for someone else's child in someone else's home. Maybe all I'm meant to be is up on the third floor watching a monitor, reading the lips of others who have part of the live action.

It's appropriate that we met in a graveyard. I am a ghost.

No one notices when I walk out of the pool area and across the paddock. I don't think about much of anything at all. I just watch the moonlight dance on the long grass and feel the wind across my arms like silk. Eventually, my feet take me to the front of the house where they carry me through the night-blooming jessamine and up to my—to *Aaron's* room.

When I hear the whine of the truck door opening, I peek out the bedroom window. Somewhere in my middle clenches when I see Locke close himself inside and drive away. He just...drives away.

I try to believe. I do. I sit on the bed and review my interactions with Locke. His steadfast assurances. His commitment to returning. But minutes pass, and I find myself packing my bag. Maybe I'll move back to Michigan. Get a quiet, little, remote house on the water. Somewhere without longhorns. Or babies. Or trucks. Or...trees.

I stop packing.

Instead, I pick up the phone. I'm not sure it will be the same number, and that may be what gives me the courage to hit *send*.

"Oh...hey...Dad? It's Emma." Silence. Except for the children I hear playing in the background. "I found out that it's OK to read the last page," I say. "So, I did. And I just want you to know that I'm glad you're alive. Even if I don't get to have you. And I forgive you for leaving. Even if you're not sorry. And I love you. Even if you don't know how to accept it. Because we don't even know how many heartbeats we get. I don't want to waste any more of mine." No response. "OK. Well? This is my number. Goodnight."

I end the call and stop pacing. That was good. That needed to happen.

Yikes! My self-congratulations are cut short when the phone in my hand rings. I fling it away like it's a scorpion. Then I quickly retrieve it. It's not my dad, though. It's Detective Wilkins.

"I just wanted to thank you for your help," she says. "We rescued twenty-seven young people this evening, both girls and boys. Families from nine different states, including your own Michigan, will be receiving their children back."

I'm saying a silent prayer that those recovered will have all the love and support they need, when three soft knocks fall on the door. It opens to reveal Locke without his usual grin.

"I need to speak with you," he says formally.

He glances around for where we can do that, and his eyes land on my bag. He fixes me with a nervous, apologetic stare.

"It's OK," I say. "We did what we were put together to do." My head bobs up and down.

"Stop it. Listen to me." Locke is absolutely serious. "I need you to hear me out. This is really—" He pulls his bottom lip through his teeth. I can see that he's struggling.

"Go ahead."

"In the envelope?" he says. I think I can guess. "Chris ran *my* DNA in a paternity test. Against Annabelle's. That toothbrush that went missing?" Locke's head falls to the side to say *that's where it went.* "Legally, now, I'm her father. I've got full rights to her. There's nothing standing in the way of me raising her, starting right now, today." Locke questions me silently to see if I understand. "She's Aaron's daughter, Em. My piece of him."

"She's a Locke." We both say it at the same time. Locke like he's arguing a case, and me like I'm conceding one.

"I understand," I say. "I—"

"You *don't* understand." He pins me with a stare that I can't meet. "I need *you* to be a Locke."

My eyes fly to his in question.

"I *need* you—to be a Locke," he repeats with different emphasis. "Annabelle's a piece of my brother, but you're a piece of me. You gave me back myself. You make me strong. You make me whole again."

Grey. Grey and pleading. And irrepressibly beautiful.

"I want you both," he says. His words pick up speed. "I know it's unfair to ask. I know you're not ready to have kids of your own. But my parents aren't in any position to raise her. And Sarah's still so young. I think it's supposed to be me, Em. I think it's supposed to be...*us*."

"Are you asking me to marry you?" My voice is as high pitched as my astonishment.

"Very poorly," he answers.

"'Cause it *sounds* like you're asking me not to."

"I want to spend my whole life with you and never be done. I want to have you for real. Please marry me, Emma."

I absorb what he's said. "And then," I say in slow deliberation, "I would adopt Annabelle? And we would be her mom and dad? Instantly? And forever? I mean, it'd have to be no take-backs. We couldn't ever be done with her any more than we could be done with each other. It would mess her up."

Locke laughs, maybe because of nerves, but also, I think, because I'm weighing the question and not running away. "Instant, forever commitment," he agrees. "Bonded for life on days when we feel like it and on days when we don't."

"And we would, what? Live in your house?"

"Unless you want us to move into your apartment."

"And you'd give me a big kitchen?"

"As big as you want." Locke's eyes are suddenly doing a lot of smiling that he's trying to hold off the rest of his face.

"And you and I would...share a bed the way we're supposed to?"

"Yeah, that part's non-negotiable."

"You should've led with that," I say.

"You'll be well-pleased on that count," he assures me. "I will be contractually bound to"—he raises his eyes to the ceiling and back—"meet your needs."

"These are the plans you've been making?"

"I didn't foresee the raising a child part. Yet."

I bunch my lips to one side and nod that I understand the conditions of the proposal. "When can we start?"

"Now?" he says. "Yesterday?" He squeezes my hands. "Really? You're sure?"

"Yes. I'm sure."

Locke fishes something out of his pocket. "This was my grandmother's and, before her, it was Annabelle's. Grandaddy told me to wait till I knew." He pushes a ring onto my finger. "That was good advice."

"That's where you went just now? To your house to get this?"

"And to pray you'd say yes."

The ring is thin gold with simple, symmetrical etchings and a small, round diamond sunk into the center. I don't react immediately, but only because I'm overwhelmed.

"If you don't like it, we'll—"

"Locke."

"Yeah?"

"Yeah."

I'm told that there are moments in life, only a few lovely moments, if you're blessed, when you feel all of the happy and none of the sad. This is one we get to share. The relief. The promise of love and a future together. The rightness of sharing that love with our baby.

Locke kisses my knuckles. "I have to learn sign," he says.

"Yes! That's right! You can learn along with Annabelle. John Mark could make a practicum of teaching you both! Maybe even his senior project if we spin it the right way."

"So, just out of curiosity..." Locke pulls me to standing and laces his fingers together at my waist. "Why does it look like you're packing all your things?"

"Oh. OK, so—" I hold up both hands before dropping them onto his chest. "I did stop. But down at the pool I suddenly realized that I was the only one around who wasn't a Locke. And then you left, for what I worried were not as good of reasons as they turned out to be. So, in a fleeting, *fleeting*, moment filled with...misguided doubt, I bought a lovely cottage on the Upper Peninsula." Locke cocks his head in a show of interest. My lips smack apart to add, "It's perfect. It's charming, and there's a fireplace. It's right on the water. But I can probably sell it. Or, you know...we'll use it to vacay."

"You were going to saddle me and Kili with the cats, weren't you?"

"Thought about it," I say.

"Can we be done now, with you packing bags and leaving me? In reality *and* in your mind?"

"Yes. All done." I rake my hands together like I'm brushing off sand and display them as proof. "I promise. I wasn't as quick about it this time, if that makes you feel any better. I sat on the bed for a good fifteen minutes to remind myself that you belong to me. But out flew the bag. It *literally* threw itself out of the closet at me. I think it may be possessed. Locke, what are you doing?"

Locke has dumped all the clothes out of the demon bag and onto the bed, and now he is crumpling the bag mercilessly between his large hands. He walks over to draw the blinds and unlatch the window. He pushes it open as far as it will go, cuts his eyes deviously back in my direction, and chucks the bag right out into the night.

"There," he says, dusting off his hands, as I had done. "Genie's lost her bottle." He advances on me, taking my face in his hands. "I belong to you. And you belong to me. Got it?"

"Got it."

He kisses me. "I will keep you until I die and, if God is kind, I will keep you after that."

"Are we writing poetry now?" I manage to say, though Locke is occupying my lips. "Are we becoming the Brownings?"

He snatches me up to himself and guides my legs around him where he stands. "Yes," he answers. "If we can do it in"—he searches for the words and finds—"kinesthetic language." He braces me against the wall and, well...

"Why don't *I* get to keep her?" Sarah fusses. We have rejoined the family, minus Locke's dad, and have explained to them that Locke will be raising Annabelle.

"You're not married," Locke answers. "It would be too hard. Trust me."

I'm looking at Annabelle with new eyes, and the baby reaches for me from where she's sitting on Sarah's hip. I snuggle her to myself as tightly as I dare. My *daughter. Our* daughter. Oh my gosh. My *husband!* I have to shake my head to hear what's being said on the outside of it. With my thumb, I feel for the ring on my left hand, and I can't help grinning. Ardea is eyeing us.

Sarah is saying, "That's stupid. Neither are y—" when her eyes brighten and her head swivels to peer at us sideways. "You're getting married."

"We are," says Locke. Sarah hurtles herself into both of our arms at the same time. Her overwhelming embrace threatens to knock me backward, but Locke corrects it.

He glances at his mom who has taken a place in the queue for hugs.

"When?!" Sarah asks too loudly.

"Soon," Locke answers. He waits for his mom to hug me. "As soon as we can."

His mom wraps her arms around both our necks. "This is welcome news," she says. "When can we tell your father?" She squeezes both our hands and holds them at once.

"*How* soon?!" Sarah demands. "How can I plan a huge, celebratory wedding *soon?!*"

Locke considers me, as I fix Sarah with what is quite possibly a look of horror. "Um, I know this is going to be hard for you to hear, Sar," Locke intervenes. "And possibly hard for you to even understand, but Emma is what they call an *introvert.*"

Sarah's nose and mouth recoil, the way they might if she'd happened upon a rotting carcass. "What are you *saying?!* There's not going to be a *wedding?!*"

I hide my face against the baby's shirt.

"How about this?" offers Locke. "Emma and I will take care of the vows as quickly and as privately as she wants to, and then you can plan as large of a party as you want to, for about"—he consults me with his eyes—"six weeks from now."

"Sure," I agree.

"OK, but I get to pick both of your outfits for both of those occasions." A shrill *aaaugh!* leaps from Sarah's throat. "And Annabelle's! I get to dress her up however I want to! She may even need costume changes. I'm going to find them right now." Sarah retreats from the room, though her voice trails behind her. "Also, I get to keep *two* of the cats!"

"Not the orange one," Locke yells after her. "That one belongs to The Hair."

Ardea is pulling out goblets so that we can toast, but she pauses to point at the desk and say, "Landon, look what came for your brother." She displays an official-looking packet addressed to Aaron. "It's from a law office in Austin. Should we ope—"

Locke snatches the packet to do the honors. As he reads the cover letter, he looks alternately bewildered and amused.

"What is it?" I ask him.

"A trust fund, I think. For Annabelle. They want more information. Her Social Security number. Her middle name."

The three of us stare at one another in bewilderment.

"Did Aaron open the account?" Ardea asks.

"I don't think so," Locke says. He's wearing an enigmatic smile. I narrow my eyes at him.

"No," I say. "Not seven *bricks* worth."

Locke nods in response.

"Chris?" I ask.

He shrugs. "Maybe it's best not to ask too many questions."

I WILL

Two Thursdays later, much like Annabelle and I, the little cats are ready for their forever homes. Since the goldens turn out to be gentle siblings, the orange kitten, Merida, and Big Mama Tac are moved into Locke's house. Sarah keeps two more in the big house, and because that very day they prove themselves to be excellent mousers, or at least halfway interested in batting things around, Locke's dad decides he can use the other two in the barns. And that is where we are headed now, to introduce the kittens to their new abode.

Locke's dad has only been home from rehab for three days, but in that time, he's taken a far more active part in the daily life around the house. I worry that a wedding on the property, even one as small as we have planned, will come too soon in his recovery and be too great a stressor. He insists that we not only hold the celebration here, but also host my out-of-town guests. "In fact," he says, "as part of my therapy, I've prepared Aaron's house for them, and it would mean a lot to me if they'd make themselves at home there."

Some of those guests are waiting for us when we return from the barns. When I spot them, I break into a run. Hannah and Noah have driven the whole family down in their camper from Michigan. And now they're stretching their legs in the driveway and trying to coax the ponies to the fence. Screaming, and laughing, and hugging, and signing commence.

It seems like everything speeds up from here. So many stories. So much wonder about the events that have taken place. I text John Mark to hurry over. Ricks and his family show up too. It's a lovely evening outside by the pool, where Sarah has procured extra seating and floating candles.

The way in which communication travels between those who speak and those who sign requires some patience, but because of that, a broader sense of understanding is won.

"You're trying to set them up," Locke accuses me. He has an arm around the back of my wooden chair, which is clothed in some kind of shabby-chic canvas material, and he's narrowing his eyes at me.

"I have no idea what you're talking about," I tell him. I really do. I just tasked John Mark with taking all the plates and cups to the kitchen. And I solicited the help of Ruth, Hannah and Noah's lovely eldest daughter. Further, I asked them to wash and dry everything by hand, which isn't strictly necessary.

"It's important that John Mark be able to converse in various settings," I say. "For the sake of his exam."

"It has to be with the prettiest girl closest to his age? He couldn't have played games with any of the younger kids instead?"

I don't answer.

"Do Hannah and Noah know about your diabolical plan?"

"Oh, honestly, Locke. Dealing with the criminal element has made you paranoid."

The next morning, before Locke can join us, I do shove the two off by themselves into the back fields. What? I want baby's breath for my bouquet. John Mark flashes me a grin and a signed *Thank you*. When he offers his arm to Ruth, she seems happy to accept.

The only grump goat of the group is Lysle, the youngest, who can't forgive Locke for marrying me. After all, Lylse had *seen me first* that day in the park when I was only fifteen, and he only five. But in the end, Locke wins him over with synchronized swimming performed by Fili and Kili in the pool, capsizing Sarah's candles, but gaining a forever friend.

Lylse is delighted when Locke uses hand signals instead of voice commands, and he declares right then and there that he's going to be a dog trainer. Locke seals the deal when, after disappearing to his house for a few minutes, he returns to gift Lylse with a whistle only dogs can hear.

My mom and my sister's family arrive in the afternoon, and my nephews waste no time exploring the farm. Their favorite thing is how Locke's dad can call the giant longhorns to himself by name. "Come on, Bill!"

My mom and her daughters claim the kitchen in the guest suite, where we set about baking pastries for the wedding day brunch. I welcome the time to visit with them in the comfortable rhythm of mixing and measuring. Annabelle mimics us from her new booster chair, where she uses her own measuring cups and flour, and she is happy to act as taste tester.

Dinner runs late into the night, out by the pool again, with the younger children falling asleep on laps, and the older ones acquiring grass stains and lifelong memories. Contented bellies. Contented hearts. I look around at the people I love, and my eyes land on Locke. He's leaning against the house with his hands in his pockets. He's been conversing with Noah, away from the group, and when he finds me watching, he winks.

On Saturday morning, once I've applied my makeup and adorned myself in the dress that Sarah picked out for me, I stare at myself in the mirror. The white gown has long lines and a longer sash. It's great. Sarah should maybe go into the fashion industry instead of cattle.

And, hey! My hair has decided to cooperate. I pull some of it back from my face and let the rest ride upon my bare shoulders.

I'm getting married today.

Although my mom and my sister and—well, really every woman on the premises—offered to help me, I just wanted a quiet morning to clear my head. Now I yearn for all those crowded wake-ups when

Locke and Annabelle were already beside me. I don't think I can bear the public greeting, all dressed up as a spectacle.

I text my betrothed. *Hi.*

And receive back *Hi, Beautiful. Are you ready to join us?*

I displace the blinds to observe our guests. They're happily munching on pastries and chatting in groups around the patio. *Is it too late to elope?* I ask.

Maybe. Should I come up?

Yes, please.

I watch him pocket his phone. He's smashing in a white button-down with sleeves rolled to the elbow and hem tucked into straight brown pants. He raps on the bedroom door, and I crack it open to peep out at him. "You look good enough to marry," I say. "What's the password?"

"I love you."

"Nope."

Locke searches the ceiling for a clue. "I do?"

I open the door a bit more and frown. "I thought we were going to say 'I *will*.' Isn't that what Pastor Ian had us practice?"

Locke levels me with his eyes—well, he levels what parts he can see of me through the opening. "Let me in, Legs," he commands.

I snicker and swing the door wide.

"Oh, my love," he says. "You are stunning." He kisses my cheek like he doesn't want to mess me up.

"Whatcha wanna do today?" I ask.

Locke sits back against the desk, folds his arms, and matches my carefree tone. "Oh, I thought we could get married. Maybe grab some cake. Hang out with friends."

"And after that?"

"After that?" he asks. I nod. "After that I'll take you home," he assures me. "Away from all the intense scrutiny. We can hide out there for as long as you want."

"But I mean, what will we do then? At home. All by ourselves."

"Oh," he smiles. "Well. Theeeen..." He checks the back of my dress and runs his fingers down the zipper. "Theeen, if you are amenable, I am going to peel you out of this beautiful dress as slowly as you will let me, so that I can enjoy every—" Kiss to one shoulder. "Amazing—" Kiss to the other. "Inch of you." He rests his forehead on mine. "And make love to you till we crash."

"Yeah, let's do that," I say, and I close my eyes against the intrusion of anyone into our private bubble.

"And after *that*," Locke continues. "I'm going to wake you up to do it all over again. Unless you wake me up first, which I give you full permission to do at any time for the rest of our lives." I hum my agreement. "But first," he says, "we have to go make it legit."

Locke offers his arm, which I tightly wrap with my own, and he leads me downstairs to where our guests are waiting. He doesn't leave my side until he takes his place at the top of the gathering when the service begins.

Outside, the day is bright with a breeze that causes the long grass in the paddock to nod in affirmation. Orange and yellow wildflowers lean in, and the two white ponies watch over the wooden fence like honored guests.

It's Noah who walks me down the aisle. The same man whose steadfast love for his wife and children had readied me for the bluebirds' concert. He and Hannah have so much room in their hearts. The extravagant grace with which they— *Quick!* I sign. *Say something funny.*

Noah stops us in front of Pastor Ian and Locke. He turns to me and signs, *I couldn't be prouder of you, Little Blue.* There are tears in his eyes! He touches my face.

That's not funny! I counter.

You're ready. You're a good match.

How do you know?

Noah lifts my chin and signs, *We've been communicating for weeks now. Did you think I'd just let you marry the first Texas cowboy you met, without vetting him?* He winks and kisses my cheek. Then he blesses me the same way he'd signed goodnight every evening for those three and a half years. *Your Holy Father, the Almighty God, will never leave you or forsake you.* He pushes the blessing into my heart. *And I'm never more than a call away either,* he signs. *You ready?*

You saved me. And that's why I'm ready. I make a sudden move to hug him. I don't mind that tears spill over. When I give him the all-clear, Noah squeezes my hand, and places it into Locke's.

Locke kisses my head. "You good?" he whispers.

From that moment on, I am. I say, "Yeah, man. Let's do this thing."

John Mark, who is acting as an interpreter, has graciously left the more private messages private, but he decides to broadcast this last statement for all to enjoy.

Then, there is Annabelle. Before the ceremony, Locke and I pulled John Mark aside and asked him to be her godfather. At first, he only answered, "Me?"

"You've been one of the only constants in her life," I said, "And a true friend to us. She's come to expect you. She's going to need your help."

But it was his coach's touching insistence—"You were put in our life on purpose. I want you to be part of this family"—that made John Mark eager to embody his new role.

After we take our marriage vows to one another, we take our adoption vows to Annabelle. She becomes our daughter as surely as if she had been born to us. Then we take vows to God on her behalf, and our daughter is baptized.

Pastor Ian procures a bewildered Annabelle, and turns so that everyone can see. Before he sprinkles her with water, he directs Locke, saying, "Father, name your child."

And Locke answers, "Annabelle Anita Aaron Locke."

"Annabelle Anita Aaron Locke, I baptize you in the name of the Father, and of the Son, and of the Holy Spirit." John Mark interprets all the words that are said and because his hands are busy, more than one tear runs off his cheek—much like the water that drips from Ian's fingers onto Annabelle's head. She moves all around to find the source of the dripping and laughs her guttural baby laugh to the delight of everyone present.

It is the sweetest, most meaningful service I could have hoped for.

Other voices can be heard all day long, echoing the sentiment. Eventually, my families begin their journeys home, and Annabelle and I take a seat by the pool to welcome the dusk. The rest of the Lockes tidy up around us, but I'm too tired to offer a hand. I make a feeble suggestion that they leave it for tomorrow, but nobody wants me to help anyway.

After Locke and his dad move a table, both his mom and Sarah shoo us away.

"Come on, Mrs. Locke," he says to me. "Let's get you home." Locke scoops up the baby and reaches for my hand. "You just tired? You're happy, aren't you?"

"Yes. A thousand yeses. I just don't gain energy from people the way you do. I have to recharge after being on for this long."

"I understand." In a somewhat deflated tone he adds, "I guess we could put the baby to bed and try to grab some sleep while she does." He's already opened the truck's door for me, when he notices that my expression has crossed into the affronted zone. "What is that face for?" he asks.

"You're aware that in Texas I can easily annul this marriage until it is consummated, right?"

"Oh, yeah?" he laughs. "Well, I don't want to give you any loopholes."

"I should think not."

"And I'm *pretty* sure that I can recharge you."

The next day, we fly to Michigan for a week-long honeymoon at Hannah and Noah's summer cottage on the Upper Peninsula. I get to show Locke the red lighthouse, and all of the trees, and quite a lot of the bedroom. It's the first time we've been able to spend uninterrupted days alone—well, not entirely alone. Annabelle comes too. Not only because she's already endured so much disruption in her young life, but also because we're family. For real. No take-backs.

AUTHOR'S NOTES

THANK YOU! For reading this. Please DO leave reviews. They are an enormous help to us, and I never forget that we are able to create words and music because of your support.

The music album: My guitar-god-of-a-husband and I recorded an album to go with the book! Songs include *Read the Last Page First*, *Keep Me*, and *Go to Jesus*. Check it out! ***Songs from The Locke Box*** can be found at JenniferDaniels.com.

ASL: The signing characters in this book use American Sign Language. I've taken the liberty to write out full sentences instead of using the proper syntax. This is merely for readability. ASL is a beautiful language. I hope that readers will feel I've treated it with respect.

Human trafficking doesn't have to look like young people being hauled across the country in windowless vans. It can be as tricky as a friendly compliment and an offer to make some quick cash. But it can spiral into other jobs too shameful or frightening to escape. Street-Grace.org offers help for victims and education for all of us.

Other Thanks:

To Jen Smith for the lovely cover design. To Scott Smith for producing the songs and bringing the story to life that way. To Mark Kelly Hall for generous time in edits. To Bob Zendejas for advice on how police stuff works. To Julie Stokes (always), Emily Wiley, Jan Michaels, Margaret Lukens, Carolyn Sunderland, Kelly Rhodes, Becky Daniels, Jeff Neal, Cornele Thomas, Crystal Sharpless, Jennifer Duran, Anna G. Joujan, Sherry Bushue.

To my songbird, Kate, for listening and laughing at the funny parts. To my creative powerhouse, Colin, for saying, "Oh my gosh! Are you working on a NEW story without having published the other ones?!" (Both of them are Young Authors Fair winners, by the way—just a proud mama talking here—so be on the lookout, World!)

ABOUT THE AUTHOR

Jennifer Daniels Neal is an award-winning singer/songwriter, author, and teaching artist. She and husband, Jeff Neal, have released nine music albums, a picture book, and two human children into the world (boy/girl twins, so...bonus!).

The Locke Box is Jenn's first novel and the first time she has released a project under her married name (not counting the kids). There are more to come! (Books and songs. Not kids.)

Jenn and the fam live on Lookout Mountain in Georgia, where there are mountain lions, excellent bike trails, and a one-hundred pound tongue inside of a black lab named Ziggy Marley.

Visit JenniferDaniels.com to learn more.

facebook.com/JenniferDanielsMusic
instagram.com/JennDanielsMusic